PROMISE ME

DIAMOND IN THE ROUGH 2

REBEL HART

Amore publishing

1

RAELYNN

"Rae, stop!"

I growled at him. "For the love of fuck, you'll let me go. Even if it kills me."

My phone stumbled out of my hand as I bit down into Michael's arm. But he released me. And I threw myself toward the edge of the bridge again. I felt him rushing for me, desperate to pull me back as I gazed over the twenty-foot drop. Sirens finally sounded in the distance. I flashed my light down there, catching yet another glimpse of where Clint was.

After slipping away from Michael's attempt to block me against the metal railing, I rushed for the tree line.

"Rae, are you thick-headed? You're going to get yourself killed!"

"I'm not leaving him down there by himself, Michael! Get over it or go home if you don't like it. I'll have an officer take me home."

I tripped over tree roots I couldn't see and forced myself to slow down. It was a very long drop to the river. A drop that would easily put me in Clint's position if I wasn't careful. But I knew he was alive. He had to be alive. Because no God in this universe was as cruel as that. I refused to believe that.

"I'm coming for you, Clint. Just hang on."

Sirens wailed as they rushed up the road. It felt like they were an eternity away. I heard the sirens, but I didn't see their headlights. And I wondered how much longer until they actually got here. I pointed the flashlight on my camera down toward the ground. I heard Michael cursing my existence as I grabbed on to trees.

They inched me down, centimeter by centimeter, until I slipped.

"Rae!"

"Shit!"

I tumbled into a tree that caught me and I almost lost my phone. I lay against the tree, catching it as the steep ravine turned into damn-near the straightest drop I'd ever seen. Vines hung from the trees, dangling above the ground. And while I considered taking the chance, none of them dropped all the way to the river's bank.

Where Clint was sprawled out.

I groaned. "Come on, Rae. Think."

"Rae! Can you hear me?"

Michael's voice echoed off the trees and I rolled my eyes.

"Unfortunately!"

"Quit being a smartass and stay there. If you move and that tree gives—"

"Didn't I tell you to go home if you couldn't stop ordering me around?"

"Maybe I give too much of a shit to let my best friend kill herself over—"

The sirens swallowed his voice and I was thankful for it. Because I was damn near ready to toss *him* over the bridge's railing. I placed my phone inside my bra, with the flashlight facing outward. With the angle I was sitting at, it meant I had a clear shot of what the downslope had for me to cling to. Some rocks. A bunch of massive tree roots. If I was careful, I could still get down there.

So I shimmied down the tree and hung on tight.

"Damn it, Rae!"

I blocked out Michael's yelling as the sirens grew closer.

"Don't make me come down there after you!"

I rolled my eyes as I slipped over the edge, placing my foot on the first rock.

"Rae, Allison is going to kill you!"

"Shut! The fuck! Up!"

I heard Michael slam his hands against the metal guardrail as headlights slowly filtered through the trees, giving me more light to work with. I touched down on the first rock and let go of the tree, digging my nails into the dirt. I reached my foot out for the first tree root I saw and caught it, slipping my foot inside it.

And just as I stepped off the rock, the tree root moved.

"Ah!"

"Rae!"

I dug my hands into the dirt, feeling my fingernails scrape across rocks. I clung to the side of the earth, looking down at the fifteen-foot drop below me. I wasn't even halfway down, and already I was struggling.

He needs you, Rae. Don't force him to be alone like he's been all his life.

I panted. "I'm coming for you, Clint. Just hang on."

With some careful maneuvering, and lots of dirt caked under my fingernails, I finally hit the halfway point. If I dropped, it wouldn't kill me. But, it would hurt. I closed my eyes and breathed, allowing the rushing water to fill my ears. I plucked my phone out of my bra and shone it down, watching as the headlights through the trees poured light down onto us.

"They're here! They're here, Rae! Stop moving!"

I wanted to shove a damn sock down Michael's throat.

When I flashed my light down against the river, what I saw horrified me. The water was rising. The river rushed harder. And I saw Clint's legs floating. If I didn't hurry up, he'd be pulled away by the current. Swept away, without a trace.

And I couldn't let that happen.

I slipped my phone back into my bra and slowly made my way down. I slipped and yelped. I ripped my nails off my fingers as I clung to the side of the earth. Trees groaned as I stepped on their roots, making a staircase for myself. And just as I hit the last rock I needed, I drew in a deep breath.

"Clint, can you hear me?"

The sound of the rushing water grew behind me as I touched down onto the bank. My feet sank immediately into the mud. The silt. The thick of it all. Making it even harder to get to Clint. I lost a shoe prying my foot out of that shit. I heard tires squealing on the bridge as the smell of burnt rubber wafted up my nose.

Reminding me of that disgusting dream I hoped to never have again.

"Clint! Can you hear me?"

I kept repeating the phrase as I made my way for him. As his body kept rising. As his legs kept floating. I saw his hips leave the ground. Then his lower back. I saw his body tilted in the direction of the current, and I was still a few feet away from him.

"Clint!"

A wave came out of nowhere, jostling his body. And before I knew it, he sank underneath the river. I threw myself at him, reaching out for him as best as I could. But it was no use. His body swept itself away, dragged with the current as the water levels kept rising. Higher and higher, like some devil from below torturing me before he killed me, too.

"Clint! No!"

I sprinted as quickly as I could. It felt like I ran above the quicksand silt as my hand reached out for him. His leather jacket trailed behind him, fluttering on top of the water. And with one last lunge, I felt the fabric against my fingers. I clutched it, tugging as hard as I could. Tears rushed down my cheeks as my feet sank ankle-high into the silt and stuck, trapping me as the river rushed with a black fury.

I wouldn't let it take me tonight, though.

Because it wasn't allowed to have Clint.

"Come on. For fuck's sake."

I groaned and grunted as more sirens approached. As more tires squealed. As Michael continued to yell and scream at me. I got Clint above the surface of the water and pulled him up the embankment, holding on to him for dear life. I reached up for a tree root, tugging on it as a tree fell over the edge of the river. I screamed as it landed just beside me. Finally giving up because of the water erosion against its roots.

But it gave me something to cling to. Something to wrap my arm around as I held Clint against me.

I drew in a shaking breath. "Just hang on, okay? Help is here."

I kept pulling on the tree, getting us higher and higher. There was a small perch. A small indent in the side of the earth that provided the dream of relief. My arm cried out for mercy. It shook with a need for rest. But I wouldn't let my body give up now. I slid my arm up the tree, hanging on to Clint as I slowly made my way for that indented earth.

And when my back finally sat against it, I breathed a sigh of relief.

Finally, a patch of dirt that didn't try to swallow us whole.

"Come on. On your back. Let's go."

I rolled Clint off me and slid him to the ground. I

CLINTON

"Clint!"

"Mom?"

I whipped around, looking down as I saw myself clad in white. A white leather jacket, a white pair of jeans, and a white fucking turtleneck. Who the hell put me in a turtleneck? I looked up as I heard the sound of soft feet falling against a tile floor. I saw my mother running toward me, arms outstretched. And when I saw her, I smiled.

"Mom!"

I rushed for her, scooping her up into my arms. I twirled her around, hearing her giggle and laugh as my face fell against her bosom. That soft, glorious place I'd sought comfort in as a child. As a young boy, wanting nothing more than to seek shelter away from my father with her.

I spun her around for what seemed like an eternity before I put her down.

I buried my face into her shoulder. "It's so good to see you."

from Clint's side, gazing down into his eyes. Holy fuck, his eyes were open. Holy fuck, he was talking!

"Clint! Clint. Clint. Can you hear me, baby? Clint?"

"R-Rae?"

I cupped his cheek. "Holy shit. I—oh, my God. Clint! Don't close your eyes, okay? Don't close them again. The paramedics are coming. It's almost over. Just—Clint!"

I tapped his face as his eyes closed, and he groaned out in pain. I'd apologize later, but not right now. Because I sure as hell wasn't about to let this miracle slip through my fingers.

"That hurts."

"Because your nose is broken. Keep your eyes open, okay?"

His reddened eyes slowly rolled over to me as the voices and footsteps grew closer. I smiled down at him, my heart filling with joy and relief as he attempted a smile back. He winced, though. I knew his nose was giving him some trouble. And rightfully so.

Because it was practically flat against his face.

water. Off the caverns underneath the bridge. I heard people crying out my name. Telling me to stay put. But I didn't give them the time of day. I placed my forehead against Clint's chest, no longer feeling his heartbeat. No longer feeling life pumping through his veins. And as I sobbed against his chest, I lay down next to him.

"No, please. Clint."

I gripped his shirt. I cried until I heaved. My fingers slid down his arm, checking his pulse at his wrist. There was nothing. No beating. No rushing. No blood pumping through his veins. He felt cold as night. As cold as that fucking water that had almost whisked him away.

"You're a fighter, Clint. Fight for this. Fight for your life."

My words were nothing but a whisper in the wind. I kept repeating them, over and over. Hoping beyond all hope that he heard me. In the distance, I heard people coming down the ravine, headed for us as my sobs filled the space around us. The words kept tumbling from my lips like a prayer, reaching out to any God that was willing to look past my indiscretions and fulfill my only wish. I curled up next to his body. His dead, lifeless body. I clutched his chest, unable to make any sounds as my grief swallowed my voice whole.

Until…

"Holy shit."

The gasp startled me so badly I yelped. I shot up

put him on his back, gazing down into his face. The flashlight from my phone poking out of my bra gave me a hard glimpse at what he looked like. And it was hard to take in.

"Clint, can you hear me?"

I tapped his face softly, but I stopped soon after. His nose was broken. There was blood all over his cheeks and pooling in his mouth from the gash in his forehead. I reached out and checked his pulse. It was weak, but there. And as my eyes continued to roam over his body, I saw his shoulder was dislocated.

"Clint, please. You have to wake up for me, okay?"

I couldn't get over the blood. How much there was. How dark it looked against his skin. I didn't know where the hell it was all coming from and I felt panic grip my chest. I tapped his neck. I placed my hand over his heart. It seemed to be beating slower and slower. Like he was slowly fading away from me.

My tears dripped against his face. "Clint, please. You can't do this to me, okay?"

Memories flooded back. The first time he sat down next to me. The first time we kissed. That night in his room, where he stripped me of my clothes and made me feel things no other boy had. I remembered waking up to him in the middle of the night. Feeling his body wrapped around mine. And the only regret I had was that I hadn't stayed that first night. My only regret out of anything was sneaking out that first night and not cherishing the time we did have together.

"Clint, please!"

My shrieking voice echoed off the trees. Off the

She ran her fingers through my hair. "I've missed you so much."

"Where the hell are we?"

"Language."

I snickered. "Thanks, Mom."

"Well, you and your father have always had such potty mouths."

I pulled back, gazing into her eyes. "Where are we?"

"Why don't you look around and see?"

As my eyes slowly gazed out over the white expanse of nothingness, I saw edges come into view. A couch. A hallway. A projector television sitting against the wall. I saw the edges of windows, looking out onto a great, big, blue sky. Clouds as white as my clothing floated high above, and the green grass of our front lawn sparkled in the sun.

I furrowed my brow. "We're home."

"We are, yes."

"But this doesn't look like home."

"Well, it's got a few changes."

"Why does it look so different?"

And when I turned around, I saw sorrow in my mother's eyes.

I paused. "What?"

Mom sighed. "Why don't we have a little talk?"

She reached her hand out for mine and I took it. She pulled me over to the couch. The one Roy and I always sat on. But it didn't feel like our couch. It didn't look like our space. It was a nice replica. Why the fuck was everything so white?

"Mom, what's going on?"

She paused. "It's complicated, sweetheart."

"I'm dreaming, aren't I?"

"In a way, yes."

"In a way?"

"Your body is giving out on you right now."

"So I'm dying."

"Do you remember much of anything?"

I nodded slowly. "I remember it all."

Mom patted my hand. "Who's the pretty girl coming for you?"

"Coming for me?"

She smiled. "Just answer the question, sweetheart. We don't have much time."

"I'm not following."

She cupped my cheek. "Who's this girl you've been spending time with?"

I felt so confused. And yet, this all still felt very natural. I nuzzled against my mother's palm, wanting nothing more than to stay here with her. Stay here, in her arms. Stay here, with her touch. Stay here, and feel her run her fingers through my hair for all eternity.

Maybe I'd get that, too. If I was really dying.

"Her name's Rae."

Mom smiled. "Pretty name. How'd you meet her?"

I snickered. "School, actually. I used to—"

And when I paused, Mom sighed.

"You used to pick on her."

I nodded. "Yes, ma'am."

"I still don't understand why in the world you run around with those kids. That Roy boy. They're such a bad influence on you."

I pulled away from her touch. "You don't understand, Mom. I can't expect you to."

"Then try. Try to explain it to me, while we have time."

"We'd have had time if you hadn't left me with Dad."

"I was in no condition to take care of you. I was hooked on so many things and—"

"And an abusive father seemed like the best route to take?"

Tears filled her eyes. "At least you would've been clothed. Fed. Had a roof over your head. I didn't have those things, after the divorce."

"You got a very nice settlement from Dad. He's still paying you alimony. What happened?"

She shook her head. "Can we try to focus on the good things? Please?"

"I want to know why you left me behind."

There was a long pause before a tear leaked down her cheek.

"Because I was selfish. Because I was thinking of only myself, in the moment. Between my depression and the medication I got hooked on, I fell into a dark hole. And I didn't want to take anyone with me. Pushing you away was the only rational fix I could come to in my pill-induced stupor, so you wouldn't fall into that hole with me. Just like divorcing me was your father's way of getting himself out of that hole. Because for a while, he was in it with me."

I chewed my lower lip. "I guess, in some ways, I already knew that."

"Because you're a smart boy, Clint. Even though you don't apply yourself in school and even though you run around with those hoodlums, you're a good kid. A smart kid. A fighter, with a strong spirit. Your father almost succeeded in dampening my strong spirit. Don't let him do that to you, okay?"

I paused. "If you're here with me, does this mean you're dead?"

She shook her head. "No, silly boy. I'm a manifestation. There isn't anything right now that we're talking about that you don't already know inside this funny little head of yours."

She tapped her finger softly against my temple and I caught her wrist with my hand. I pulled her palm to my lips and kissed it. Over, and over, and over again. I didn't care if it wasn't real. I didn't care if this wasn't really her. It felt like her. And smelled like her. Just like I remembered.

And I didn't want it to ever go away.

"You're a fighter, Clint. Fight for this. Fight for your life."

I shook my head. "I'm tired of fighting, Mom. I don't want to do it anymore."

"She's waiting for you, sweetheart."

"You're a fighter, Clint. Fight for this. Fight for your life."

I furrowed my brow as my mother's voice distorted itself.

"You're a fighter, Clint. Fight for this. Fight for your life."

"Mom?"

Her body started floating away, and I reached out for her.

"Mom!"

"She's waiting for you. Don't let her down like your father let me down."

"Mom! No!"

"You're a fighter, Clint. Fight for this. Fight for your life."

"You're a fighter, Clint. Fight for this. Fight for your life."

"You're a fighter, Clint. Fight for this. Fight for your life."

Then I drew in a deep, resounding breath.

"Holy shit."

A yelp hit my ears and made me flinch. All the white had faded away. The warmth of my mother's touch was gone. And for some reason, I was soaking fucking wet. I shivered as I gazed up at the night sky. A stark juxtaposition to my dream. Or my limbo. Or my purgatory.

Or whatever the fuck had just happened.

"Clint! Clint. Clint. Can you hear me, baby? Clint?"

I coughed. "R-Rae?"

Something warm cupped my cheek. "Holy shit. I— oh, my God. Clint! Don't close your eyes, okay? Don't close them again. The paramedics are coming. It's almost over. Just—Clint!"

I felt her tap my face and a blinding pain shot through my skin. I groaned and lobbed my head over toward her, taking in her blurry form. The blackened outline gave me comfort. Much like the comfort I'd just experienced with my mother.

Or the vision of my mother.

"That hurts."

Rae snickered. "Because your nose is broken. Keep your eyes open, okay?"

That explains a lot.

I heard footsteps off in the distance. I saw flashes of light and heard sirens above me. Rae settled against me, warming me with her presence as she gazed into my eyes. It was hard keeping my eyes open. My lungs felt like they were burning and drowning at the same time. She smiled at me. That tender, sweet, relieved smile she always had when she laid eyes on me.

And while I tried smiling back, my nose only let me go so far before I winced.

I groaned. "Yep. That's broken."

Rae sighed. "Your shoulder's dislocated, too."

"Explains the back pain."

"Well, lying on a rocky river bank will do that, too."

I snickered. "I suppose it will."

She whispered. "I'm so glad you're talking to me."

"I know you are."

"Because you—"

I nodded, ignoring the disorienting pain. "I know."

"You know?"

"I saw my mother."

"You... you did?"

I scoffed. "Yeah. Crazy, right?"

"Maybe when this is all done, you can tell me about it."

She cupped my cheek and I fell into the warmth. I lobbed my head over, trying to seek out as much of her comfort as I could. Holy hell, she felt fantastic. I almost didn't want the moment to end. Had it not been for the blinding pain that made me sick to my stomach, I would've cried out for everyone to leave us alone.

But I needed a damn hospital.

Before I died again.

"I promise you're gonna be okay."

Rae's lips pressed a kiss to my ear and I moaned. I didn't even try holding it back. Over and over, she pressed kisses against me, warming me from my toes to my nose. I felt my legs come back to life. I wiggled my toes as the sounds of sliding rock and dirt sounded above us. I felt sprinkles of the earth battering against my face, the smallest specks sending ricocheting pain signals all the way to my brain.

"It's okay. I'm right here. I'm going nowhere, okay?"

I sputtered. "How did you——? Are you okay?"

I couldn't speak through the pain anymore. It was excruciating. How the hell did Rae get down that steep cliff? Was she hurt? Had she fallen over, too? What the fuck was happening around me?

I couldn't crane my neck enough to see. All I felt were people gathering around us as Rae's lips left my ear.

"No, no, no. Come back."

"I'm right here, Clint. Just right here. Take my hand."

I felt her fingers curl around my wrist, but it wasn't enough. I needed her lips. Her body. Her warmth. Her presence. I needed more of her. All of her. I didn't want her to leave me like my mother had.

I drew in a shaking breath. "Please, don't leave."

"I swear to you, I'm going nowhere. I'm going straight to the hospital with you, all right? Just let the paramedics do what they do best."

I heard a count off before my body was lifted. I cried out in pain as the world around me flashed. In an instant, the dark world was gone. Replaced by the white of my dreams. Or my purgatory. I saw my mother's face smiling down at me. Clad in that beautiful white summer dress of hers.

"Don't let her down like your father let me down."

"Heave up!"

"Shit!"

"Clint, it's okay. I'm meeting you at the top, all right?"

"Heave up!"

"Fucking hell."

"Clint? Can you hear me?"

Every time someone called out 'heave up' my body jostled. I tilted my head off to the side, spitting up bile as the pain took over my body. I stopped fighting it. I stopped trying to make it better. And instead, I became one with it. The paramedics heaved me up from the ravine. A straight shot of absolute hell before pulling me over the edge of the bridge. I heard Rae scrambling for me. Telling me to keep my eyes open as lights flashed in them. I felt something prick the tops of my hands. I felt a mask come down over my face. I was overwhelmed. And scared.

Until I felt Rae's hand in mine again.

"I'm here. I'm back, baby. Okay? Can you hear me?"

I nodded my head, becoming one with the aching migraine as my eyes rolled her way. I saw her walking alongside me. Our fingers interlaced together. She was all I saw. Her dark outfit. Her dark hair. Her dark skin. Her dark eyes. Dark, like the night. Dark, like the water. Dark, like the abyss I'd fallen into. Dark, like my heart.

And somehow, I'd still fallen in love with her.

"Start a morphine drip. Get this kid some relief."

"Do it before you set his shoulder."

"Are you riding with us? Or him?"

Rae looked down at me before she kissed my cheek.

"See you at the hospital, okay? There's too many paramedics in the back to ride with you. They all need to work on you."

I nodded slowly, but I wasn't happy with the situation. But when her lips pressed against my forehead, I hung on to that feeling. That sensation. Those butterflies in my heart.

"See you soon," she whispered.

Then the morphine drip kicked on, causing my body to go limp as her hand slowly fell away from mine.

3

RAELYNN

Michael gripped my shoulders. "Come on. We can follow the ambulance. The paramedics have to work on him while driving, otherwise it's not going to be good."

My chest jumped as my hand fell from Clint's. I hated leaving him. I hated not being by his side. But Michael was right. They were all right. It was all hands on deck to save his life at this point. Especially since his heart had already stopped once. The second I told that to the paramedic, his eyes widened. They all leapt into action, like I'd just shot them to DEFCON-5 or some shit like that. I didn't like it. I didn't like how they reacted one damn bit.

But I let Michael guide me to his SUV so we could hop in.

"You have to breathe for me, Rae. Okay?"

I nodded. "I'm—trying. I'm—I-I-I-I—"

"It'll do us no good to have a panic attack. Take my hand. Here."

I slid my hand into his as we pulled off the bridge. We followed the speeding ambulance back through the woods, passing those neighborhoods and all those tire tracks. Which only served to make my panic worse. The world curled in on itself. I had to close my eyes to keep from getting sick. My chest felt as if it were caving in and my heartrate skyrocketed.

"Tell me five things you smell."

I furrowed my brow. "What?"

"Now, Rae. Five things you smell."

I tried sniffing the air in broken intakes of air. Trying to latch onto the world around me.

"Uh, I uh—I smell rubber. And—and oil."

"Three more. Hit me with 'em."

I snickered. "I smell your cologne."

"Good."

"And dirt."

"One more. You're doing great, Rae."

"And… and sweat."

"Okay. Give me four things you hear."

I trained my ears out onto the world, locking on to the sounds.

"I hear your car engine."

Michael snickered. "All right. Good one. Three more."

"I hear your classical music turned down. And your tires on the road."

"One more. You can do it."

I drew in my first steady breath as the sound hit my ears.

"I still hear the sirens behind us."

Michael paused. "Three things you taste."

"Taste?"

"Yep. Taste. Go. Now."

I drew in a deep lungful of air. "I taste dirt. Saliva. And…"

Michael squeezed my hand as he waited for my final answer.

"And metal."

"Okay, Rae. Open your eyes and tell me two things you see."

I slowly slid my eyes open and the world didn't tilt. It wasn't curling in on itself or spiraling outward. It was still, and the ambulance with its silent, flashing lights was still in front of us.

"I see the ambulance, and its flashing lights."

"Good. You need to do one more?"

I shook my head. "Nope. I think I'm grounded enough."

"You did good back there, Rae. You need to know that. Clint's alive because of you right now. And he's in capable hands."

"And to think you didn't want me down there."

Michael chuckled. "There's the Rae I know and love."

I turned my head toward him. "Love?"

He squeezed my hand again. "You know you're one of my best friends. Sometimes I hate you for things —but I'm never going to stop being your friend."

"Really?"

"Really, really."

I felt tears crest my eyes before another thought hit me.

"I should call Clint's parents."

"Do you have their number?"

"I've got Clint's home number, yes."

Michael nodded. "Then I'd give them a call. They need to know what's going on."

I reached down for my purse, shocked that I still had it. I smiled a thankful smile over at Michael and he nodded his head. And for the first time, I felt like things were finally resolved between us. I dug out my phone and scrolled through my contacts, coming upon Clint's home number. He'd given it to me in case of an emergency. But for the most part, he'd told me not to call it unless I absolutely had to.

And this was pretty much the biggest emergency on the planet.

I sighed. "Here goes nothing."

I dialed the number and the phone rang in my ear. It rang and it rang, and I almost hung up. Maybe his father and stepmother were out on another trip. Not even in town. Which wouldn't have shocked me a bit. Then, on the last ring, the phone picked up.

"Who's this?"

His father's gruff voice filled the phone and my mind pulled me back. Back to that morning where he found us leaving the house to go to school. That wild, empty smile. Those mean, villainous eyes. My stomach turned over as his voice filled my ear, and I almost couldn't speak.

Until Michael cleared his throat at me.

"Hi. Yes. Mr. Clarke?"

He paused. "This is he. Who is this? Why are you calling my phone so late at night?"

"This is Raelynn Cleaver. I don't know if you remember me, but—"

"Can you cut to the chase? I'm a bit busy with work over here."

"Clint's been in an accident. He's headed for the hospital."

The phone call fell silent before a sigh emanated over the phone.

"A crash on his bike?"

I paused. "More like someone ran him off the road and he fell over a bridge."

Michael quirked an eyebrow at me as my voice started to flatten. It sounded like his father was more annoyed than anything. There wasn't the slightest hint of worry in his tone.

"Well, that's what my son gets for pissing off half the city. What hospital are they headed to?"

My jaw dropped open. How the hell could he be so calloused?

"Um, they're headed to—"

I looked over at Michael as he mouthed the name of the hospital.

"—Dignity Health," I finished.

"How far out was he? That's clear across town."

"It was a bad wreck, Mr. Clarke. His heart stopped

there for a while on the bank of the river. You really should get to the hospital."

And with a groan, his father hung up the phone.

"Son of a fucking bitch," I hissed.

I tossed my phone to the floorboard as my body vibrated with fury. I felt Michael staring at me as we came to a stop at a stoplight. I mean, the ambulance blew through it. But we weren't sure we could. Even if we were following it.

Then, he cleared his throat. "I take it the call didn't go well."

I snickered. "When I told him his son's heart stopped, he groaned and hung up on me."

"He what now?"

I nodded. "Yeah. I mean, I get that you don't like Clint because he's a dick. But his father makes him look like a saint."

"Sounds like it."

I leaned back against the leather seats of Michael's SUV and gazed out the window. Maybe I shouldn't have called his father at all. I didn't know. I wasn't sure if I'd made the right decision. So much had already happened tonight, and my head felt like it was still spinning. Michael took my hand again, holding it until we pulled into the hospital parking lot. I saw the ambulance crew hauling Clint out as we pulled into the parking garage, and I told Michael I'd pay for the ticket.

Then I shoved myself out of his car and took off.

"Rae! Wait up!"

I heard Michael racing after me as I kept my eyes

trained on that ambulance. I hopped over railings and darted through medians. Car horns honked at me as I cut them off. I'd be damned if I let them stop me, though. I saw the ambulance pulling away from the hospital E.R. doors. Michael caught up with me, heaving for air as we charged through the automatic doors.

Just as they rolled Clint down the hallway, a nurse stopped us.

"You here with the crash victim?"

I nodded breathlessly. "Clint Clarke. Yes. I need to see him. I told him I wouldn't leave his—"

"He's being rushed into surgery. They prepped him in the ambulance. If you wait here—"

"Look, Nurse. I know. I get it. But I have to see him before that surgery. I told him he wouldn't do this alone, and I couldn't ride with him in the back."

The nurse sighed. "Girlfriend?"

I looked over at Michael before I nodded.

"Yes. Clint's my boyfriend."

She sighed. "I can only update you on so much since you aren't family. But what I can tell you is this: in less than two minutes, he's going to be on an operating table. And any time we waste, there's a higher chance he won't make it out of surgery. He'll understand once the surgery is over. Now, I need you to sit here and try to remain calm for us. Can you do that for me?"

I drew in a quick breath. "What do you mean, you can't update me on much? His family doesn't give a shit about him!"

Michael sighed. "Rae, take a breath for me."

"No! I'm done with the breathing. His father doesn't give a damn about that boy. And his step-mother is just some trophy at his side. And you're going to update them before you update me?"

"It's protocol. I'm sorry. I'll tell you what I can, but nothing more."

And with that, the nurse turned on her heels and went back to the intake desk.

I hissed to myself. "Bitch."

"All right. Let's sit you down before you get us thrown out of this place."

Michael guided me to a chair before he left. I watched him turn a corner, disappearing from sight, only to emerge with two bottles of water. He sat down beside me and handed me one, and I tossed him a thankful look. I didn't feel like talking anymore. I didn't feel like using my voice. It was going in and out already. Hoarse, before coming back mightier than ever. So the two of us sat in silence and sipped on our water.

Until Michael broke the silence.

"All we can do is wait. And in the meantime, maybe we can call Allison. Get her to bring us some food."

I shook my head. "I don't wanna bother her with this. Bothering you with it is enough."

"You're not bothering me. Okay?"

I nodded slowly, refusing to argue with him. "I still don't want to call her, though. I mean, if she gets in touch with you, don't lie to her. But I'm just…"

Michael rubbed my back. "I know. I know."

I nodded as I took another sip of my water before Michael spoke again.

"What about your mother?"

I snickered. "You mean the woman who's probably already made up with D.J. and is with him right now?"

He paused. "Wait, I thought they broke up for good."

"All I know is that Mom's still got money to pay bills even though she hadn't secured a new job yet. And the only place I know of where that money can come from is him."

"Shit. I'm so sorry, Rae."

I shrugged. "It's her life. Not mine. If that's how she wants to live it, then so be it. If anything, the fact that she hasn't called and asked me why I'm not home yet tells me all I need to know. She's making up with D.J., making plans with him, and doesn't have enough sense to realize I'm not home yet."

"I guess you and Clint do have some lifestyle similarities, then."

That statement said a lot, coming from Michael. Because I knew him well enough to know that was the first step in Clint being accepted into the fold. I mindlessly sipped on the water, refusing to break for the restroom just in case something with Clint popped up. I kept shifting us down, seat by seat, until we were stationed right beside the nurse's unit. This way, I could eavesdrop. Pick up bits and pieces of Clint's condition, hopefully.

Because apparently, being the girlfriend and the

one to help him out in his most dire time wasn't enough merit to earn information on his condition.

Michael shifted. "When do you think his parents will show up?"

I shrugged. "Part of me isn't expecting them to show up at all."

"Seriously?"

"Seriously. His father's a damn nutcase. And his stepmother doesn't ever step in on anything until it's getting too violent. It's insane, what he puts up with."

"No wonder he's angry all the time."

I nodded. "You're telling me."

"Where's my son?"

The booming voice forced me to whip my head around. I looked at the emergency room doors, watching Clint's father barge straight through them. Cecilia was behind him, her hair fluttering down her back and her pristine heels clicking across the floor. Clint's father gripped her hand tightly, tugging her along as he bellowed for information.

"Clinton Clarke is here, and I want to know what the fuck is happening with my son!"

And as nurses rushed him, waiting on him hand and foot as they shoved information down his throat, I saw tears in Cecilia's eyes.

Tears I hoped were for Clint.

4

CLINTON

"C lint!"
        "Rae?"

I turned around, taking in the bright blue color that surrounded us. I saw Rae in the most gorgeous dress. One that fell off her shoulders and fluttered just above her knees. She ran for me with the biggest smile on her face, and I held my arms out for her. She lunged at me, wrapping her entire body around me. And as her warmth encompassed me, I spun her around.

Around, and around, until we fell into the soft blue grass below us.

"Hi there, handsome."

She kissed my cheek and it shivered me to my toes.

"Hey there, beautiful."

"I'm glad you're okay."

I nodded. "Me, too. And I like this dress on you. You should wear stuff like this more often."

She giggled. "You mean you don't like my brown pants and my baggy black shirts?"

"*I mean, they do nothing for your form, no. But, if you're comfortable wearing them, then it's fine.*"

"*You just want to stare at my tits all day.*"

I grinned. "*And you know you like it.*"

She laughed and snuggled next to me, using my arm as a pillow. Her leg slid between mine, and together, we stared up at the sky. The sky that matched our clothes. Matched my light blue leather jacket. Matched the light blue grass we lay on and the light blue trees swaying in the cool summer breeze. White clouds moved above us, dancing for us and morphing into shapes right before our very eyes.

Rae pointed. "*Look. That one's dancing.*"

I smiled as the elephant got up on its hind legs and started shimmying.

"*Holy shit, it is.*"

She giggled. "*And that one looks like a heart. See it?*"

I smiled. "*I do see it, yes.*"

"*Oh! The butterfly! It's flapping its wings!*"

I scanned the clouds. "*I don't see it.*"

"*No, not the clouds. Over there, silly.*"

I turned my head to where she was pointing and I saw it. The biggest butterfly I'd ever seen in my life. Easily as big as my stomach, and it had the most beautiful wings I'd ever seen in my life. Intricate light blue and white patterns as it lifted off toward the sky. It sprinkled us with something. A sparkling dust of some sort. And as it floated toward the sky, covering us in this dust, I felt peace come over me. I felt Rae relax into me.

I felt my lips loosening.

"*I love you, Rae.*"

Her hand cupped my cheek and she pulled my face toward hers, smiling brightly at me. As bright as the clouds hanging in the sky. Her thumb smoothed over my cheek and I leaned forward, capturing the sweetness of her lips. I rolled her over on the grass, kicking up more of that dust as we found ourselves smushed inside a patch of light blue and white wildflowers.

"I love you too, Clint."

I grinned. "You do, huh?"

She nodded. "I do, yes."

"Do you love me enough to stay by my side?"

"I do."

"Do you love me enough to deal with my shit?"

"I do."

"Do you love me enough to make love to me whenever I ask?"

She snickered, swatting at my chest. "You're about to lose brownie points here, handsome."

"Oooh, and what do these points get me?"

I slipped my hand underneath her dress as giggles fell from her lips. I captured them with mine, swallowing her sounds as her skin puckered underneath my fingertips. Her legs parted for me, allowing my body to sink between them. And as her womanly scent wafted up my nostrils, I felt my cock hardening. I felt my body tightening. I felt her rolling against me, ready for my fingers to fill her as I danced over her bare pussy.

My eyebrows rose. "No underwear?"

And when that salacious little smile crossed her cheeks, I filled her pussy with my fingers.

"Oh, Clint."

"So wet for me."

She gasped. "Shit. Just like that."

"I've got you, Rae. I'll always have you. I'll never disappoint you like my father disappointed my mother."

"I know. I know. And it'll be all right, Clint."

I gazed down into her eyes, watching as a flash of darkness took over her face, muting her presence before bringing her back. My fingers stilled. My brow furrowed deeper. And as her hand cupped my cheek, I watched the light blue quickly fade into the darkest shade of navy I'd ever seen.

"It's going to be all right, Clint."

She disappeared from underneath me and my world tilted. The warmth of her pussy around my fingers were gone, and pain unlike any other raced up my spine. I cried out, watching as the world tilted me onto my back. I heard the rushing sounds of water. I smelled the scent of burning rubber. I heard someone calling my name in the distance as I gazed up at the navy blue sky. Dotted with stars that twinkled for my delight.

Trying to ease me through the pain.

"You're a fighter, Clint. Fight for this. Fight for your life."

As I lay there, a reel played out in the sky. Like the projector screen back inside the hellhole that was my father's mansion. I watched everything play out on screen. Like some kind of sick, twisted horror movie. As the water rushed over my legs, trying to carry me downstream, the movie played out. Those four drunk boys, rolling up on Rae and me in the parking lot. Them taunting her. Threatening her. Licking their lips at her and wanting to make her their meal for the night. I saw me harassing them, getting them to chase me while Rae hopped the fence to get away from them. I watched the car chase play out with horror filling my body. I felt my eyes widening as my nose ached. I felt my toes tingle as my shoulder slowly moved itself out of socket.

"Holy fuck!"

I roared out into the expanse of nothingness as the water

lifted my body. I kept my eyes trained toward the sky as that damn phrase kept repeating itself. Over and over, from a disembodied voice that haunted me from the depths of the water.

"You're a fighter, Clint. Fight for this. Fight for your life."

I'm so fucking tired of fighting, though.

I saw the wreck. How the car slammed into my bike. I saw myself stumbling over toward the woods, trying to get away from the beer bottles those damn boys threw at me. I watched myself turn around. I watched that damn bottle clock me right between the eyes. I felt my head throbbing. Aching. Spilling with blood as the car rushed me again in my stunned stupor.

Before he ran into me completely, pushing me over the edge of the bridge.

"No!"

I saw my own body coming at me. I tried reaching out to catch myself, but I couldn't move. Just as my own body reached me, it turned into nothing. It felt like my soul had slipped into my body before the water whisked me away. I sank underneath, wrapped up in its cold nature. Sinking to the bottom as screaming filled my ears.

I felt the water dragging me away as my lungs refused to breathe.

"You're a fighter, Clint. Fight for this. Fight for your life."

I felt my back fall against the rocks at the bottom of the river, my legs dangling helplessly in the water. My heart was giving out, my blood slowing. And as the world faded to black, I felt something snag against my coat.

My body stopped moving. But not soon enough.

"Holy shit."

My eyes ripped open and I panted for air. I stared up

at a popcorn ceiling, listening as the sounds of beeping machines dawned on my ears. The smell of disinfectant filled my lungs. With every breath I took, it rooted me to the most uncomfortable bed I'd ever slept on. And as I licked my chapped lips, it confirmed my theories.

I was in a hospital. In a bed. Staring up at my room's ceiling.

It was silent. A silence I didn't expect to get. Where was Rae? She promised me she wouldn't leave me alone through all this. Wasn't she supposed to be here? Was she all right? Had something happened on the journey to the hospital?

Wait, what day was it? What time was it? Maybe she was simply at home, sleeping. I mean, I didn't know how long I'd been out. How long I'd been dreaming.

I reached my hand out, hoping Rae was there to take it. Maybe she was preoccupied. Or she was speaking and I simply couldn't hear it. I tried moving my neck, but couldn't. I tried darting my eyes around, but they moved too slowly. My body felt lighter than air. I wiggled my toes, and even tried bending my knees. There wasn't any pain. But there wasn't any feeling either. And as my eyes fell onto the morphine drip, that answered my questions.

Shit. I was still drugged to the high heavens.

A hand slipped into mine, but I didn't recognize it. It was soft, but not necessarily warm. Not like Rae's. Or my mother's. I felt ring bands against my skin, nails softly scratching up my arm. I grimaced at the feeling and it quickly stopped, and that movement told me who it was.

"Welcome back, hun. How are you feeling?"

Cecilia.

My stepmother was in the room.

My eyes lobbed over as her chair scooted across the floor. She came into view, her hand still holding mine. I heard the clicking of her manicured nails, the scraping of her Louis Vuitton heels against the floor. Even in the hospital, her hair was perfect. The perfect face of makeup. Contoured with precision and glistening against the expensive diamonds my father showered her with. Her clothes were designer, in the middle of the fucking night. Just like my father always wanted with his women.

Wait, it was still the middle of the night, right?

Cecilia didn't say anything, so I didn't strike up a conversation. Because while it was nice having her there, I was still disappointed that she wasn't Rae. Where was she? Had my father scared her off? Holy fuck, if my father had scared that girl off, he'd be dead.

Once I could get out of this hospital bed.

My eyes slowly panned back up to the ceiling. Cecilia kept a grip on my hand, her grip growing stronger every minute that passed by. It didn't shock me one bit that my father hadn't surfaced yet. He was probably at work, doing some shit. Or taking work phone calls. Or booking their next vacation getaway.

You know, doing more important shit than tending to his son.

"Where's Rae?"

Cecilia sighed, and it gave me all the answer I needed. I felt my blood boiling. My fucking father with his fucking antics. The beeping machines around me began spiking. Cecilia gasped as she stood up from her chair. She leaned over me, her hair curtaining us off from the rest of the world. I heard something beeping close to my ear before something warm dripped through my system, making me feel like I was damn near peeing myself.

"Is everything okay in here?"

"What happened? Why did he spike?"

"Let me check his vitals."

Cecilia sighed. "I've already pressed the morphine button. Just give him a second. He's a strong boy. Stronger than he should be."

There was a sadness to the last part of that phrase. That last little sentence she tacked on there. I felt my eyes growing heavy as the drugs rushed my system. They settled my heartrate and my blood pressure back down. Nurses poked and prodded. They shone more lights in my eyes. One of them set themselves to the task of changing out my I.V. bag while another tugged on something that made my dick jump.

Shit. I had a catheter in.

Fucking grand.

"It's okay. I'm right here, sweetheart. Can you still hear me?"

I swallowed. "Yeah, Cecilia. I can hear you."

"Good. The nurses want you to stay awake through this morphine rush. So try to keep talking to me. What do you want to talk about?"

I want to talk about what the fuck my father said or did to Rae.

But, I settled on a better question. One that still required an answer.

"Where the hell is Dad?"

5

RAELYNN

Michael hissed. "Rae, we have to go."

I held up my hand as we crept through the hallways of the hospital. We dodged staff, racing around corners as I tried to get to Clint's ICU room. I sure as hell wasn't allowing his father to chase me off like that. I didn't give a damn how he felt about my being there or what he'd said to me to try and get me to leave. He didn't want to be here. He didn't give a shit about his son. The only thing he cared about was his businesses. How much money he pulled in.

How hard he could sock his son in the fucking jaw.

Michael grabbed my arm. "Rae, stop."

I ripped away from him. "If you don't want to be here, then go. I'll catch a ride back somehow. But I'm not leaving. Not until I know how Clint's doing."

"And if his father catches you sneaking about? If the doctors catch you?"

I shrugged. "What's he going to do? Hit a girl?"

Michael's face fell and I moved down the hallway again. Doctors had whisked them away to a room that had already been set aside for Clint after he came out of surgery. Which meant things didn't look very good. I wanted to know how the surgery had gone. Or was going. Or whatever his status was. I'd waited for almost two hours to find the opening I needed to sneak through those metal doors. To get back to Clint. To see if I could pick up on any information I wanted. Anything to soothe my worried soul. I wanted to know exactly the kind of condition he was in. But when I saw Clint's father pacing up and down the hallway with his cell phone stuck in his ear, I paused. Taking in the scene. How apathetic and unapologetic the man looked.

And the kicker was that it didn't shock me one bit.

"No. No. I need you to do it the way I said for you to do it. You're costing us money. And a great deal of it. I won't be paying your paycheck if you don't do as I ask!"

His father's voice boomed down the hallway and I shook my head. I peeked back at Michael, watching his face fall. Then we hid around the corner of the empty hallways of the hospital as I tried my best to listen to what his father was saying.

"Is that man really doing work right now?" he asked.

I nodded. "Yep."

We tucked ourselves away, hiding as a doctor came around the corner. We pressed ourselves into a dark space, and I even held my breath so no one would hear us. The doctor passed, leaving the hallways bare and empty again. We clamored right back up to the corner. Right back to where we'd been.

I watched as the doctor approached Clint's father, and even I could see the frustration in the doctor's shoulders as they tensed.

I watched his father hold his fucking hand up to the doctor, telling him to hush while he continued working. I wanted to strangle the man myself. I wanted to beat him into oblivion so he could know exactly how he'd made Clint feel all these years.

Then his father finally put his phone away.

"What's going on with my son? Will he be okay?"

Michael murmured, "Like he cares."

"Shh!" I said curtly, turning my attention back down the hallway.

"Sir, your son is going to be okay. Surgery was touch and go there for a while, but we fixed him up and he should be coming out of it at any second. This is the room he'll recover in for a while. We wanted to go ahead and get him moved so we could hook him up to the pain medication he'll need. Your son will be in a great deal of pain for a few hours."

His father sighed. "How long will he have to be here? I've got a trip planned in a couple of days I really don't want to cancel."

Michael snickered. "He's really being serious, isn't he?"

I rolled my eyes. "If you don't shut u—"

The doctor shook his head. "I'm not sure if he'll be out of here in a couple of days. Three, maybe. If things go very well. But not under forty-eight hours. Your son sustained a great deal of trauma. And, there's a criminal investigation open right now, since it's pretty clear your son was run off the road."

Clint's father's eyes fell beyond the doctor and I knew he spotted me. Even as I tried to hide behind the corner, I heard his footsteps tearing toward me. Michael grabbed my arm, pulling me down the hallway as the footsteps came around the corner. And as his voice thundered down the hallway, all eyes were on us.

"What are you doing?"

Michael froze before I slowly turned around, watching Clint's doctor appear beside his father.

"I'd like to know the same thing, actually."

I sighed. "I just wanted to know how Clint was doing."

The doctor furrowed his brow. "And you are…?"

His father snickered. "No one important."

I glared at Clint's father. "I'm his girlfriend. I'm the one that found him. You said he's going to be okay, Doctor? Like, really okay?"

Clint's father stepped up to the plate. "He needs space. From you. Because I have a feeling you got him into this mess in the first place."

I shook my head. "That isn't what happened. Those boys approached us, sir. We had nothing to do with it."

The doctor held up his hand. "This sounds like a statement for the police in the E.R. waiting room. Where the two of you should be."

"Please," I begged, "I care about Clint. Deeply. And I'm worried about him. I don't have to see him. I just want to know what all he needed work on. I know his nose was broken. I think his shoulder was dislo—"

"Back off and let us handle this. Now. Before I have you escorted out."

I snapped back. "Or you'll what? Slug me like you enjoy slugging your son?"

His father lunged at me, causing Michael to step in front of me. His father began ranting. Raving. Screaming down the hallway as the doctors and nurses held him back.

"You don't know shit about how this works! You don't know a damn thing! Get the hell out of here before I have you arrested and put in handcuffs and charged with attempted murder, you stupid little girl!"

Michael groaned. "Did you really have to spit that out?"

I pushed him away. "Maybe now someone will investigate it and arrest that man for all the things he should be thrown into jail for."

"Sir, calm down, or you'll be escorted off the premises."

"Sir, I'll have to sedate you if you don't stop."

"Get that girl out of here. She's not welcome around my son any longer!"

Tears rushed my eyes as a woman poked her head out of the recovery room. And when my eyes landed on Clint's stepmother, sorrow filled her face again. She mouthed how sorry she was to me. And for a moment, I thought maybe we understood one another.

Until someone grabbed my arm.

"You can't be back here if you're not family. I'm sorry, but romantic partners don't count. Come with me before you get into any more trouble."

I freely went with the nurse as she led me back out into the E.R. waiting room. And as Michael came up behind me, I started gathering my things. I'd lost my shoe along the way somewhere. Also, my phone. I picked it up and headed for the exit doors, not bothering to hear what Clint's father was still screaming down the hallways. People stared. Some gawked. Others eavesdropped in order to get their daily dose of gossip. I hopped out of the E.R. doors as I put my shoe on, then tucked my phone away in my bra.

As silent tears streaked my cheeks.

Michael placed his hand between my shoulder blades, silently leading me toward his car. But all I wanted to do was go and sit by Clint's bed. I couldn't stand this. I couldn't stand not knowing. What all did they have to do in surgery? How many stitches did he have? What kind of medication was he on? Would he fully recover? Would he be able to ride his bike again, if he wanted?

I needed to see him. Touch him. Place my ear against his heart and still hear it beating. I needed to know, without a shadow of a doubt, that he really was all right.

But his father wouldn't even give that to me.

I mean, what else did you expect, Rae?

Michael opened up his car door for me and helped me in. He closed the door, and I leaned my forehead against the cool glass. I let the sounds of the world fade into the background as I watched as the hospital disappeared in the rearview mirror while we drove away. I moved and weaved with the twists and turns Michael took. And after he pulled up to a drive-thru menu, his voice pierced the silence.

"You hungry?"

I shook my head, but my stomach betrayed me with a mighty growl.

"Medium Coke, large fry, and a chicken wrap?"

I shrugged. "Sure."

I didn't even bother moving to get my wallet. I knew Michael would insist he pay, so I didn't fight him. I didn't have the energy to, anyway. Part of me wanted to turn this car around and storm back into that hospital. Part of me wanted to spew everything I'd witnessed regarding Clint's father until that man was in fucking handcuffs.

The only thing that stopped me was Clint.

Because I wasn't sure if that was something he'd want me to do.

Michael paid for the food and handed me my bag. I sat up enough to reach for my drink before mindlessly sipping on it. The food stayed by my feet as he pulled into a parking space in the empty parking lot, pulling out his burger to devour.

Then I heaved a heavy sigh.

"None of this shit is fair."

Michael swallowed hard. "You just have to be patient. There's a reason why hospitals have rules like this. It's to protect the patient."

I scoffed. "And if the patient's father is an abusive dickweed?"

He shrugged. "Maybe the comment you made and how riled up his father got will prompt them to look into it. But, for right now, all you can do is hang tight and wait until Clint gets out of the hospital."

"Maybe his stepmom will reach out to me."

"By the sounds of it, she won't even be here in a couple of days."

"I mean, who's going to sign for Clint's discharge, then? Isn't that how that works?"

Michael shook his head. "At eighteen, a kid can sign for their own discharge. He's eighteen, right?"

I nodded. "He is, yeah."

"Then he'll check himself out. I guess."

"Such bullshit."

"I know. But you can't get so upset and frustrated over things you can't change. It is what it is, and even though it isn't good, it's also not in your control."

"And what was that thing about the doctor saying something about me talking to the police?"

"Oh, you were pretty out of it when we walked out of the E.R. When the police need your statement, they'll find you."

I sighed. "Great."

I didn't have the stomach to eat. Michael, however, inhaled his food. I wasn't even sure he tasted it. And as he backed out of the parking space, I clutched the food between my feet. My mom hadn't called me once. Not a single time to figure out where in the world I'd gotten off to. Which meant I was most certainly heading back to a house with D.J. in it. Michael made his way back to the school. And with each turn he made, I felt myself growing sicker and sicker in my stomach. Sipping on the Coke didn't help. Smelling the greasy food on the floorboard of his car didn't help, either.

"Stop the car."

Michael slammed on the brakes. "What? What's wrong?"

And as worry took hold, I threw open his SUV door. I leaned out, heaving in the middle of the road as we sat there in front of the high school.

Letting my body finally career itself out of control as my stomach leapt into my throat.

6

CLINTON

The question hung heavily in the room as Cecilia smoothed her thumb over my skin. I didn't know what day it was. What time it was. I felt disoriented. Drugged. And all I wanted to do was sleep.

Cecilia squeezed my hand. "Keep those eyes open."

"Then tell me where Dad is."

She sighed. "He stepped out for a little bit. Just... needed some air."

I snickered. "You're a terrible liar."

She giggled. "That obvious?"

I lobbed my eyes over to take her in. Even though I couldn't move my neck.

"I don't think I've ever heard you laugh."

She sighed. "To be honest, I don't do much of it nowadays, unless I'm with friends."

"Then why stay?"

"Hmmm?"

"If you aren't laughing, then you aren't happy. And if you aren't happy, then why are you still here?"

She shrugged. "I guess because it's familiar. Because I do love your father. And because I do love you."

"You don't have to tell me what I want to hear, Cecilia. Just tell me the truth."

"Why is that so hard for you to accept as truth?"

My eyes gravitated back toward the ceiling. The rush of warmth was gone, leaving me shivering, even though I was covered in blankets. Cecilia stood up, tucking the blankets along my legs as she spoke with the nurses. My eyes finally slid closed as their voices wafted around me. I felt Cecilia patting my leg, forcing me to stay awake through it all this time. Part of it was endearing, and part of it was annoying as fuck.

Then, once the nurses left the room, she sighed.

"Just tell me where Dad is. Because all you're really doing is confirming what I already know."

She sighed. "He's stepped out to make a few business calls."

I snickered. "Of course he has."

"Your father works hard. He's got four different businesses under his belt. Three of which are booming right now. He's got a lot on his—"

"I know, I know. His businesses are important. It's to provide the life I've got now. That's why he travels so much, because he loves me enough to provide for me. His love equates to money, and all that bullshit. You can spare me the lecture. I already know it."

"He does love you, Clint."

"Well, he's got a shit way of showing it."

My flat tone blanketed the room as Cecilia sat back down. I chewed on the inside of my lip as I lay there, practically trapped in this damn hospital bed. I didn't know when the hell I was getting out of here, but I had a feeling Dad wouldn't even be around to help me with it. At this point, I was more prone to the idea of my stepmother staying behind and helping rather than my own father.

Who I hated even calling 'Dad' at this point.

I sighed. "That man is a basket case."

Cecilia snickered. "I know."

"Then why the hell did you marry him?"

She shrugged. "Because he made me laugh. He made me feel special. It was easy to fall in love with him, though sometimes I wonder if I ended up falling in love with someone more like my own father."

I paused. "What do you mean?"

"Ah, we don't have to get into all that. Right now, we need to focus on—"

"Cecilia."

My curt tone shocked her into silence, and I heard why. I sounded like my father. My voice filled the room like my father. I closed my eyes, trying to swallow down the taste of my father's voice within my own.

"I'm sorry."

She took my hand. "It's okay."

I shook my head, ignoring the dull pain I still felt. "It's not."

"You just wanted me to—"

"I sounded just like him, and that's not okay.

Because my father isn't an okay kind of man. You and I both know this."

Damn it, I wished I could fucking look at the woman. To read her face. To look in her eyes. To let her know she wasn't alone in all this.

I licked my lips. "What do you mean, he's like your father?"

Cecilia paused. "I'm not sure if I should really be talking about something like that with you."

"Why? Because Dad told you not to? Or because you don't want to?"

And when she fell silent, I knew the reason why.

"Don't let Dad be that control freak with you, okay? He gets it enough with me," I said.

She squeezed my hand. "Your father can be a bit off the wall, can't he?"

I snickered. "That's one way to describe it."

"My father was a bit off the wall, too."

"How so?"

"Oh, you know. Randomly yelling over things. Never quite sticking to the rules he set out. One day, my sisters and I couldn't wear dresses that came above our knees. And the next day, it was full-length dresses only. No boys' eyes should be on us. And if they were, it was somehow our fault."

"Yikes."

She giggled bitterly. "Yeah. It was a very traditional household. The women kept their heads down. Dressed modestly. Head to toe, if Dad preferred it that way. No makeup. No jewelry. No hair products. My father didn't believe in those kinds of things. Material possessions and all that."

"Were you raised Amish or something?"

Then the giggle was real. "We might as well have been. Though that still might be an insult to the Amish people as a whole."

And that comment made me chuckle.

I squeezed her hand as the awkward conversation slowly started to flow. And in the back of my mind, I wondered why I hadn't taken the time to talk with Cecilia sooner than this. I mean, she and my father had been married for a few years. And in those years, there were things about her I'd never known. Like her laugh. Her bright smile. The way her touch felt against my own. I didn't know these things about her and she was my fucking stepmother.

Cecilia's sniffing ripped me from my mind.

"What's wrong?"

She swallowed hard. "I tried convincing your father to stay. I really did."

I paused. "He's not even at the hospital right now, is he?"

"I mean, I don't know for sure. But I do know your father. And it's been well over an hour since he's come back to the room."

"Yep. He's left for his office or something."

"I'm so sorry, Clint. I told him to put that damn phone away and pay attention to what was happening. Be present. But he just gets worse and worse with that work stuff of his."

"Cecilia, I hate to break it to you, but he's always

been that way. There's no 'it' getting worse. It's just you figuring out that this isn't behavior that'll change."

She sighed. "I suppose you're right."

I paused. "Are you okay?"

She snickered. "I believe that's the question I should be asking you."

"Doesn't mean I can't ask you."

"You know, I don't know how to answer that question. I mean, your father and I have been together since you were fourteen years old. And now you're lying in this hospital and I'm sitting here holding your hand and I realize I don't know a thing about you."

The silence that followed that admission was deafening. Because she was right. She didn't know anything about me, and I sure as hell didn't know anything about her. I tugged her hand, pulling her up from her seat as she sat down on the edge of the bed. She leaned over me, placing one hand on one side of my body as I continued holding the one in my hand I already had.

"All right. Good to know," I said.

She furrowed her brow. "What?"

I snickered. "Your eyes. I didn't even know they were hazel."

"We're a sad bunch, aren't we?"

I shrugged. "We do the best we can."

Tears rushed her eyes. "I really did beg for him to stay."

"It's fine. I know the kind of man my father is. There's no use in begging with him, either. At least do yourself a favor and keep your dignity."

"There are so many times where I should have—"

"It's okay. There's no use dwelling on the past, either."

She wiped her tears away. "Again, isn't this the kind of thing I should be telling you?"

"Eh, I'm sure we'll get there."

That made her smile. Which made me smile. And slowly, the burden of the hospital room lifted from my shoulders. The two of us talked for a little bit. I found out more about her home life as a child. How drastically different it had been from mine. And yet, how similar our own fathers were. I told her about my mother. Every question she asked, I answered. Including why my leather jacket was so important to me. For the first time in years, we opened up to one another. Learned more about one another. And the more I learned, the more I wondered how the hell my pathetic excuse for a father had snagged such a bright, beautiful, candid woman for a second wife.

"You're way too good for my dad."

She giggled. "Maybe so. But he does have a softer side."

I rolled my eyes. "I'm sure he does."

"I know that sounds cliché and trite, but he does. At least, he did. I see it sometimes when we're on vacation."

"Well, tell him to send some of that softness my way. I could use some of it."

We stared at one another and my eyes lingered on her face. Her hazel eyes stared back at me from a full face of makeup that seemed almost luminescent. She didn't have a wrinkle on her face, courtesy of the botox

I was sure Dad pumped into her skin. Her fake breasts were sky high, propped underneath her chin without any sort of effort. Her hair was pulled back in a modest fashion. Probably a habit she hadn't broken from her childhood. And as I lay there, studying her, I realized something.

She reminded me a bit of Mom.

Guess Dad has a type.

"Do you need anything?"

Cecilia's voice filled my mind and I shook my head.

"Nah. I'm good for now. Though I'd really like to see——"

A knock on the door interrupted my sentence, and I hoped it was Rae. Cecilia slid off the edge of the bed, whipping around to see who it was. I knew she wanted it to be Dad. While I wished it to be Rae. But instead, we were both disappointed as a man in a white coat came strolling in the door with a clipboard underneath his armpit.

My heart sank as he walked toward us. And I had a feeling Cecilia's heart was doing the same thing.

"Hey, Doc," I said.

Cecilia sat back down, quickly falling into 'her place.' She got out of the way of the man, making herself as small as possible as the doctor came to stand at my side. He silently checked my tubing. My I.V. My morphine drip. A few other things, before finally standing upright. I saw his eyes lingering on Cecilia for just a few seconds longer than was appropriate. Then he turned his attention back to me.

"All right. Since you've had an evening to rest and

recuperate out of surgery, I think it's time we discuss what you're looking at in terms of your recovery."

I nodded. "Fair enough. How long do you think I'll be in the hospital?"

The doctor peeked back at Cecilia before answering. "Three days, at least. But the nurses have examined you all through the night and you seem very stable. If today goes well and we don't run into any issues, you'll be transferred out of ICU and into a regular room."

Cecilia sighed. "Thank the Lord."

"But your recovery is going to be daunting. You'll be on pain medication for a while. And there are police officers who are clamoring out here to speak with you once you're able to recall your side of events from last night."

I nodded. "You can send them in once we're done talking."

The doctor paused. "Do you want to wait for your father?"

Cecilia stood up before coming to my side. She found her voice as she reached for my hand, cradling it within hers. She looked that doctor straight in his eyes, even though I felt her hand trembling with nerves. Finding her place beside me when Dad should have been there himself.

"I'm here, and whatever you tell me I can relay to my husband," she said.

And damn it, I was proud of her for finding her voice.

7

RAELYNN

After I got sick on the side of the road, Michael made the executive decision to keep driving around. And I was thankful for it, because I couldn't go into my house like that. I'd still been too shaken up to deal with being alone. For all I knew, I'd walk right in on Mom and D.J. in the living room, and I'd erupt. Just completely unload all the stress and anxiety and worry on my shoulders off onto them. And they didn't deserve that.

I mean, D.J. did. But not Mom.

We drove around and Michael made me eat my food. Despite the fact that I was convinced it might make me sicker, he convinced me otherwise. And again, he'd been right. The saltiness of the fries settled my nausea, and eating the chicken wrap leveled out my blood sugar. For the most part, my trembling stopped. The shaking in my hands ceased. Some of the nausea in my stomach abated, giving me a bit of rest.

Then Michael drove me out to that park.

We sat there on the bench where Clint and I had sat a few weeks back. A few weeks. Holy shit, it felt like a few months. A few years. I ran my fingers through my hair and kept sighing. I gazed off at that bright star between the trees, wondering if Clint was all right. And the entire time, Michael stayed by my side. Even though Allison bombarded him with phone calls. Even though she begged him to tell her what was happening. He didn't tell her, and he didn't leave my side.

Which pushed even more tears down my face.

I cried on Michael's shoulder as we sat in that park. I ranted his ear off as I paced around in front of him. I regaled him with how Clint had found me out here. How much I wanted to shove his face into the dirt before he opened up randomly about his home life. Prompting me to talk about mine. I kept telling him story after story. How we made it back to Clint's house. What happened. How he made me feel. I spilled it all out to Michael and he listened while nodding his head, drinking it all in.

And not once did he criticize me for it.

As the remnants of the sun began blossoming over the tops of the trees, Michael finally took me home. I was shocked when I didn't see D.J.'s car in the drive-way. But it didn't matter. Nothing mattered, at all. Nothing except Clint's health and happiness. His healing and what he'd have to do for his recovery time.

"See you at school?"

Michael's voice pulled me from my trance, but I shook my head.

"Not if I can help it."

I gathered up my garbage and slid out of his car. I closed the door behind me, listening as he backed out of my driveway. I'd have to find a way to thank him later. But not now. Right now, I couldn't focus on anything else. Especially after I threw my trash away in the trash can out front.

Because the second my hands came into view, I saw I still had Clint's blood on me.

"Shit."

I unlocked the front door and pushed my way inside. I closed it behind me, leaning my forehead against it. A sound pacing down the hallway made me jump. The footsteps grew closer, then they grew frantic. I whipped around, watching my mother rush me. Watching her robe flutter behind her with her hair wild and maniacal around the crown of her head.

Then her eyes fell to my clothes.

"What the—? Rae, where the hell have you been? Are you all right? What are you—is this your blood!?"

She ran toward me, her slippers sliding across the floor as she took my hands within hers. She tugged me into the kitchen, murmuring to herself in Spanish as she sat me down at the kitchen table. Her hands ran over me, checking for wounds or gashes. Anything to explain the blood I'd completely forgotten I was covered in.

"It's not mine," I whispered.

Mom paused. "Then whose is it? Where have you been? I've been up all night, worried sick about you."

I nodded slowly. "I'm sorry."

She pulled up a chair. "Rae, look at me."

I slowly turned my head to find her eyes, but I didn't try holding back my tears. Mom wiped them off my face, brushing away more crusted blood as she grimaced to herself.

"Talk to me, princess. What's going on?"

My lower lip quivered. "He's so hurt, Mom. He's in the hospital, and I can't know anything."

"Who's hurt? Michael?"

"No."

"Allison?"

I shook my head. "Clint."

She paused. "That the boy from school you talked to me about?"

I nodded. "We—it—happened so fast, Mom."

"Are you hurt, Raelynn?"

"I wish I was, instead of him."

"Oh, sweetheart."

She wrapped her arms around me and I sobbed against her. I heard myself wailing. I felt my chest heaving. It was almost like an out of body experience. My heart fluttered so wildly I thought I'd burst out from my chest and take off toward the rising sun. My legs locked up, shaking and trembling as my stomach slammed against my ribcage. It felt like my entire body was rebelling. Fighting back after years of being caged.

I shook against Mom, soaking her robe with tears as she stroked my back.

"I'm right here. It's okay. It's going to be okay."

"They ran him off the road, Mom. They wanted to kill him."

"Who did, sweetheart? Who wanted to kill him?"

"Those dumbass drunk boys!"

I shrieked it so loudly that Mom clung to me tighter. She stood up, pulling me against her as she slowly moved us from the kitchen to the living room. We fell to the couch and she pulled me into her lap, cradling me the way she used to do when I was a small girl.

She kissed the side of my head. "Tell me what happened."

I shook my head. "I can't—can't—can't ta—"

"Sh-sh-sh-sh-sh. It's okay. Deep breaths for me, princess. In through your nose, out through your mouth. Okay? Like this?"

I tried to do as Mom asked, but my breathing was choppy. Weak. I couldn't breathe out as much as she was and I had a hard time drawing in air. But she worked me through it. She counted softly in my ear as I sank against her. Sank into the warmth and comfort I'd always remembered about my mother. My tears slowly dried and my body quietly calmed down. And after a few minutes, my breathing evened out.

"There's a good girl. That's my princess. I'm right here, sweetheart. I'm not going anywhere."

I sniffled. "Clint came to hang out with me after work last night. He wanted to hang out before bringing me home on his bike."

She nodded. "Sounds like a good enough plan. What happened?"

I sighed. "Four boys drove up to us in some car. It was obvious they were drunk, too. A couple of the guys

Clint knew from a fight that happened at school a couple days back or so. I don't know. I can't really remember the timeline anymore."

"It's okay. You can talk about whatever you want."

"It all happened so fast. It's such a blur. I just—they kept saying things to me. Looking at me. Licking their lips at me. Clint got them angry with him so they'd leave me alone. He told me to run, and I did. I hopped the fence to the elementary school playground and he took off on his bike."

"My God, princess."

"Next thing I know, I'm calling Michael to come get me. Calling 9-1-1 and telling them they have to get out there. We're driving up and down roads with tires squealing in the distance. And then we come upon Clint's bike."

I felt my voice catching in my throat as Mom tucked my head into the crook of her neck.

"Where was his bike?"

My chest jumped. "Crushed into the metal railing of a bridge. Momma, he fell into the river. Twenty feet, down onto the bank. It was terrible, Mom. He looked absolutely mangled. He stopped breathing. There was water. Michael kept screaming at me. There were sirens and I kept calling out his name, trying to get him to wake up. I just couldn't leave him down there like that, Mom. I couldn't let him be alone. Please don't be mad at me. Please."

"I could never be mad at you. Ever. I'm just so thankful you're okay."

"Please don't be mad. Please. Please, Mom. Please."

I cried into her, wrapping my arms around her neck. I clung to her tighter than I could ever remember, and she rocked me side to side. I heard her singing a song in my ear. A Spanish lullaby she'd always sung to me as a little girl. It calmed my soul and soothed my fears, quieting down my tears.

Then a knock came at the door.

"Raelynn Cleaver?"

The man's voice stunned both my mother and myself. Until it dawned on me.

The police.

The knock came again and Mom stood up with me. I slid to her side, walking with her toward the door as she cracked it open. I peeked around the corner with my tear-stained cheeks, studying the two officers standing on our porch.

Wow, Michael really wasn't joking.

"Can I help you?" Mom asked.

They brandished their badges. "I'm Officer Talbot. This here is Officer Williams. We need to speak with your daughter about an incident last night. A motorcycle wreck, supposedly involving a car full of boys?"

I piped up. "Not supposedly."

Mom held her hand up, signaling for me to be quiet.

"You are more than welcome to come inside and sit. I can make us some coffee. But before you speak with my daughter, she's going to get herself a hot shower."

The officer sighed. "Ma'am, I'm afraid this is urgent."

Mom stood her ground. "Well, so is her shower. She's covered in blood and still shaking from trauma. You can take it, or you can leave it. But if you take it, it comes with coffee, courtesy of me."

She held the door open, waiting for the officers to choose.

"Either way, I'm going to go run my daughter a hot shower before placing a call to her school. She's in no condition to go to classes today. Give us thirty minutes, and we'll be with you. Or find another time. I'm good either way."

And as my mother stood there, stronger than I'd ever seen her, I leaned my forehead against her shoulder. I kissed her robe, hoping she felt it through her clothing. Her hand came up, running through my hair as the officers murmured between themselves.

"All right, ma'am. We'd enjoy the cup of coffee."

Mom smiled. "Great. Let me get my daughter in a shower, then I'll brew a pot while placing that quick phone call."

8

CLINTON

"I already pushed back the trip, Cecilia. Just what exactly do you expect me to do about it?"

"I expect you to cancel it, Howard. Because your son is going to need you in the coming weeks."

I felt myself waking up, but I didn't open my eyes. The second I heard their voices, I stayed silent. I kept my breathing even. I wanted to listen in on their conversation. On what they were arguing about. And as their hushed whispers grew to faint growls, I wondered if my father would ever give a shit about me.

"I'm not canceling anything, Cecilia. This meeting is too important."

She scoffed. "Then do it via video conference. From your laptop, or your home office. My God, Howard, you've got one but you never use it."

"Because I have to be there in person. I'm the owner of the damn thing. I can't just not show up to a meeting everyone is expecting me to be at."

"Well, when you tell them your only child has gotten himself into a life-threatening accident. I'm sure they'll change their tune."

He snickered. "CeCe, we don't know the details of that crash. The police are still trying to sniff things out. For all we know, this was Clinton's fault!"

"And why does that matter?" she hissed.

"It matters because if he put himself in this situation, he can get himself out of it. It one hundred percent matters, if you knew anything about raising a boy like him!"

"So you think that even if he did cause this accident, he wouldn't need his father? Howard, he's staring down the barrel of weeks of physical therapy. Weeks of strenuous activity before he's walking normal and riding his bike and moving without assistance. He needs you at home. He's a boy, Howard."

"He's my boy, and don't you forget it. I know what I need to do in order to parent my son, Cecilia. You, of all people, don't need to educate me on that."

"Then step up and be the father he needs."

I waited for it. I braced for the cracking sound of his hand against her face. I mean, I knew it was coming. It would have been coming had I said something like that to him. Cecilia was brave. Braver than I could have ever been. I was proud of her for standing up for what she believed. And honored that she was standing up for me.

But I heard the door of my hospital room whip open, stalling out the moment in its tracks.

"Take it outside, if you have to fight. Clint needs his rest, and I won't have you two ruining it with your bickering. Understand?"

The doctor's voice was curt. Pierced. And I would have given anything to see my father's face. The argument halted in its tracks before Cecilia apologized. But all I heard from my father was the lumbering of footsteps, murmuring and stumbling. Cursing. I heard the clicking of Cecilia's heels as they left the room.

"Howard. Get back here!"

I let my eyes fall open as I stared at the ceiling. The doctor walked around me, checking vitals and shining that godforsaken light in my eyes. I wanted to rip that damn flashlight out of his hand and bash him over the head with it. Or shove it up his ass. One of the two.

"The talk with the police wear you out?"

I shrugged. "Got it over with."

"Sometimes that's the best course of action."

"What day is it?"

He chuckled. "Still Friday. Just after lunch. Almost two, I think? Have you eaten?"

"No."

"Well, I'll get the nurse to run down to the kitchen. The lunch trays have already gone by, but I'm sure she can pick you up something that is suitable for your current diet."

I sighed. "Ah, yes. The boring, no fun foods diet."

He snickered. "I've been on that diet before. It's more or less so nothing interacts with the medications you're on. Like food dyes and such."

"Just don't have anyone attempt to mix up white rice and a banana again. I don't know who decided that was a good thing, but it isn't."

The doctor took a few notes, then pressed my morphine button. I was on my last pump of it. After today, no more morphine. I wasn't sure how I'd take that. How my body would react to it. Or what kind of pain I'd be in. But any step down was a step closer to home. And a step closer to Rae.

Which was where I wanted to be.

I heard the doctor talking to Cecilia outside. But I didn't hear my father. No shocker there, of course. He probably stormed off and used this fight as an excuse to get more work done. And if it was up to me? He'd stay gone. He didn't help. He wasn't supportive. And, apparently, this accident was all my fault. At the very least, I didn't deserve an ounce of pity until it was proven that I didn't cause my almost-death.

He could fuck off with all that bullshit.

"Clint? Can you hear me?"

I nodded as I cleared my throat. Cecilia sat down beside me again, taking my hand like she had this morning.

"Dad's gone again, isn't he?"

"You know how he is."

I snickered. "Yeah, yeah. I know how he is."

That seemed to be the excuse for my father more days than not nowadays.

"How are you feeling, Clint?"

I sighed. "Better. But the doctor also just pressed my morphine button, so…"

"I was on morphine once, you know. A little ball drip thing fastened around my waist in a fanny pack."

"That when you got your boobs done?"

I didn't catch the question before it flew out of my mouth. But I was kind of glad I didn't. Because it launched Cecilia into another story of her life I would have never expected from her.

"Actually, yes. It was a reconstructive surgery I got when I was twenty. Saved up almost my entire life for it."

I paused. "Reconstructive surgery?"

She giggled. "Yep. I left home when I was seventeen, after graduating high school early. And in between part-time classes at the local community college, I took on a job. Saved up as much as I could while living with three other girls in a two-bedroom apartment to save up enough money to have it corrected. And boy, was that a surgery."

"What was the defect?"

"Its technical name is 'tubular hypoplasia,' or something like that. It essentially means the base of a woman's breast is much narrower than it should be, causing a tissue deformity and nipple malformation during puberty."

"So much more than I ever needed to know about my stepmom."

"And yet, here we are."

The two of us laughed softly before she patted my arm.

"Hell of a surgery. Nine hours under, lots of sawing and suctioning and tugging about. And when I came out of it in recovery, I had this compression bra on and a fanny pack of morphine around my waist with tubes running into the tops of my chest."

"Yikes."

"Yep. I still don't remember those first two weeks of recuperation. Because morphine wasn't the only drug I was on during that recovery time."

I smiled. "Holy shit. I don't blame you on that one, then. This morphine's got me fucked up enough as it is."

"You know, part of me wants to tell you 'language.' But, here I am. Cursing up a storm along with you."

It almost felt surreal. Like this was simply another dream. The shy, timid, soft-spoken stepmother I'd become accustomed to was anything but. And it made me wonder why the absolute fuck she'd settled for someone like my father. Then again, I knew why. We both knew why. She'd grown up in a life of conservatism. And my father, well, wasn't. He gave her all the things she wanted. And even things she didn't want. That would be attractive to any woman. Even a woman with her head seemingly screwed on straight.

Money talked nowadays.

"So, weeks of physical therapy?"

She paused. "You heard that?"

I shrugged. "Bits and pieces. I was still waking up and falling back asleep."

"You're a shit liar, you know."

That made me laugh hard. "All right. All right. You caught me."

"I'm sorry, Clint."

"Don't be. You stuck up for me. No one's ever done that before."

"I should've started doing it sooner."

"Well, something tells me you've at least been trying."

"I'll get him to stay behind, though. Don't worry."

"At this point, I'd rather him go."

She paused. "Really?"

I nodded. "He's useless during shit like this. In his mind, this is my fault. So the medical bill will be my fault. For all I know, since I'm eighteen, he'll write me up some sort of an official loan document and expect me to pay him back for it. Either that, or he'll feel guilty after the fact and buy me a new bike to try and make things better."

"I'm sorry, Clint."

"Not your fault, Cecilia."

As I lay there, holding her hand within mine, I felt the crushing weight of an unwanted burden settle against my chest. I closed my eyes, hoping sleep would sweep me underneath its warm current again and rid me of the insanity of my mind. What in the world had I done to make my father hate me so much? Why couldn't he just love me? Accept me? I mean, I was his only child. It wasn't as if there was another child to play 'favorites' with.

Did he just not want me?

Had he ever wanted me?

"I'll be here with you, okay?"

Cecilia's voice pierced my thoughts, and my next question flew out faster than I could even process it.

"But why? You don't owe me anything. And I'm pretty sure you don't love Dad. So, you aren't sticking around for him."

And after a beat of silence, she sighed.

"I'll be here because I want to be here. And you'll just have to deal with it."

She didn't comment on my other insinuation. On the other comment I'd made. And I couldn't blame her.

I mean, how the hell could she love a man like that?

"I feel tired."

"Then get some rest. I've got a book I'm reading, and I'll let you know what the doctor says—if anything —once you wake back up."

I sighed. "What are you reading?"

She held up the book in front of my face. "Finding The Spouse You Married."

I would have laughed had my heart not randomly started aching for her. This beautiful woman, full of love and interesting stories and lessons to pass on, was reading some bullshit self-help book on how to make my dad treat her the way she wanted to be treated. It was sickening, and yet very telling of what my mother must've gone through with Dad.

I wondered if she'd ever tried reading books to fix what had become so broken.

"Want me to read you a page? The anecdotal stories are pretty funny."

I smiled, closing my eyes. "Sure. Go ahead."

"All right. This particular chapter is about getting the two spouses on the same page. Listen to this. There are two people in the story, Mary Margaret and James. And I'll let the story tell the rest."

I settled into bed as she launched into this story. A ridiculous story of some imaginary married couple that had drifted apart because James thought he wasn't getting enough sex. And Mary Margaret thought James had gotten lazy about sex. I chuckled as Cecilia giggled through the story, and before she could wrap it up the two of us fell apart in laughter. The story was so ridiculous, and had almost nothing to do with them getting on the same page. I mean, I'm sure it did, eventually. But Cecilia and I were laughing so hard we couldn't actually get to that part.

"It's so ridiculous. I still can't finish this chapter because of the story."

My chest jumped with laughter. "How the hell can you read shit like that?"

Cecilia kept giggling. "I don't know. It's so insane. And all the stories are like that. I guess I just…"

Her sentence trailed off and I coughed, trying to calm down my laughter. Because hers had shut down, like someone had flipped a switch inside her head.

"You just what?" I asked.

She sighed. "I guess I'm just desperate to get back the man I married, I guess. And maybe, if I read enough of these books, the answer will jump out at me and I can fix what's been so very broken for so long."

And in that moment, I didn't know which I hated

more: my father, for putting her in this position, or the damn author of that book, for preying on women like her and draining them of their money, only to feed them shit I could sum up with one sentence.

It can't be fixed if the other person doesn't feel like they need fixing.

9

RAELYNN

"Why don't you come make brownies with me? We can have them for after dinner tonight."

"Want to try our hand at making fresh ice cream to go with them?"

"Let's go out to eat tonight. Come back to the brownies and have a movie night."

"Want to put on pajamas, too? We could go out to eat in our pajamas."

I knew my mother was trying the best she could to cheer me up. To get my mind off things. But all day yesterday had spiraled into my Saturday, and I still sat up in my room. By the window. Hoping someone might come over and give me information on how Clint was doing. His father, even if he yelled it at me. His stepmother, even if I had to pull it out of her. Hell, even the police officers, even if they had more questions for me to answer.

I'd take any update I could get.

I sighed, gazing out over the dirt we had for a front lawn. The rain drizzled down, creating a sheen of mist over everything as clouds rolled above. The sun hadn't peeked through once. So, apparently, it and I were on the same wavelength. The weather matched my mood perfectly, and I found myself brooding at my windowsill.

Until a knock came at my door.

"Hey there, sweetie."

I sighed. "Hey, Mom."

"I brought you some lunch. Leftovers from last night."

"Thanks."

"You mind if I eat in here with you? The bread-sticks look tempting."

"You can have them, if you want."

I heard her sit on my bed, but I didn't move. I wasn't hungry. Even though eggplant parmesan was my favorite. I wanted to be at the hospital with Clint. By his side, assuring him I'd be there for him. I'd made him a promise. I'd told him I wouldn't leave his side. And yet I couldn't get past his fucking father.

At Clint's side was the only place I wanted to be.

And his father didn't give a shit about that.

Mom cleared her throat. "You sure you're not hungry?"

I nodded. "I'm sure."

"You want to come downstairs and watch Judge Judy with me?"

"Maybe later."

"It'll give you a chance to yell at the television for a while."

I shrugged. "Not really in a yelling mood."

She sighed. "Sweetheart, I know you're worried about him. But——"

"Mom, please. I just…"

I heard her stand up before her hand came down against my back. I closed my eyes, feeling my empty tear ducts try to churn out more salted tears. But there were no more for me to cry. My pillow had soaked all of them up last night. They burned without recompense as Mom rubbed my back, trying her best to continue distracting me.

I was tired of the distractions, though.

I wanted to know how Clint was doing.

"I made him a promise."

"I know you did, sweetie."

I sighed. "And I'm not there, like I promised."

"I'm sure he's a smart boy and has figured out why you aren't there. Especially if he doesn't have a good relationship with his father."

"I just don't get it. All I want to do is be there, and his father's being a——"

Mom sat down, wrapping her arms around me. She pulled me against her and I felt my frustration growing. The more I thought about it, the angrier I became. I mean, why they fuck did his dad have to be such an absolute asshole? I'd confided in Mom with just about everything. The first time I ever met his father. What he did. The bruises Clint came to school with. The life he really led with his father behind those massive mansion doors.

Her party tricks were wearing thin as my worry for Clint grew.

"Maybe he's not at the hospital anymore," I murmured.

Mom kissed the top of my head. "At any rate, it's best if you stay here and wait for an update. The last thing you need to be doing is storming in there and getting yourself into trouble. Especially after already dealing with the police."

"It wasn't his fault, Mom."

"And I believe you. But, until things cool down, you know I'm right."

I hated that fact, too.

The doorbell rang downstairs and I scoffed. I didn't give a shit who it was, but I wanted them to leave. Mom kissed me one more time, then ventured downstairs. I heard her whistling to herself, like the sunshine poured out of her ass in that very moment. I rolled my eyes. I hunkered back down by the windowsill and watched the misty rainfall coat my window.

Until I heard familiar voices racing up the stairs.

"Hey! Girlie!"

"Your mom said you're up here!"

"Get dressed, we're heading out."

I whipped around at the sound of Allison and Michael's voices. They barged into my room, all smiles and dressed to the nines. Well, not really. But Michael stood there in a pair of khaki pants with a polo shirt tucked in and Allison was in one of her bright ensembles.

I furrowed my brow. "What are you guys doing here?"

Allison rolled her eyes. "Does that matter? Come on. Get cleaned up. We're heading out."

I stood. "Where are we going?"

Michael grinned. "Pretty sure there's someone in a hospital waiting to see you."

My eyes bulged before I started rushing around my room. I threw clothes around while Allison giggled at me, then I stumbled out of my pajamas. I heard Michael leave the room, leaving me to undress as Allison tossed me my clothes. And after I'd pulled on a fresh pair of jeans and a T-shirt, I rushed to the bathroom.

"Give me five minutes!"

I brushed my teeth and splashed some water in my face. I ran a brush through my hair before piling it on top of my head in a bun. I grabbed my chapstick and charged out of the bedroom, tucking it into my back pocket.

I found Allison and Michael at the bottom of the steps with my cell phone.

"Ready to go?" he asked.

I leapt down the steps, taking my phone from him. And as I tucked it away in my bra, I looked over at my mother. She smiled at me, blowing me a kiss as I stood there with my two best friends. My heart went out to her. I rushed over to her, giving her a massive hug before I pressed a kiss against her cheek.

"I love you," I whispered.

She patted my back. "I love you, too. Now, get going. I want to know how that boy's doing, too."

We rushed out toward Michael's car and hopped in. I crawled in back, anxious to get out of this driveway and on the road. I knew Mom had called Michael and Allison. Probably to try and pull me out of my funk.

But had she called the hospital as well?

I licked my lips. "Does anyone at the hospital know we're coming?"

Michael shrugged. "Does it matter? They can't expect you to just sit on your hands and wait without hearing a word. You were at the crash site."

Allison nodded. "It's absolutely ridiculous. You saved him. You're the one that found him. You deserve to know what's going on with him."

"He's got a bastard of a father, but that shouldn't stop him from updating you on his son's condition."

"If anything, he should be thanking you. Because you're the reason Clint is still alive."

I nodded slowly. "Thank you guys so much."

Allison reached back, taking my hand. "That's what friends are for."

I sniffled. "I take it Michael filled you in?"

She nodded. "On everything. Especially once you didn't show up at school yesterday."

"I'm sorry I didn't tell you. I just—"

She squeezed my hand. "No need to apologize, crazytown. I'm not upset. I'm just glad you guys are okay."

"Even Clint?"

Michael nodded. "Even Clint."

Allison had the bright idea of picking up fast food and sneaking it into the hospital for Clint. Which shocked me, because that was something she'd do for me. Was it possible they were finally considering Clint part of our group? A friend, even? I hoped so, in the pit of my soul. Allison stuffed the food into her purse after we were done eating, and even managed to prop up a soda in one of her pockets so it wouldn't tip over.

And after sneaking through the hospital corridors, we finally found Clint's room.

"Holy sh—"

I held up my hand, stopping Michael's sentence in its tracks. Clint was fast asleep, and no one was in his room. This couldn't have been planned any better. My eyes ran along him as I slowly walked into his room. His ICU room.

"Oh, Clint," I whispered.

I walked over to his bedside with my hands trembling. He was in rough shape. Even rougher than I remembered. Both of his eyes were blackened, along with his jaw. His nose had been set, so he had a brace around it, taped down to his face, which had red marks where it wasn't bruised. He had his right arm in a sling, and his neck was braced. Unable to move. He had tubes running in and out of his nose. In and out of his hands. His arms. Even from underneath the covers.

My lip quivered as I sat in a chair beside his bed.

I reached out for his hand, placing mine against his. I settled it softly, feeling how cold he was to the touch. The second I touched him, his eyes popped open. I yanked my hand back, but only partially. Because he moved with lightning speed, wrapping his hand around my wrist.

"Rae?"

I looked over at Michael and Allison as they stood at the foot of his bed, beckoning for me to talk to the boy.

"I can't move my neck. Please tell me that's you."

Tears rushed my eyes as I stood up. I slowly maneuvered myself into his view, listening as he breathed a sigh of relief. I sniffled and smiled, gazing into his bloodshot eyes.

"Hey there."

He grinned. "Hello, beautiful."

His fingers slipped between mine, our hands lacing themselves together. I wiped at my tears with my free hand as I sat on the edge of his bed. My eyes kept dancing over him. I knew there were probably injuries I couldn't see. And, as if he'd read my mind, he began rattling them off to me.

"I've got a concussion, too. Which is why my neck is braced like this."

I nodded slowly. "What else?"

He sighed. "Well, I broke my collarbone. Which didn't help my dislocated shoulder. My ribs are pretty bruised. But not broken, miraculously."

"Yeah."

"There was minor internal bleeding, though. They found it during surgery. I've got some stitches in places no one should have stitches. But it is what it is. If I have a good day today, I get moved out of ICU. They say the concussion is almost gone. So at least it wasn't a bad one."

"Oh, Clint."

Michael walked up beside me. "Jesus, man, you look rough."

Clint looked surprised, but didn't skip a beat. "I'd say I've had worse. But that would actually be a lie."

Allison walked around to his other side. "Can we get you anything?"

I smiled. "Are you able to eat?"

Michael nodded. "Because we brought you a burger and fries from a joint up the road."

Allison started pulling the food out. "With a Mountain Dew. Rae said it's your favorite."

Clint smiled. "That's my girl."

And my heart soared with delight.

Allison handed him the food as I navigated the controls for his hospital bed. I got him sitting up without moving his neck too much, then he took everything over. He seemed happy to see us. Having Allison and Michael with me didn't kick up too much tension. I kept smiling while Clint talked. While he chewed. While he swallowed. So many small things about him I'd taken for granted. Things no one ever thinks about enjoying on another person.

Until there's a fear of no longer having those things.

Michael cleared his throat. "Well, Allison and I should probably go stand guard."

Allison nodded. "Yeah. In case your parents come back."

Clint furrowed his brow. "My parents?"

I leaned in. "They don't exactly know we're here."

His eyes darkened. "What did my father say to you?"

I sighed. "We can talk about that later, okay? I promise I'll tell you why I haven't been here. I just wanted you to know I hadn't abandoned you. If I could have gotten to you, I would have."

He brought my hands to his lips to kiss. "I know. I know you would have. I know you better than that."

And as my two best friends slipped out into the hallway, I sighed at the touch of his lips against my skin.

A touch I hadn't been sure I'd ever feel again, thanks to the events of Thursday night.

10

CLINTON

I couldn't stop staring. I hadn't seen those eyes in what seemed like an eternity, and my blood boiled at the idea of my father robbing me of them. I heard my heart monitor ticking up. I felt my blood pressure rising. Rae's worried eyes darted to all the machines around me before dipping her lips down against my ear.

"Breathe for me. It's okay. I'm here. Just breathe."

I wrapped my arms around her, pulling her close to me. I didn't care what part of me hurt. I didn't care what part of me cried out for mercy. I needed to feel her. I needed to hold her. I needed to be close to her, just in case someone came to remove her. I closed my eyes, breathing along with her as she coached me through my breaths. I slid my left-hand fingers through her hair, trying to be ginger with my right arm in its sling. She curled up against me, snuggling into bed.

Her warmth overcame me and the scent of her filled me with life.

I wanted nothing more than for her to stay here with me. Like this.

She drew in shuddered breaths and I wanted so badly to kiss her. To lean down and kiss the top of her head. She sniffled, wiped at her tears and snuggled deeper into me as I tried so hard to keep my groans of pain at bay. I wouldn't rob her of this. I wouldn't rob either of us of this moment.

Because it had been a long time coming.

"Thank you so much."

I furrowed my brow. "For what?"

She sniffled. "For doing what you did. For leading those assholes away. Had you not, they might've—"

I gripped her hair softly. "Never, on my life, would I have ever let something happen to you. Never. Not while you're around me. Do you hear me?"

She nodded softly. "I just can't help but think that this is all my fault."

"If I could shake my head fervently right now at you, I would. This isn't your fault. None of this would've taken place had those assholes just stayed at home. Passed right by us instead of coming into the parking lot. They started this. Not you, and certainly not me."

She paused. "The police came to talk to me yesterday morning."

"I've talked with them, too."

"Is everything going to be okay?"

"Once they find those dickweeds and arrest them, I'll feel even better. But, yes, beautiful. Everything is going to be okay. Thank you for talking with them. I'm sorry I couldn't have been there to support you through it."

She scoffed. "I'm sorry I haven't been here since the accident. I made you a promise and—"

"—and my father got in the way. Like he always does. This isn't your fault. I had a feeling my father had done something, even though my stepmother wouldn't tell me what he'd done."

"So they've been here for you? Through all this."

I sighed. "Eh, more or less. I've woken up to Cecilia instead of my father. The only time I woke up to the sound of Dad's voice, he was arguing with her."

"Arguing? About what?"

I scoffed. "A business trip Cecilia wanted him to cancel."

Rae rose up, looking into my eyes. "Are you fucking kidding me?"

I shrugged, groaning at the pain. "That's how he is. Work comes before everything. He thought he was doing everyone a favor by pushing the trip back once already."

"Your father's an absolute asshole."

I chuckled. "You don't have to tell me."

"You should tell the doctors what he does to you."

"By the sounds of it, someone already has."

Rae blushed, but all I did was laugh. I pulled her back down to my side, feeling her curl around me. Her leg slipped between mine, and it was the closest I'd felt to her in a long time. I drew in a deep breath as my fingertips stroked her arm, sending goosebumps puckering her skin for me to touch.

"It just kinda slipped out. I'm sorry."

I grinned. "Ah, worse things have happened. I'm eighteen, so there isn't much people can do now except look into my father. And he'll pay them off. Like he usually does. Then we'll go on about our lives and he'll buy me something out of guilt to make things okay again."

"So this has happened before? Someone reporting him?"

"Yep. I reported him once."

Rae sighed. "This is such shit."

"The way I see it, I've got less than a year. Then I graduate and I'm free to go and do as I please. Just need that high school diploma, even if it isn't enough to get me into a community college or whatever."

"Speaking of graduation, what does your recovery look like? You're going to walk and all that, right?"

"Well, I'm pretty beat up. I know Dad wants me out before he goes on this fun business trip. But just because my concussion is clearing up doesn't mean I'm out of here. If things go perfectly, I might get released in a couple days. But, realistically, I'm looking at another week in this hospital. At least, before they release me."

"What happens after they release you, Clint?"

"The usual. Physical therapy. Exercises. In home, and in an office somewhere. That will help fix my back and the movement in my arm, once my collarbone heals."

She paused. "Wait, your back? What happened to your back?"

I grinned. "I fell twenty feet down a ravine and landed on a bunch of rocks. My vertebrae have slipped out of place. My back's crooked from the impact."

Her eyes rose to meet mine. "You didn't tell me that."

"I'm sorry. I guess, in the grand scheme of things, it's easier if I tell you what's *not* wrong with me."

I laughed, but she didn't find that funny.

"Not a cool joke, Clint."

I cleared my throat. "Sorry, beautiful."

I watched her sit up, and already I missed her warmth. She placed one arm over me, propping herself up as her body hovered over mine. I gazed into her eyes as I sat there, staring at her. Propped up for the first time in days as I gazed upon the most beautiful face I'd ever come to know in my short life.

I smiled. "I'm really glad you're here."

Rae blushed. "I'm glad I'm here, too."

"You're eighteen, right?"

She paused. "Yeah. Why?"

"I'll have a talk with the doctor about putting you on my HIPAA form."

"Your what now?"

I chuckled. "It's a release form that designates who can know about my condition. Since you're technically a legal adult, I can put you on the list so the hospital can call and update you on how I'm doing."

"Or I could pick up your school work and bring it to you so we can study together. Which means your father looks like an absolute asshole if he stands in the way of your studies."

"I like the way you think, Cleaver."

She winked. "And here I thought you'd keep calling me 'beautiful.'"

My smile faded. "You'd really do that for me?"

"Do what?"

"Bring my schoolwork and help me study?"

"I mean, why wouldn't I? You're going to be here while school is still happening. You'll still have tests and shit like that. If you want to graduate, you have to at least not fail things. So, yeah. Of course I'd do that for you."

I felt overwhelmed by her words. This beautiful young girl really was willing to bend over backwards for me. Which was such a refreshing change of pace from my father. I blinked back tears, feeling like a great big pussy as a smile crossed Rae's face.

"We'll blame it on the pain you're in, okay?"

I snickered. "Yeah. Sure. Good thinking."

I looked up and saw Michael staring inside the room at us. And I could've sworn he and Allison were holding hands. He gave me a thumbs-up, I guess signaling to me that the coast was still clear. I reached my arm out for Rae again.

"Come here, gorgeous."

She smiled. "Oh, I like that one much better."

"I figured you would."

She lay back down in my arms and I closed my

eyes. This was how I wanted things to be. Her, nestled against me, while I closed my eyes and slept. The food sat well in my stomach. Greasy, fatty food that helped me wake up a bit. All this healthy shit the hospital fed me—bland foods like rice and unbuttered toast—was getting old. And now that they had me off the morphine drip, why couldn't I have a nice burger?

Even if it came back up on me, it was still worth it to see Rae. To hold her again. To smell her again. To be next to her again.

"You saved me."

I snickered. "No, gorgeous. You saved me. And I owe you my life for it."

She kissed my chest. "You owe me nothing."

"I owe you everything, and you'll like it that way."

She giggled. "You're a mess, you know that?"

"A mess you like."

"A mess I—"

She paused, and my heart skipped a beat. Surely she hadn't been about to say something like that. What I wouldn't have given in that moment to look down at her. To read her face and gaze into her eyes. Fucking hell, this damn neck brace. I needed it off, and now.

But when she buried herself into my side, I knew. I knew what she almost said.

And I hoped one day, she knew I felt the same way.

"Get some rest, Clint. I'm sure you're exhausted."

I stroked my fingers up and down her back. "I don't want to miss a second with you."

She wrapped her arm around me. "I promise, I'll be back. I'm bringing your homework, remember? I've become your study buddy. Plus, you're putting me on that 'HIPPO' form."

"HIPAA."

"What?"

"HIPAA. With an 'A'."

"'HIPPO' sounds better."

I chuckled. "It does, doesn't it?"

"Yep. You can't get rid of me that easily, handsome."

I smiled. "Trust me, I don't want to."

She paused. "I like sappy you. It's very romantic."

"Don't give away all my secrets at school now. Can't have all the guys being as smooth as me. Someone might steal you away."

She snickered. "I'd like to see them try."

"I'll punch them in the throat if they try."

"You and what army?"

"Me and the left arm that can still move."

She giggled. "Let's not break the other arm, okay?"

"Technically, it's my collarbone. My right arm was just dislocated."

"Oh. Oh. Yeah. Totally better then, Mr. Internal Bleeding."

I laughed. "Are we really making jokes out of my injuries?"

She reached up, kissing my jawline. "Do we really have any other reaction to this situation?"

My face fell. "I guess you're right."

And as she tucked herself back against me, my eyes fell closed. Sleep began drawing me under. I felt myself succumbing to the darkness. And as my body relaxed, I hoped with all my might Rae would be here when I woke up. I hoped with all my might my father wouldn't give her any other trouble. But if he did, I hoped with all my might Cecilia would find her voice again.

Long enough to put him in his fucking place.

11

RAELYNN

Clint's soft sleeping sounds lulled me into my own sort of trance. I knew Michael and Allison wanted to get back on the road, since they'd been standing in the hallway for well over an hour. But I couldn't relinquish Clint. I kept wrapping myself around him. Clinging to him. Simply thankful to be in his presence again.

I have to go, though.

I sighed as I slowly untangled myself from his body. I reached up, pressing a soft kiss against his bruised cheek. His face looked like a mess. Every time I gazed up into it, there seemed to be a new bruise. Or a spreading bruise. Or another part of his face swelling. It made me sick to my stomach.

Let the boy sleep, Rae.

"I'll be back soon."

I whispered the words against the shell of his ear, then slipped off the bed. I peeked out into the hallway, watching as Michael and Allison stared at me. I sighed before nodding my head, signaling to him that I was ready to head out.

Until Clint jerked awake.

"Rae?"

I whipped around. "What is it? I'm right here."

"Rae? Where are you? Rae!"

I rushed back to his side, lunging myself into his face. I crawled back up onto the bed, straddling him as I blocked off his view of the rest of the room. Michael and Allison rushed in. I pressed my lips against Clint's, trying to stop his yelling. If he spooked the nurses or one of the doctors, we'd be thrown out.

"Sh-sh-sh-sh-sh. It's me. I'm right here."

His lip quivered. "I'm sorry. I—I felt you leave, and—"

I shook my head. "Your father isn't here. It's okay. I figured since you'd fallen asleep—"

"Dad's already gone."

He blurted out the words and I heard the hurt in his voice. I looked back at my two best friends, watching as they flicked their hands out at me. Telling me to stay as they made their leave again. His statement didn't shock me, but it hurt me. Mostly, because I saw how much it hurt Clint.

"What was that?" I asked.

He grimaced. "Dad's already gone."

I slid off to his side. "But, I thought you said—"

He sighed. "He and my stepmother got into another fight last night. I mean, a really good fight.

The hospital threw them out. I haven't seen either of them since."

"Then maybe your father is still in town. Just not allowed back in the hospital."

"He called me to let me know he'd be back before I was released."

The flatness of Clint's voice turned my stomach. I took his hand, lacing our fingers together as I rested my head against his good shoulder. He drew in broken breaths, trying so hard to stay strong when I knew all he wanted to do was be weak.

I kissed his arm. "It's just me. You can let it out."

"He fucking left me, Rae. To rot in this hospital bed. And Cecilia isn't allowed back in the hospital. At least until tomorrow morning. And I have no one. Just the doctors and the nurse staff who come in here with their pitiful glances and their small talk."

"You have me."

He snickered. "Thank fuck for that."

I nuzzled against him. I watched his chest jump as his voice hiccuped. I gazed into his face, watching as tears rushed down his cheeks. I sat up, wiping at them softly with my fingertips. I grabbed his drink and put the straw to his lips, giving his trembling lip something to do.

"I'm right here. I won't go anywhere if you don't want me to."

He swallowed down the liquid. "I just—don't understand."

I rubbed his arm. "What don't you understand?"

He closed his eyes. "Why my father doesn't love me."

I didn't know how to answer him. I didn't know what to tell him. The only thing I could do was be there for him, so I settled deeper into his side. I watched him cry silent tears as he held his sounds back, his chest hiccupping with pain and anger and sadness.

"Clint, I—"

He sniffled. "For years, it's been this way. For years, my father has seen me as nothing. But, I mean, even the last time I was in the hospital, he was here. Present. Sure, typing away on his laptop and taking phone calls. I'd fallen out of a fucking tree and jammed my neck. And every time I woke up, he was at my bedside. Working, yes. But here. And now? He's nowhere to be found. On a jet somewhere, or chilling on some island with a cocktail in his hand while the only person who's been at my side since I was admitted to the hospital sits at home, by herself, because of him!"

I cupped his cheek. "I'm so sorry, Clint."

"My father is a good-for-nothing piece of shit. And he thinks that, for some reason, being back before I'm discharged is good enough. Like, sure. I'll leave you while you're in the hospital. While you're hooked up to tubes and in ICU. But, at least I'll be here by the time they take your fucking catheter out."

I leaned his bed back as he closed his eyes. Something in the pit of my gut told me he wanted to lean back, so I laid him down. I tucked the blankets around him tightly because I really didn't know what else to do.

Other than listen, of course.

He murmured, "Thanks."

I shook my head. "No thanks needed. I just wish I had something to tell you. Or advice to give."

He snickered. "There's no advice when it comes to my father. He treats me like a nuisance rather than a fucking son."

"I'd do anything to take your pain away, Clint. All of it. Physical. Emotional. Mental. All of it."

"I know you would. But I wouldn't let you. I've been dealing with this for a long time. I can do it for a few more months."

"If it makes you feel any better, you're right. He's a piece of shit human being who doesn't deserve the type of son you are in his life."

He scoffed. "I'm not anything special. It's not like I made things easy on him."

I nodded. "I'm sure that's true. But at one point in time, you were nothing but an innocent boy. A boy who missed his mother and didn't understand the world. Anger begets anger, Clint. You are this way and you act this way because you've learned to survive your father. Not thrive alongside him. And that's your father's fault."

His eyes found mine. "Since when did you become so smart?"

I smiled softly. "You forget we both have Daddy issues."

He chuckled. "How is it that you can make me smile, even in this kind of situation?"

I shrugged. "Consider it my superpower. Making

people smile and laugh when they're on the brink of destruction."

"Says a lot about what you've been through."

"Yeah, well. I can cry on your shoulder about it a different time."

"Deal."

I squeezed his hand tightly. "I hope you know this isn't your fault."

"Rae, don't."

"I'm serious, Clint. None of this is your fault. It's got nothing do to with you. Some people just don't know how to be parents. Your father doesn't know how to be a parent. He only knows how to be a business-man, and everything else is a nuisance. Including your stepmother, I'm sure."

"I hope she comes back tomorrow. I've liked having her around."

I smiled. "That's good. I take it you guys have been talking a bit?"

"A bit, sure. I mean, it's been awkward. We don't really know each other, despite the fact that she's been around for a while. But, it's been nice waking up and having her around. She's helped a lot with the doctors. Relaying information. Shit like that."

"Sounds like she's finally figuring out how to step up as a parent."

"And she doesn't berate me for things like my father does."

I swallowed back my growl. "If I could get your father in a room for just a few minutes..."

Clint smirked. "I'd like to hear what you might do to him."

"For starters, I'd sneak in a baseball bat."

"Old school. I like it."

"His kneecaps wouldn't."

The two of us laughed softly as my eyes danced between his. Then Clint closed his eyes.

"I guess I just always wondered if he loved me or not. But now I guess I have my answer."

I snuggled against him, trying to be his rock while his foundation eroded from underneath him.

"And the funny thing now, Rae, is that I'm starting to regret ever wondering at all. I guess ignorance really is bliss, at times."

I looked back over my shoulder and saw Allison wiping at her tears. Even Michael's eyes were glistening. I didn't know what to say. As I looked to them for guidance, all they did was shrug their shoulders. None of us knew what to say. There were no words for the situation. I turned back around, finding Clint staring at me as I sighed.

"You can go, if they need to go," he said.

I nodded. "If they need to leave, they can come back around and get me. Or I'll catch a cab once a doctor kicks me out."

Allison piped up. "Actually, you've been okayed to stay in here for a bit."

I furrowed my brow. "Really?"

"Well, once we get you on this HIPAA form, yes."

I turned around at the sound of the strong voice. A man in a white coat came into the room with a clipboard and a pen. He handed it all to Clint before sitting him up in the hospital bed, using the controls that had taken me damn near ten minutes to figure out.

The doctor quirked an eyebrow. "While we're not fans of how you guys sneaked in—or brought him food —the truth of the matter is that neither his father nor his stepmother are allowed in here right now. So, as long as it's one person at a time, we can overlook some things for a few hours."

I smiled. "Thank you, Doctor. I really appreciate it."

Clint groaned. "What do I do, Doc?"

"Have this young woman put her name, address, and phone number down. Then you sign at the bottom. That's all you need to do."

Clint handed me the clipboard. "Rae?"

And with a smile on my face, I took it from him to fill in.

Anything that got me one step closer to never being pushed away from his side again.

"All right, Mr. Clarke. It's that time again."

I smiled coyly. "Hello, Nurse Nina. Time for me to show you my nooks and crannies again?"

She giggled. "You better stop that flirtatious nonsense. My husband'll come in here and give you a piece of his mind."

"The more, the merrier."

"Hey, now! I saw that cutie patootie that came in here yesterday to visit. I also saw how she made your heartrate monitor rise and fall. You can't tell me there isn't something there."

I chuckled. "That's Rae. And she's a saint. Literally, my guardian angel. She's the one that found me in that ravine."

"Well, thank the Lord for that. Because without her, I wouldn't be accosted by you on a daily basis."

"And you know you'd miss it."

Nurse Nina was always a refreshing face on the

ICU floor. An older lady with a spunky personality and a lovely meet-cute story she enjoyed telling people about. Everyone on the hall knew the story of how she and her husband met. And I had to admit, I didn't mind hearing it multiple times a day. She always had a smile on her face and a giggle on the tip of her tongue to offer someone. An infectious sound. One that reminded me a lot of Rae's giggle.

Thank fuck for Rae.

Nurse Nina sighed. "All right. Ready?"

I looked up at the ceiling. "Just be gentle with me. I'm tender, and sensitive."

She giggled. "You wish."

She pulled my blankets off, exposing me to the harsh cold of the room. And after she flipped up my hospital gown, she got to work. I had bandages covering stitches created during surgery. Multiple entry points where the surgeons had explored, cauterizing veins or whatever the fuck it was they did to stop the internal bleeding.

"All right. Things look nice."

I grinned. "Just nice, Nurse Nina?"

"Oh, stop it, you little hellion."

The humor detracted from the fact that she was literally raising my cock up to inspect me. Because out of everything else, my balls had also been bleeding when I came rolling into the E.R. She finished her inspection before changing my bandages. She ran this numbing salve over my wounds before covering them back up with new gauze. She taped everything down and flipped my gown over my hips. Then she changed my blankets out for these nice, warm sheets that made me moan as they hit my skin.

"Fresh out of the dryer. Why do you always flirt with me like this?"

Nurse Nina laughed. "I plucked them out just for you. It'll help you relax a bit."

But I knew the real reason she was doing it.

Does everyone on this damn hall know my father abandoned me?

I closed my eyes as she continued checking my vitals. I felt my tubes being finagled with, and I held my breath for it. I hated it when they shifted the ones going up my nose. It always pinched a bit more than I wanted. I listened as she whirled around the room, whistling to herself and trying to bring a bit of cheer into my life.

Then I heard the clicking of those heels.

"Uh oh. I think I hear someone coming down the hallway."

I opened my eyes as the nurse leaned up my hospital bed. And my heart exploded with delight when I saw Cecilia come into the room. Thank hell, the hospital had let her back in. Because this Sunday was creeping by slower than I wanted it to. She clutched a bag of food and it made me smile. Plus, she had some books in her hands. She pulled up a chair and sat down next to me, sitting the books in my lap.

"I found those on your bookshelf. They had various bookmarks in them, so I figured you might want to continue reading them to pass the time."

I grinned. "I appreciate that."

Cecilia unpacked the food. "I also brought lunch. There's this cute little cafe on the corner just a couple blocks down from here. Massive salads. And great soups. I got you a steak salad with extra meat, and then some thick tomato bisque soup and some of their freshly-baked bread to dip in it."

"Thank you, Cecilia."

"I also snagged you a lemon bar, if your sweet tooth starts acting up."

She said it as if she had some sort of dangerous secret she were carrying around. And the tone of her voice made me chuckle.

"That's more than enough food, thank you. Really. I'm glad you made it back today."

She sighed. "I'm sorry I let your father get to me like that. I couldn't stop thinking about you yesterday."

I reached out, taking her hand. "I'm glad you stood up for yourself against him. Even if it did get you tossed out."

"I should have kept a cooler head for you. You were here all alone yesterday. That isn't right. I shouldn't have been so selfish."

I squeezed her hand. "It's fine. Don't beat yourself up over it, okay?"

I wanted to tell her about Rae, but I figured… baby steps. I thanked her for the food and the books, then dug in while she ate beside me. I looked at the books in my lap and sighed with relief. I'd been painfully bored in this place. And while I usually would've been upset that she rifled through my room, she brought me four books I had been wanting to secretly devour for weeks now.

"I'm sure those books will help. And if there's anything you want from the house, just let me know. I'll do my best to find it."

I took a large bite of my salad. "Thank you. Really."

"Oh! I have exciting news, too."

I looked over at her as I chewed my food, watching as she set her salad down. She looked at me with pride in her eyes, and I wondered what had her so worked up in all the best ways.

"I talked with your father. And meetings are going well. He said he's going to video conference in tonight and hang around with us. I have the laptop in the car, I'll just have to go out and bring it up here once he tells me he's ready. He's going to text, I'll get the laptop, then boom! Howard's here with us."

She beamed with happiness, and I tried to give her the kindest smile I could. But I knew how my father worked. He'd get busy with something, or pissed off at something, and suddenly he'd forget all about me. I didn't have the slightest bit of hope he'd video conference in, much less remember to text Cecilia about it. But she looked so happy about it. So bright and vibrant with hope.

I didn't have the heart to destroy it.

"That sounds great. It'll be nice to see him."

She picked her salad back up. "He's been asking about you. Updates and such. I know he's worried, even though he isn't here right now. His flying out was a knee-jerk reaction to us fighting. Not you, Clint. I hope you know that."

Yeah, sure. "I know."

"Good. Very good. And to celebrate, I'll go out and get us something nice for dinner. You know, so you don't have to keep suffering through all this hospital food. This is going down easily enough, right?"

I nodded, taking another bite. "Like butter."

The two of us continued eating and her vibrance filled the room. I knew she'd take it harder than me when Dad faltered on his word. But I knew how things rolled around here. I didn't want to say any of this to my stepmother, though. She seemed so happy, and I wanted to enjoy that happiness for a while. So I chose to enjoy her company and eat with her instead of pin-pricking her happiness.

After all, my father did enough of that.

Ask her why.

I pushed the thought away from my mind. For days now, I'd been wondering why she loved my father. Why she was with my father. And while I could conjure a decent-enough answer, something about this entire situation I wanted to hear it from her mouth. Wanted to hear her open up and say it. Maybe it was all of our discussions, or somehow getting to know one another. But something inside me wanted to hear her admit why she was still with my father.

Then again, it also wasn't any of my business.

Plus, you don't want to piss her off and have her leave you alone in this place.

No. I really didn't want that. If Cecilia left, this

hospital stay would be even more lonely than it had already become. No. It was better to keep the peace and let her be ignorant for a little while. Keep that blissful nature about her that filled up whatever space she might have occupied. She cured my loneliness. She made this stuffy ICU room more bearable.

Minus Rae, of course. Rae made this place shine. Hell, Rae made any place shine. Rae could've made the bowels of hell itself shine with her presence.

Thank fuck for Rae.

And maybe someday, I'd feel confident enough to indulge Cecilia with stories of my girlfriend.

13

RAELYNN

As I sat in my English class just before lunch, I felt everyone's eyes on me. I heard them whispering. I felt their minds wondering. I smelled their confusion and their questions. Their snickers made me upset. Their scoffs made me want to punch them. All day long, people had been staring. When Michael, Allison, and I walked through those school doors. Every time I walked to class and paused by Clint's locker. Every time I got up to do anything, everyone watched my every move.

It felt like even the teachers were out to get me.

"I heard he fell over."

"I heard he was pushed over."

"Do you think she pushed him over?"

"Maybe he jumped over because she won't leave him alone."

"I don't know, I heard there was a car involved."

"Her car?"

"No, no. I don't think she has a car."

"So she rides on the back of his bike? Lucky."

You're damn right I'm lucky.

As the day progressed on, I tried my best to keep my head above water. To stay out of the gossip and ignore the slivers of voices I heard wafting around me. Every transition to class made it a bit more difficult, though. Every bathroom break I took, the girls would stare at me. Silence themselves. Like they were talking about me before I walked up. I shook my head and made my way into the stalls, wanting a bit of peace and quiet. A safe space to breathe before going back out into the shark-infested waters of Valley High School.

I hated this fucking place.

I knew everyone was familiar with what happened. The crash. The boys. The car. Clint's bike. How he was in the hospital, and not due to return to school for a while. Everyone gossiped about it. I had to stop Allison from interjecting into their conversations. I had to hold Michael back a few times, seeing as he lunged at people trying to come up with asinine excuses as to why I was there.

"It's okay, Michael. Come on. We just need to get through the day."

In some ways, I was thankful for them. They wanted to leap to defend Clint. To defend me. And in other ways, I was upset. I was there. I brought Clint back to life. I was the one that got him into this situation, yet I was the one holding other people back?

Why did I always have to be the strong one for everyone else?

"No, for real, guys. Clint's really bad off."

"I heard he broke his collarbone."

"And a concussion? Poor guy. I don't know what Rae's doing here at school."

"Yeah, I'd be by his side every second if I was his girlfriend."

The only thing that made me smile was the school referring to me as 'his girlfriend.'

I didn't like anything else, though.

"Rae, can I ask you—?"

"Rae, what—?"

"Rae, do you have an update on—?"

"Rae, I heard you—"

Every time someone stopped to ask me a question —to actually own up to their curiosities—someone stepped in my way. Michael. Allison. A teacher. The principal. And I was thankful for it. I'd talked about it enough to the police. To the doctors. With Clint. With myself. I didn't want to talk about it with anyone else. I didn't want to keep reliving it. It happened, it was over, and all I wanted to do was focus on Clint's recovery.

And how to tap-dance around his father in the process.

The school lunch bell rang and I sighed. I gathered my things and rushed to my locker, exchanging one set of books for another. I held back tears as I twirled the dial to unlock it. At this point in my day, Clint would have come up and put his hand on my shoulder. Spun me around. Grinned down at me with that shit-eating grin of his before offering to carry my books. Yet his touch didn't come. That grin didn't appear. I stuffed my books into my locker and grabbed the ones I needed for the back half of my day, feeling my stomach growling out for food.

But I wasn't hungry.

I didn't have the energy to eat.

Michael walked up to me. "Ready for lunch?"

Allison giggled. "There you two are. I walked into the cafeteria and was like, 'Whoa, where is everyone?'"

She let out a forced giggle and I sighed. I closed my locker door and gave my best friend a polite smile, trying to thank her for her efforts. Then she put her hand on my shoulder. Much like Clint would have had he been there.

"He's going to be okay, Rae. I promise."

Michael took my books. "Yeah. He's strong as hell, and stubborn. He'll pull through this."

"I know. I know you guys are right. It just… hurts. The murmurs hurt. The rumors hurt. And make me angry. I just wish this school wasn't what it is, you know?"

Allison snickered. "You and me both. Now let's go get some food."

Michael sighed. "I'm starving. Is it pizza day yet?"

They managed to make me smile as we walked our way through the cafeteria. We got our food and sit down in our usual spot, with my books piled beside me. I only picked at a few things, though. Softly sipped my soda. What I wanted was to go back to the hospital. What I wanted was to be eating with Clint. What I wanted was to not be reminded constantly of what happened to him. What happened to us. What happened that night.

But every single student wanted a slice of the pie. A sliver of the drama all to themselves so they could feel important.

"Well. I wasn't sure if you'd show up today or not."

Roy's voice made the hairs on the back of my neck stand on end.

"Especially since you weren't here Friday."

And of course, there was Marina's voice. Right alongside his.

Allison scoffed. "You guys can just walk away."

Michael nodded. "Yeah. Leave her alone for now. This is serious."

I turned around, catching Roy's grin. "Oh, I know it's serious."

Marina giggled. "I hear he's busted up pretty badly."

I shrugged. "Then I don't know why you're smiling. Or laughing. Or even over here in the first place."

Roy chuckled. "Just wanna know, is his face busted up as badly as everyone says it is?"

Marina licked her lips. "There are a lot of rumors going around. Broken nose. Black eyes. Dislocated jaw. No teeth. Lost tongue."

"Guess he's not gonna be such a looker anymore, huh?"

I shot out of my seat. "You want to try running that by me again?"

"Rae, no."

"Rae, sit down. They aren't worth it."

Roy nodded. "You should listen to your posse."

Marina smiled brightly. "I heard he's on a liquid diet for the rest of the school year because his body got mangled with that drop."

Roy laughed. "You think he can still get it up, sweetheart?"

"I don't know, baby. I'm more curious to know if Rae will stay with him if he can't."

"That's it!"

I lunged at them, but Michael stood up. Marina took a step back and cradled into Roy's side, as he shot me a death glare. I swiped my hand out, catching my nails across Marina's face as she cried out in pain. And as the blood surfaced on her skin, Roy hissed at me.

"You'll pay for that, you freak."

Michael pressed his lips to my ear. "Calm down. Stop it. That's enough."

Allison stood up. "We need to get out of here. Teachers are coming."

Michael threw me over his shoulder as Allison gathered my books. They rushed me out of there as Marina whimpered like the bitch she was in some corner. Probably ready to suck Roy's dick to make herself feel better. Hot tears of anger raced down my cheeks as Michael jogged me down the hallway. Like I weighed nothing. Like I was nothing.

I am nothing.

I fell limp to his movements. I heard Allison huffing as she carried my books in her arms. They took me down to my history class before Michael put me back down on my feet, with Allison dropping my books to my desk.

And again, my eyes fell to the seat Clint sat in every class. Every day, after lunch.

"He's not here," I whispered.

Michael rubbed my back. "He'll be back before you know it."

Allison took my hands. "And until then, you have a promise to keep."

Holy shit, that's right.

I had to talk to Clint's teachers.

I spent the rest of my lunch break going around to his classes. I sat down with his teachers and told them exactly what was going on. Gave them the story everyone else wanted. And to my surprise, they listened with an open ear and were more than willing to help him.

"I want him to stay on track to graduate. I know if he applies himself, he can still get out of here with just shy of a 3.0 GPA. Which is still good enough to get him into most community colleges."

"Of course I'll give you his work. Let me send him a note, too. Let him know he's missed."

"Make sure he reads, too. I'm holding you account- able for the accuracy of his pop quizzes. Can you do that?"

Their generosity and understanding were over- whelming.

I gathered everything I needed from his first two periods and slipped it into my backpack. And while I usually kept that thing in my locker, I carried it around with me for the rest of the day. The principal allowed me access to his locker to get the books he needed for his classes. And the inside of his locker shocked me. I expected it to be in disarray. Filled with trash and disheveled with his books stacked on the small floor of it.

However, what I found gave me pause.

"Wow," the principal said.

I stared at a picture of myself. A yearbook picture of me from freshman year. It had obviously been torn out of a book, and it was taped to the inside of his locker. And beneath my face, a heart. A simple, black ink penned heart. I ran my fingertips along it. I felt tears cresting my eyes. I gazed along his organized locker, taking in his alphabetically-arranged textbooks and his notebooks neatly stacked and named.

I sniffled. "Oh, Clint."

"It's kind of you, you know. To help him stay on track with his grades."

The principal's voice caught me off-guard and I quickly wiped at my tears.

"I'd like to think he'd do the same for me."

He snickered. "You seem to bring out a different side of him. A side I've never seen before."

I nodded. "He's a good kid. He's just a bad home life."

"You'd be surprised how common that is."

The statement made me sick to my stomach.

"I mean, I know Clint isn't the most well-liked kid on campus or anything. But I'm really glad you guys are helping me out with this. I know he wants to graduate. If anything to get away from—"

I paused before I said anymore. And I watched as the principal nodded from the corner of my eye.

"Don't worry. I'll make sure his teachers work with you. And him. You know, to try and get him graduated."

I snickered. "And get him off your plate?"

"And get him going in the direction he needs to be in. A direction he deserves."

"You're right about that."

I finished gathering his books and the principal closed his locker. The bag was heavy, but I didn't care. A small price to pay for helping Clint recover and do what I know he wanted to do. My only regret was that I had to work tonight at the grocery store. Which came with its own set of worries and hesitations.

Like what the hell the manger would think—or say to me—once I walked through those doors.

I'll be there soon, Clint. I just have to get through work.

And I hoped with all my might I wouldn't be scared closing at work again after school.

14

CLINTON

Cecilia clicked her way into the room. "Guess who's calling!?"

Oh, goody.

I groaned as she sat on the edge of my bed, jostling me around. A laptop got flopped into my lap, and right there on the screen was the face of my father. Stoic. Cold. Still as stone. And I saw him analyzing me even from his laptop. Even though he'd overshot the video conference by an entire day, hey. At least he was calling, right?

"How's he feeling?" he asked.

I sighed. "He's feeling fine, Dad."

"Cece said you had physical therapy today. How'd that go?"

I shrugged. "My neck's out of that brace, so that's nice. Still hurts to move, though."

"Guess that's what happens when you throw yourself off a ravine."

I fluttered my eyes over to Cecilia, and she urged me to keep going with a nod of her head. I didn't want to do this. I didn't want to talk with my father. But it seemed like it made her happy. And out of all the people who had been the most supportive of me through this trying time, she'd been one of them.

So, why not make her happy?

"Yeah, well. I'll try not to do that next time."

Dad nodded. "What did they have you do in physical therapy?"

I licked my chapped lips. "Uh, some stretches with my back. Trying to get these vertebrae to straighten out on their own. Some leg work. Not really arm work, since my collarbone has to heal first."

"Can you see out of your eyes?"

"Yep. I can see your disapproving stare just fine."

Cecilia sighed. "Clint."

Dad's face fell. "Well, if you weren't always doing such disappointing things, there would be no need for the disapproving stare."

"Howard!"

I shook my head. "He's fine. It's whatever."

I felt myself still sweating from the physical therapy. And holy shit, that'd been rough. Walking around made me bust a sweat. But with all those exercises I felt like I was a young child again, relearning how to do everything. Moving my legs took effort. Propping myself up took time. I bent my back every which way, flexing my muscles like I hadn't moved them in years.

My body was damaged. My soul, weak. And I had a very long road of recovery ahead of me.

Cecilia cleared her throat. "Well, they said his first try at physical therapy went really well. They even gave him a few back stretches most people coming out of something like this can't even attempt. They think he's going to do really well."

Dad grunted. "How many weeks of physical therapy are we talking about?"

I mouthed to my stepmother, "He wants to know the money."

Cecilia shook me off. "They say six to eight weeks. Then, a re-evaluation to see if he needs another course of it."

Dad sighed. "Great. I'll get started on finding a home nurse or something. Which'll cost me an arm and a leg."

"Howard."

I shot Cecilia an 'I told you so' kind of look. For my father, it was all about money. How much I cost him. How much he spent on me. How much it took to apologize. What he had to dip into in order to cover the cost of something I'd done. I had no idea how to speak with my father. Well, scratch that. I knew exactly how to talk to my father. I just didn't care to. This entire time, all I'd wanted was for my father to come home and take care of me. Come home and visit. Field the doctors since he knew the bulk of my medical history.

But, now? Even just this video conference changed my mind.

He could stay wherever the hell he was for all I cared.

Cecilia whispered. "Howard, be kinder to your son. He's laid up in a hospital and you're nowhere to be found. I'll shut this laptop if you don't."

Dad snickered. "More time for me to work, then."

I shook my head. "Do you always have to win every fight?"

The room fell silent as my eyes fell to my father's on the computer screen.

"Because I really want to believe that you aren't the sorriest sack of shit I've ever known. That you say these things just to—"

"What did you say to me, boy?"

I raised my voice. "Any other half-decent father would be here with their child in the hospital. I almost died, Dad. Actually, I did die there for a little while. I've been resuscitated twice, and you act like I've stolen your last damn cookie from the fridge."

Cecilia took my hand. "Clint, take some breaths. Your heartrate is climbing."

"Yeah, because I'm talking with Dad. So now I'm done talking with Dad. You can take the laptop away."

My father glowered. "You're lucky I'm not there, son. Because a hospital bed doesn't protect you from the whooping you deserve."

"And I believe I've heard enough."

The doctor's voice rose from the corner of the room and I looked over. That man looked me square in my face before nodding his head softly. I wasn't sure what he was thinking, but damn did I ever want to know.

"Who's that?" my father asked.

Cecilia paused. "The doctor, honey. It's the doctor."

The man in the white coat walked over. "And this conversation is done."

"I'll let you know when I'm done speaking with my son."

I scoffed. "No worries. I'm done talking with him."

The doctor nodded. "You can remove the laptop now, Mrs. Clarke."

My father got in one last glare before Cecilia picked up the laptop. I heard him making remarks to himself as she carried the laptop out of the room. Typical remarks from my father. 'He's asking for something like this to happen.' 'How much did that doctor hear?' 'Maybe he needs something like this to teach him a lesson. He drives that bike much too recklessly for my tastes.'

I mean, did my stepmother have the damn volume turned up all the way on that thing?

I sighed as the doctor sat down on the edge of my bed. He patted my knee, holding his hand there as I stared at the wall. I heard him and my stepmother bickering. Again. Over the computer, out in the hallway. Pissing off people, including me.

"If your heartrate gets any higher, I have to sedate you."

I snickered. "Good."

The doctor paused. "You know, there are services for adults, too."

I slowly turned my head toward him. "What?"

He shrugged. "You don't fall under the protection

of child services anymore. But there are adult services. You know, if it's always like this with your father."

"I'm good, thanks."

"I don't think you are."

I shrugged. "Then, that's what you think. But I know how to handle my dad. And in a few months, when I graduate, I won't have to at all."

"You know damn good and well that boy had a hand in what happened, Cecilia!"

"He's just a kid, Howard. Go easy on him. Your son almost died. Don't you have a heart anymore?"

"Right, of course it isn't his fault. It's never his fault when you're around. He had no hand in it at all, and it's all me. All the time."

"Yeah, well. Maybe you should heed my advice for once."

"He's my son. Not yours. Can it, or leave. You know the drill."

The conversation out in the hallway took me aback. I wasn't sure what to make of it but—but it sounded like Cecilia was standing up for me.

Like she had stood up for me in the past.

"I'll be right back," the doctor said.

With one last pat of his hand, he got up. He stormed out into the hallway, walked right up to that laptop, and closed it in the middle of my father's sentence. I snickered. Oh man, if there was a mushroom cloud in the distance, I knew why. I sighed with relief as I eased myself back into the hospital bed, thankful to have some peace and quiet.

Then I felt Cecilia's hand fall against mine.

"I'm sorry, Clint."

I sighed. "Not your fault."

"I really thought he'd—"

"Give it a few more years. You'll stop expecting so much from him."

She squeezed my hand softly as a nurse came in and hooked me back up to a few things. She got my I.V. drip going again. Got the oxygen tubes seated in my nose. And as the nurse tucked me in, I felt my eyes flutter closed. Dad was partially right, though. I did have a hand in why I was run off the road. But not in the way my father thought. I hadn't instigated anything this time. I'd prevented it. I'd saved Rae from harm by throwing myself in harm's way. That shit was noble.

Right?

Don't second guess yourself because of that asshole.

Part of me wanted to tell my father. But I knew how he'd see it. If I told him it was to save some girl, he'd call me soft. He'd tell me Rae probably deserved whatever was coming to her, and that I needed to let her learn her lesson instead of babying her. And I wasn't sure I'd be able to keep myself from murdering him if I heard those words come out of his fucking face. Sure, I might have been able to tell Cecilia, but I knew if I told her she'd eventually tell my father. Because she was still in those years where she wanted to please him. Make him happy. Make him proud.

Whereas I'd abandoned those ideals around the time I was fifteen.

Dad won't understand the idea of defending a woman like that.

Cecilia patted my hand. "Get some rest. I'll be here when you wake up."

I nodded. "Sounds good."

"I'm really proud of what you accomplished today in PT."

"At least someone is."

"Your father's proud in his own way."

I snickered. "No, he's not. But, I'm glad you still think so. Means he hasn't gotten to you yet."

And when she didn't answer, I knew she knew I was right.

15

RAELYNN

I smiled as I walked through the hospital doors, not bothering to ask for Clint's room number. I knew where he was, and I was anxious to get to him. I tossed my shoulder pack around behind me, feeling it bounce against my legs. I moved as quickly as I could without running through the hallways, navigating the corridors before coming to his room.

I had a pep in my step and a giggle on my lips as I approached his door.

I looked around for his father. Or his stepmother. But there was no one except a nurse coming out of his room. I had all his homework. All his textbooks. And I was eager to dive into everything. I jogged down the hallway, slipping in my old tennis shoes along the freshly-waxed floors. The smell of disinfectant hung heavily in the air, but soon I stopped in my tracks.

When I saw some male nurses wheeling Clint out of his room.

"Where are you taking him?"

"Rae?"

I rushed to his side, taking his hand as he smiled at me.

"Hey, you're here."

I laced our fingers together. "Of course I'm here. What's wrong?"

He shook his head. "Nothing's wrong. I just get a normal room now."

"A normal roo—wait. Where's your neck brace?"

The nurse giggled. "Old handsome here's no longer got a concussion. Did well with his physical therapy today. So he gets a normal room and no more catheter."

Clint rolled his eyes. "She could've done without that part, Nurse Nina."

I furrowed my brow. "So you're doing okay? Nothing's wrong?"

"How could anything be wrong when you're here?"

I smiled at him, holding his hand as the nurses navigated his bed down the hallway. With this 'Nurse Nina' at the helm, directing traffic. She kept shamelessly flirting with Clint and he flirted right back. And while part of me was jealous, part of me was also thankful he had that kind of banter going on with someone here at the hospital.

Someone who made him smile whenever he didn't have anyone else.

"Wow. A regular room. I wonder what it's like. Does it have a cotton candy machine? Floor to ceiling windows? A nice tub for me to soak in?"

I giggled at Clint as we came to a stop in front of another hospital room.

Nurse Nina smiled. "Well, Cee, this isn't the DoubleTree. You get a private recuperation room with your own window, and a toilet that doesn't stink."

I quirked an eyebrow. "Cee?"

Clint winked. "That's what she calls me when her husband isn't around."

I nodded playfully. "Oh, okay. And here I thought I was supposed to be jealous."

"What? You mean you're not jealous, beautiful? I'm hurt."

And as the two of us laughed together, the male nurses got him situated into his new room.

I turned my back so the nurse could relieve him of his catheter. I took the time to set up our station for schoolwork, pulling out history, the one still fresh in my mind. I knew exactly what he'd missed and what he needed to get done before Friday. I flipped open to the page and things like that as the nurse walked beside me. She patted me on the back, causing me to look over at her. And with a friendly smile, she nodded.

"He's ready when you are, lucky girl."

"Thank you. For everything."

The nurse snickered. "Don't thank us yet. PT only gets harder from here. I'm sure he'll be cursing my name before too long."

Clint chuckled. "Never, Nurse Nina! How could I with that pretty face?"

I shook my head at the two of them as I turned around. And even after only a couple of days, Clint looked worlds better than he had. His neck wasn't braced. He didn't have oxygen tubes running up his nose. He only had one I.V. as opposed to two. And his face seemed a lot less swollen. I walked over to the edge of his bed and sat down, taking his hand within mine. And as I brought it to my lips to kiss, I felt him bend over. Freely.

To kiss me on top of the head.

I smiled. "You look amazing."

His lips lingered in my hair. "I feel amazing, now that you're here."

"Do you want to get started on history first? Or math?"

"First, I want to hear all about school. I'm sure there's been a circus act you've had to field."

I snickered. "I mean, whatever you're thinking is probably right. Roy and Marina have approached me a couple times, too."

"Oh, I'm sure they've had lots to say."

I rose up, looking into his eyes. "I think Roy has kind of become the schoolyard bully now. He's picking a great deal on Michael and Allison and me. Of course, with his girlfriend at his side. I mangled his face pretty badly, though."

He paused. "How so?"

I rolled my eyes. "She made a comment about how injured you were. That maybe you couldn't—"

I was hesitant to tell him. But he urged me on.

"You can tell me. Talk to me. It's okay."

I sighed. "Roy made a comment about you not having a nice face any longer. Then Marina backed it up with a comment about you not getting it up anymore. So, I lunged at her and raked my nails across her cheek."

He grinned. "That's my girl."

I blushed. "Well, she deserved it. Damn bitch."

"Are you okay, Rae?"

I shrugged. "I'm getting by. I'm really thankful the teachers and the principal are cooperating with me in terms of getting your schoolwork. Whatever it takes, you're going to graduate with us. Okay?"

"How are Aly and Mike?"

I paused. "Oh. Allison and Michael."

He nodded. "Yeah. How are they?"

Cute nicknames. I like them. "They're good. Worried about you. They're excited for the update when I see them tomorrow."

"We could call them, if you'd like."

"Oh, no, no. You're not getting out of schoolwork, sir."

"I mean, I've got other ways of getting out of schoolwork. But I think my heart monitor might give us away."

His hand slid slowly down my body and I shivered at his touch. I scooted closer to him, our foreheads falling together. Him joking around was a good sign. Moving a bit on his own. No longer chained to his bed. Our noses nuzzled together as his hand slipped to my lower back, inching me even closer to him.

And just as his lips hovered over mine...

"I think we should start with history."

He groaned. "Okay, okay. You win."

I smiled. "Great."

"What's up first?"

"Reading. There are three chapters we have to catch you up on. I can give you notes on the first one. Then, I actually have to read the other two. So try to stay with me. After that, two worksheets. Then, we're done for the night. We can move on to math."

"Wonderful."

"I'll pretend that's a good exclamation."

I maneuvered myself in bed with him, staying above the covers. He wrapped his arm around me, leaning his head against my shoulder. And as I cracked open the textbook, I gave him the condensed version of chapter four. I talked him through the biggest points and told him I'd get him a copy of my notes. Then I turned to chapter five and began reading.

I read for a few pages before he sat up, groaning as he moved.

"Can you give me a second?"

I nodded. "Of course. Take your time. Do you need water?"

He sighed. "I just need a minute. The head hurts."

I leaned back in bed with him, watching as he closed his eyes. I took his hand, feeling him squeeze it as he breathed through whatever he was experiencing. I kissed his cheek and whispered sweet nothings in his ear. The book soon fell to the floor, plopping open and crinkling the pages as he relaxed against me.

And five minutes later, the first snore erupted from his face.

Yikes.

I lay there with him for a little bit, staring at his face. His snores grew to exponential proportions, so I reached over and started finagling with some of the switches on his electronic bed. I finally got him going down, hitting that sweet spot where his snoring stopped.

And after I slowly inched away from him, I picked up the book off the floor.

"I'll just make some notes for him to go over."

A quick notation summary of Chapters Five and Six turned into me doing the worksheets for him. Quick answers that sounded like Clint before I moved onto his math homework. I intentionally got a few wrong, trying to make it look like I wasn't actually doing his work for him. And an hour later, I moved on to my own homework.

I stayed in that hospital room for almost three hours before Nurse Nina finally poked her head in.

"I hate to do this to you, honey. But, visiting hours wrapped up a few minutes ago."

I nodded. "Thanks. I'll get my things together."

"I can buy you maybe fifteen more minutes. But that's when the doctor comes back from his break."

I smiled, whispering, "I really appreciate it."

She crept in and took a quick look at Clint's vitals, then rushed back out. I quickly gathered my things, shoving our homework into my bag before I made my way back to his side. I took his hand, gazing into his sleeping face. The bruising from his broken nose was spreading. But the swelling had gone down a great deal. I smiled softly to myself, leaning forward to kiss his cheek. I let my lips linger, feeling him mindlessly press into my warmth before hunkering down further in bed.

And queuing up that damn snoring.

How did I ever sleep beside that?

"I'll see you soon," I murmured against his skin.

Then I picked up my things, threw the backpack strap across my back, and slowly made my way out of his room.

Wishing the entire time I could stay the night with him.

16

CLINTON

"Guess what day it is? Guess what. Day. It. Is."

I quirked an eyebrow. "Are you doing a parody of those commercials?"

Nurse Nina drew in a deep breath. "It's discharge day!"

My eyes widened. "Wait, what?"

"Surprise!"

Nurses and doctors jumped out of every orifice of my room. I had barely woken up. Just gotten out of the bathroom, literally hopped back into bed. And all of a sudden, my room was filled with people. I smiled as tears crested my eyes. Nurse Nina came over and hugged me, bending over my body. Her warm arms wrapped around me and I held her close, pressing my lips against her ear.

"Thank you so much. For everything."

She patted my back. "You did this yourself, Cee. We just came along for the ride."

The doctor walked up beside me. "Your official discharge paperwork. As well as a few other things you might need in your future. You know, just in case."

Nina backed up and the doctor looked me square in my eyes. I knew what he was talking about, too. I took the folder from him and peeked inside, taking in the paperwork. How to take care of my stitches. My body. How to schedule physical therapy and when to come see them next to get evaluated.

I also saw some brochures in there for adult assistance programs. And it made me sigh.

"Thanks, Doc. I really do appreciate it."

He patted my shoulder. "My number's in there. You call me anytime, day or night, if you need anything. And I mean anything. Okay?"

And without thinking, I reached out and wrapped my arm around his neck. I pulled him into a hug, feeling him brace himself against the bed. He chuckled against the side of my head before patting my back, and I sighed with relief.

"Thank you for everything you've done for me."

He shook his head. "Don't get it twisted. You did this. You fought, all week, to recuperate to this length. You're the fighter. We're simply the assistance in that fight."

Nurse Nina clapped her hands. "So, ready to get out of here? We have a few things to do, like gathering your prescriptions and scheduling your physical therapy. Then I get to wheel you out of here in a chair."

I smiled, pulling away from the doctor. "Does that mean races?"

"Do birds fly?"

I chuckled as they all helped me get out of bed. It seemed like it took a team of nurses to get me unhooked from all the tubes and machines. But, in reality, I was glad they were there. This staff had helped me around the clock for the past week and a half. They made Rae feel comfortable, they stood up for me with my father, and they encouraged my stepmother to keep speaking up for herself. It felt nice, having people in my corner.

Especially people like them.

"Your chariot awaits, Cee."

I grinned. "Oh, Nina. You really shouldn't have."

I flopped down into the wheelchair, clutching the folder of discharge paperwork in my lap. And away we went. I heard the doctor calling after us to slow down, but it only made me throw my hands in the air. Nina ran down the hallway with me, whooping and hollering as we careened around corners. She rushed me at that pace all the way down to their pharmacy, huffing and puffing as she sat with me. Waiting with me to get my medication.

"You got a ride home, kid?"

I nodded. "Stepmom's coming to get me."

She patted my knee. "She's one of the good ones. You make sure to keep her around."

I shrugged. "If my father stops being an asshole, she might actually stick around."

"What I wouldn't give for five minutes alone with that man."

We sat there, with her hand on my knee, and I

settled my hand over hers. I squeezed it softly, reluctant to let it go. They called my name too soon for my prescriptions. She walked me through how to take them a little too fast. I had an entire support network in this hospital, and I wasn't ready to let them go.

They'd been so good to me.

And I wanted to find a way to thank them for that.

Nina rolled me out to the roundabout in the front of the hospital and I saw Cecilia drive up. Nina helped me out of the wheelchair as my stepmother parked the car, rushing around to help. I stood up and turned around. I saw my doctor as well as the rest of the staff standing there, softly clapping for me. I stood strong. I stood tall. And with a smile on my face, I cleared my throat.

"Thank you, guys. For saving my life. And I know you'll stand there, telling me I'm the one fighting. But, without your surgery and your I.V.s and your knowledge, I'd be dead and you know it."

Silence fell over everyone before I sighed.

"I'll never be able to fully thank you or ever pay you back for what you did for me. And my stepmom. But I'm going to find a way to try."

The doctor cleared his throat. "Take care of yourself. That's what you can do."

Nina smiled. "And keep up with your therapy."

I grinned. "Don't want me coming back to visit."

A resounding 'no' rose from the crowd.

All of us started laughing before everyone came to give me hugs. They clapped my back softly and murmured words of encouragement. Nina reminded me the order of my pills, then made me recite it back to her. Then, my doctor—once again—told me to call. Anytime. For anything.

And I hugged him a bit longer than I should have.

Climbing into the car was hard. Driving away from that support system was even harder. But the second Cecelia took my hand, I felt at ease again. I relaxed against the leather interior of her car, my eyes fluttering closed as the car swerved softly with the roads. I didn't wake up until we'd pulled into the driveway of my home. I didn't say anything until Cecilia helped me inside. She settled me on the couch with a drink and a snack, then started writing out my medication schedule on a pad and a piece of paper as I rattled it off to her.

But the best part was that my father never came up in conversation.

Not once.

"All right. So, it's one of the painkillers in the morning, two of the anti-inflammatories after food at lunch. No later than two. Then another half a painkiller at night to help you sleep."

I nodded. "Right."

"Then, after one week, we add in the vitamin. Once the painkiller runs out."

I nodded. "Mm-hmm."

"And that vitamin is once in the morning up through the end of your first cycle of PT."

I grinned. "You got it."

"Perfect. I'll get this on the fridge so I can remember which ones to set out for you."

"You know you don't have to do that, right?"

She scoffed. "Nonsense. I'm going to help you out around here. I might not have to wipe your butt or anything. But that doesn't mean I can't get you your medication whenever you need it."

I smiled. "I appreciate it. Thanks."

"You need anything right now?"

"You mean other than a nap?"

She giggled. "Yep. Other than that."

I paused. "Oh! Yes, actually. A friend of mine is bringing my homework and stuff to me from school. She's helping me keep up with my studies."

"She, huh? Anything special about this... she?"

I snickered. "We're just studying."

She winked. "For now."

I chuckled. "Is that all right, though? If she comes by? I don't know if she will. She works sometimes. But I think this is her weekend off."

"If she pops by, she's more than welcome. I'm going to cook dinner tonight, so she can stay and eat with us."

"Dinner? I didn't know you cooked."

"What in the world do you think you've been eating for the past four years?"

"Uh, takeout?"

She cackled. "Well, glad to know my food tastes like takeout. I think."

"Wait a second, is that really your lasagna I've been eating?"

She nodded. "Oh, yeah. One of the many things my mother taught me was how to make most every traditional and popular recipe from scratch.

That's my lasagna and breadsticks you've been eating."

My jaw dropped in shock. "Holy shit. I mean—"

She laughed. "You're fine. It's okay."

"Well, damn then. That's some insane cooking skills you've got."

"In another lifetime, maybe I would have done it professionally. But I'll settle for blowing you and your father's socks off."

A silence fell over us and she cleared her throat. She patted my leg before getting up, then made herself scarce. I heard her humming to herself in the kitchen, piddling around in there. Probably figuring out what to make for dinner. I pulled my phone out and crafted a text to Rae. Hoping she didn't have to work tonight.

Me: Hey. If you want to come over tonight, you can. Stepmom's cooking dinner, and you're more than welcome to come eat with us.

I stared down at the text message and paused. Had I ever invited a girl willingly over to my house before? I raised my head, staring off at the wall. Holy shit, this was a first for me. A first with a girl. Willingly inviting her into my world. I smiled as I looked back down at my phone. I sent the text message off with excitement rushing through my veins.

And a few minutes later, my phone vibrated.

Rae: I'd love to. Be over there after school?

Me: Sounds like a plan. I can't wait.

And I meant every word of it.

"Hey, Clint!"

"Yeah, Cecilia?"

"I'm about to make myself a little frozen banana milkshake. You want one?"

"Uh, yes please. That sounds fantastic."

She giggled. "I thought it'd go well with a movie. There's supposed to be an action movie marathon on this afternoon."

I paused. "You like action movies?"

"Are women not supposed to like those?"

"No, no, nothing like that. You just strike me as a—"

The whirring of the blender cut me off and I started laughing. I craned my neck back, peeking into the kitchen as her playful glare fell onto my face. I laughed harder than I had in a while with her. I clutched my ribs, coughing and laughing through the pain as the blender turned off.

Then, my stepmother's voice filled the room again.

"If you tell me I look like a romantic movie junkie, you'll get this milkshake down your shirt."

I chuckled. "That might actually feel good with how hot my ribs feel."

"Are you okay? Is your skin red or anything? Because that's supposed to be one of those things we look out for."

I lifted my shirt. "Nope. I don't see red. They just feel internally hot."

"Let me get a thermometer really quickly."

She whirled around me, bringing me the milkshake before jamming a thermometer under my tongue. She sat there, looking like a worried mother until the damn thing beeped. The relief on her face told me I wasn't running a fever. Which was a relief to me, too. Because after settling in on this couch, I sure as hell didn't want to move.

"Okay. Well, we'll keep an eye on that."

I nodded. "Sounds good to me."

She handed me the remote. "Find that marathon and I'm going to get my milkshake."

"And take off those heels?"

She paused. "I suppose I could do that."

"Are you not supposed to walk around without your heels on or something?"

The mere fact that she had to think about it told me all I had to know, too.

"Want a snack?" she asked.

I nodded slowly. "Whatever you want is fine with me."

"Wonderful. Because caramel popcorn goes great with a banana shake."

"Am I supposed to be having all this junk?"

"Don't worry. I'm cooking a healthy dinner, and there's no dessert. So we can just have dessert now."

I chuckled. "I don't know if it works like that."

She called out from the kitchen, "Hey! It's how I've kept my figure all these years. And it's not like you haven't been eating greasy burgers behind my back."

"Wait, how did you know about that?"

"You fart in your sleep, Clint. I know all things!"

I threw my head back in laughter as I turned on the projector television. Cecilia came in a few minutes later with a milkshake in one hand and a bowl of caramel popcorn for us to share in the other. I lifted my feet, watching her sit down before I settled my legs onto her lap. And as I flicked through the channels, trying to find this marathon, I felt at peace.

"Thank you, Cecilia."

"For what?"

"For looking out for me this past week and a half."

She smiled. "We look out for each other, right?"

I nodded. "Always."

"Oh! There it is. Fast and Furious 4. Not my favorite. But it's a good one."

As we settled into the movie, I found myself staring at her, not the television. I mindlessly sipped the most incredible milkshake I'd ever put in my face, and I gazed at the woman who'd had my back since the ambulance was called. This must be what it felt like to have a parent in my corner. An adult who looked out for me.

It felt refreshing. Nice. Supportive. Natural.

And I really hoped I didn't do anything to make her hate me like my father.

17

RAELYNN

I rushed home after school, bursting through the front door. I ignored the car in the driveway. I ignored him calling out my name. I didn't want a damn thing to do with D.J. while he was over at the house. The only thing I wanted to do was quickly get ready for Clint's house and get the hell over there.

I was eager to spend time with him.

I closed myself off in my bedroom, blocking out the sounds of D.J. and my mother. Whether they were arguing or making out, I didn't know. And I sure as hell didn't care. I took my hair down from its ponytail and tried to find another way to fix it. I stripped down to nothing but my underwear, then rifled through my underwear drawer. Did I have anything else that looked even remotely nice? Something other than morphed training bras and fucking cotton panties?

I dug to the bottom of my drawer before settling on a pair of panties that I'd technically outgrown.

They were a bit tight around my hips, but showed off my ass cheeks nicely. I slipped them on, pairing them with a new bra Mom had managed to pick me up a few weeks ago. It wasn't a nice color or anything. Just a plain tan bra. But it had pretty little flower designs over the cups of them and lifted them off my chest a bit.

"Man, this thing is comfortable," I murmured.

I rifled through my drawers and pulled out my best pair of jeans. A bit tight, a bit low-riding, and exactly what I was looking for. I hopped myself into them, jumping around before I fell to my bed. I wiggled my ass into those things and sucked it in, wanting nothing more than to get them buckled.

"Come on. You can do it. Just a little—there we go!"

I stood up and bent down, trying to stretch them out a bit. I swiveled my hips, feeling them loosen before I looped my fingers in the belt loops. I worked them up a bit higher. Just enough to cover the top of my panty line. Then I rifled through my T-shirts until I found my favorite one.

A bit too low cut and a bit too tight around my breasts.

"Perfect. Ha-ha!"

I slipped it over my head and fluffed out my hair. And I had to say, I looked great. I smiled at myself as I ran a brush through my hair, trying to figure out how to fix it. I usually wore it in a ponytail. Just a simple one. Nothing special. But, tonight? I wanted to do something special. This was the first evening I'd be spending with Clint in a while. And without him being in the hospital. I knew we had schoolwork to do. I knew we had things to catch up on.

But part of me hoped his hands might do a little exploring, as well.

"Rae?"

A soft knock came at my door as my mother's voice trailed in front of it. I debated on not opening it. Mostly because I didn't want to chance seeing D.J. behind her. She knocked on the door again, calling out my name as I ran my fingers through my hair again.

"D.J.'s still downstairs, honey."

Well, in that case…

I opened the door and let her in, watching as she walked through the threshold. And when she turned to face me, she grinned.

"Getting dolled up, I see."

I shrugged. "Maybe a bit."

She turned me back toward my mirror. "Know what you're going to do with your hair?"

"Not yet. I'm still trying to figure it out."

"Can I try something?"

I nodded and she started tracing her hands through my hair. I closed my eyes, feeling the comfort of her warmth I remembered from my childhood. For years, my mother had done my hair. Brushed it out after baths and put it up into pigtails during middle school. She always talked about how envious she was of my hair. How thick and shiny and luxurious it felt. I leaned into her a bit. I settled against her, drawing in a deep breath as she worked out the last of the knots.

"You've always had such gorgeous hair. I don't know why you keep it in that ponytail."

I shrugged. "Easier in the mornings, I guess."

"You're excited about tonight, aren't you?"

I nodded. "I am, yes. It's been a few days since I've seen him. You know, because of work and stuff."

"Well, you take your time tonight, okay? No need to rush back home."

"Thanks, Mom. I appreciate it."

I felt her hands pause. "He's a good boy, right?"

He's better than D.J. "Yes, ma'am. He's a good boy. The best of boys."

"Good. That's very good."

I opened my eyes and watched her in the mirror. I saw the worry in her face, but I didn't know what to say in order to get her to calm down. So, I didn't say anything at all. I let her put my hair up into a half ponytail, with my hair pouring down past my shoulders. She fluffed the remains of it out then hugged me from behind, settling her chin against my shoulder.

"You got a ride over there?"

I shrugged. "Figured I'd walk. Or ride my bike."

"Well, I can drive you. D.J. said I could borrow his car while he watches the game."

I nodded. "Thanks, Mom. I appreciate that."

"Let me just get my purse and we'll head out. I'm doing the food run while D.J. stays here."

The two of us made our way out of my bedroom and down the stairs. And even though I peered into our living room and saw that sorry sack of shit sitting on our couch, he didn't even acknowledge my presence. He didn't look at me. He didn't say 'hi' to me. He didn't say anything about my outfit or ask me where I was going. Not that I'd want to tell him anyway. But, still.

Dick.

Mom tapped me on my shoulder. "I'll be right back with food, D.J."

He nodded mindlessly. "Sounds good."

"I'm gonna drop Rae off for the night, then go get it."

"Uh huh."

"You want anything else tacked onto your regular order?"

"Not if it gets you out the door quicker."

I wanted to punch him in his nutsack. But Mom simply giggled. She laughed at him. Like he was making some sort of a joke.

"Be back soon, sweetheart."

D.J. nodded. "Uh huh."

What an absolute asshole.

We made our way out to D.J.'s car and I quickly slipped in. I wanted to get away from this house, and fast. Even if I couldn't stay over at Clint's for the night, I'd end up at Allison's. Because I sure as hell wasn't coming back home until D.J. left.

I pointed. "Take a right here."

"On it."

I talked to Mom all the way to Clint's house and she whistled lowly to herself. I saw her staring up at the massive mansion, her eyes widening as we parked in the roundabout driveway. I unbuckled my seatbelt.

I leaned over and kissed her, thanking her for the ride.

Mom winked at me. "My daughter really knows how to snag 'em."

I snickered. "Have a good evening with D.J., Mom. Okay?"

My eyes found hers and she nodded slowly.

"I will. I promise."

I let myself out of the car and watched Mom drive away. I waved at her, wanting nothing more than to go right back to the house while she wasn't there and give that man a piece of my mind. I hated that she was back with him. I hated it, because I'd actually believed her the last time she told me it was over. I felt like we'd bonded over that moment. Bonded over our hurt and our pain. Yet, here she was, giving him another chance.

Then again, I'd given Clint a lot of chances, too.

I walked up to the front door and knocked. While I was nervous about meeting Clint's stepmother for the first time, formally, it didn't abate the butterflies in my stomach. I was anxious to see him. Anxious to hold him. Anxious to be in his presence again.

And when the front door opened, Clint smiled at me.

"Hey there, beau—oh!"

I threw myself into his arms, unable to contain my laughter. I wrapped my arms around his neck, holding him close as his body cloaked itself around mine. His arms hugged my back. He pulled me into the house, kicking the front door closed with his foot. I buried my face into the crook of his neck, feeling how much stronger he already was.

"You're upright."

Clint chuckled. "And you're here."

I giggled. "I am. Thank you for inviting me."

"Are we going to stay like this until we get to the kitchen?"

"Depends. Do we have to go to the kitchen right now?"

He snickered. "Nope. Not yet."

I drew in his scent, clinging to him as he held me tighter. His strength shocked me. Especially after such a terrible accident. I kissed his neck. His shoulder. His jawline. I nuzzled my nose against his as I slowly pulled away from him. His hand cupped the back of my head as his emerald eyes danced between mine.

And as he fisted my hair softly, I pressed my lips against his.

"Mmm, hello there, gorgeous."

I smiled. "Hi, handsome."

"I'm really glad you're here."

"Me, too."

"Ahem."

I jumped at the sound of the female voice, but Clint kept his arm wrapped around my waist. I saw his stepmother standing there, clad in a beautiful yellow dress and a crimson red apron. She smiled at the two of us before she came closer, her bare feet padding on the floor. She held her hand out to me, taking mine within hers. And I smiled at how warm and welcoming she became.

"It's nice to finally meet you, Rae. I'm Cecilia, Clint's stepmother. I've heard a great deal about you, too."

I paused. "You have?"

Clint chuckled. "Over the past few hours, at least."

I nodded. "That sounds about right."

Cecilia giggled. "Don't worry, he's not hiding you."

I shook my head. "I never would have thought that."

Clint squeezed my side and I leaned closer into him as Cecilia dropped my hand.

"Well, why don't you two come on into the kitchen? The lasagna just came out of the oven and the salad's ready. Plus, by the smells of it, the garlic bread is about to come out of the oven."

Clint chuckled. "You haven't lived until you've had her lasagna. Ready to eat?"

I shrugged. "I'm ready whenever the food's ready."

He kissed the side of my head. "A girl after my own stomach."

Cecilia laughed as she turned around, beckoning for us to follow her into the kitchen. And the smells that greeted me once we got there made my stomach growl out loud. It was a beautiful home-cooked meal, and the table was set with fine china and actual silver-ware. Not the plastic stuff we used, and not the fake silver stuff found in most stores. Genuine silver utensils.

"Rae, what would you like to drink?"

Cecilia's voice pulled me from my trance. "Um, soda or something is fine."

Clint pulled out my seat. "We've got Mountain Dew, Diet Dr. Pepper, and Coke."

"Um, Coke's fine. Thank you."

Cecilia was a brilliant host. She cracked open the can of Coke and poured it into the ice-filled crystal glass. Right in front of me. I'd never been treated this way before. Home-cooked meals in my house were microwaved meals and pre-cooked oven meals my mother slapped into the oven or something like that. With canned vegetables on the side. This was a spread. Lasagna. Fresh salad. Multiple dressings. Freshly-made garlic bread in actual loaf form.

Clint whispered in my ear, "And there's blueberry crumble for dessert."

And oh, the growl my stomach let out.

18

CLINTON

"**O**h, holy sh—itake mushrooms."

I chuckled at the way Rae edited herself. "Good, huh?"

She groaned, taking another bite of the lasagna. "It's heaven. Where in the world did you learn to cook?"

Cecilia smiled. "My mother. She taught me a lot of homemade recipes. Macaroni and cheese. Basic noodles."

Rae's eyes widened. "You made these noodles?"

"Yes ma'am, I did."

Cecilia beamed with pride and my heart felt fuller than it had in a long time. Rae kept devouring the food like she hadn't eaten in weeks, and I loved it. I adored a girl that wasn't afraid to put carbs in her system. Not like the other girls at school, who walked around with fiber bars stuffed in their purses and ate nothing but fruit and yogurt for lunch.

"So, Rae. Are you a senior, too?"

Rae nodded. "Mm-hmm."

"Any plans after graduation?"

I waited with baited breath as Rae swallowed her food. For some reason, I was now wondering what her plans were. I mean, it hadn't been important before. But now that Cecilia had formally brought it up, I wanted to know the answer.

And quickly.

"Well, I've been saving back money from the grocery store. And if I play my cards right, I'll have enough to share an apartment with Allison once we graduate."

Cecilia nodded. "And who's Allison?"

"Rae's best friend," I said.

She nodded. "Yep. Known her for years. She's been accepted into UCLA's architecture program early."

Cecilia smiled brightly. "Nice. So you'll still be close. You hear that, Clint?"

I snickered. "I do. Thanks."

"Are you wanting to go to UCLA, too?"

Rae shrugged. "I was thinking more of a community college. I don't want to get into loans or anything like that. Maybe work part-time, go to school part-time. Or work out something like where I work full time a year then go to school full time a year or something like that."

"That's noble. I admire you for that."

Rae paused. "You do?"

Cecilia nodded. "Mm-hmm. I graduated early

from high school when I was seventeen and left home. I did part-time classes at a community college not too far from where I grew up and took on a job in between classes and such. Saved up as much as I could while living with three other girls in a two-bedroom apartment. It wasn't easy, but I wouldn't trade it for anything."

"What did you get your degree in?"

"Medical transcriptioning. A nice little work from home position that would have eventually paid an hourly wage equivalent to that of a full time job, plus benefits."

Rae nodded. "Then you got married?"

Cecilia smiled. "Well, a few other things happened in between there. I did work for a while. Struggled, but made it through. I met Howard about six years ago, so I lived a lot of life between that job and now."

"Is there a reason you graduated early?"

Cecilia looked at me from across the table and I shrugged. To be honest, I was simply excited they were getting along. Hitting it off. I was glad Cecilia didn't hate Rae, or vice versa. I was content with taking a backseat and letting them get to know one another. Because things felt calm this way. Peaceful. There was no tension or anger like there would have been had Dad been around for this dinner.

Then again, this dinner wouldn't have happened at all had Dad been here.

"I grew up in a very conservative home. And while I loved my parents, I knew there was a great deal more out there for me to experience. They did a lot of things while I was younger. Tried marrying me off at sixteen. Grounded me by locking me in my room and not letting me do things like to go school and have meals with the family."

Rae sighed. "I'm so sorry."

I furrowed my brow. "I didn't know that, Cecilia."

She giggled bitterly. "It's not really something you talk about. Especially with guests over. But she asked the question so I figured, why not answer it?"

Rae cleared her throat. "I mean, at least they taught you how to make awesome food. Plenty of grease pans to throw in their faces for later."

Cecilia snickered, almost blowing her water through her nose. Rae fell apart in a fit of giggles, and I quickly joined in, though it still hurt my ribs to laugh that much. Cecilia's head fell back as she barked with laughter, snorting and covering her mouth. Which only made us laugh harder. I'd never heard her laugh like this. Which meant I'd never heard her snort. And as we all leaned back into our chairs, I finally knew what it felt like.

Home.

I finally understood what the word meant.

"Oh, my gosh. I haven't laughed like that in ages."

Rae giggled. "You should hang around Clint more often, then. Some of the situations he can get himself into are hysterical."

I paused. "Hey, now. Sometimes a guy has to blow off steam."

Cecilia heaved for air. "You don't blow off steam. Otherwise you wouldn't be so full of hot air."

I playfully glared at her. "I think you're confusing me with Dad at this point."

And soon, the girls were falling over in their chairs with laughter.

The jokes continued through the night, even as we sat down with coffee and blueberry crumble. Tears crested our eyes from the hilarity of it all, and the worries of the accident quickly fell away from our memories. Cecilia looked comfortable in her own home. I felt comfortable in my own home. And Rae looked perfect in this home. With her red face and her silent laughter and her frazzled hair puffing out the redder her face got.

She was perfection in a bottle.

And I wanted to drink her down.

"All right, you two. I'm going to clean up. I'm assuming Clint has some homework to get done, so you guys might as well get to it."

I sighed. "Ready for torture hour?"

Rae got up, rolling her eyes. "You're such a drama queen when it comes to homework. Come on. It's not going to kill you to get caught up."

She took my hands within hers, helping me up from the chair. I playfully grunted, feigning absolute exhaustion and pain as I threw my arm around her shoulders.

"I can't make it. Rae, I just—say good things at my funeral. Tell them how loved I was. Make them remember!"

And as I fell with my body weight against her, she caught me in her arms. Giggled into my chest. Pulled me down the hallway before pushing me up the stairs. She grabbed a sack of books I didn't even realize she'd brought with her. An old, brown sack sitting in the corner by the stairs.

"Need me to get that?"

She shooed me away. "Come on. Up we go. I'm good. Let's go, Tiny."

I paused. "Tiny?"

But all she did was giggle to herself.

We found our way to my bedroom and I closed the door behind us. She hopped on the bed and started pulling out books. I couldn't stop staring at her. The way her hair poured down past her shoulders. The way it fell in her face. The way her breasts protruded from that tight T-shirt and the way her panties played peek-aboo with me from the top of her jeans. I licked my lips as I made my way for her. I hopped onto the bed, watching the books and papers bounce.

"All right. English or math first?"

And as Rae looked up into my eyes, I grinned.

"What if we have dessert first?"

She rolled her eyes. "We've already had dessert."

I tucked a strand of hair behind her ear. "What about second dessert?"

"Clint, you're not using sex to get out of home-work. Come on. I'm tired of doing it for you. Let's go."

I paused. "You've been doing my homework for me?"

She blushed, and my world came to a grinding halt. Had she actually been doing my homework for me? Why?

"We really should get started on this."

I smiled. "Didn't realize we'd made it to Guantanamo."

Rae rolled her eyes. "You done with the torture jokes? Because if we get started, it's less than an hour's worth of work."

"And then second dessert?"

"Math. Now."

She thrust the notebook and a pencil in my hands and away we went. She helped me through the problems I stumbled on and had some great explanations for me whenever I got hung up and frustrated. I'd always hated math. It was that course in school I almost always failed, even with tutoring and extra credit. It took me forty minutes alone just to stumble along through the one-page worksheet. And we hadn't even touched the history reading yet.

"Fucking hell."

Rae rubbed my back. "We'll take a break and then maybe I can read to you. Okay?"

I snickered. "I don't need you to read to me. I just need this shit to not exist."

"I know. But it's important. I know how much graduating means to you. So we'll get through it and then we can... do whatever else."

And when I caught her eye, she winked at me. Making fire surge through my veins.

I felt my strength coming back, so I pressed on. While the one-hour's worth of work took me almost three, Rae got me through it. Not once did she get upset or frustrated. Not once did she berate me for it or call me 'stupid' like my father used to. She didn't even comment on how long it took me to get all that shit done.

But, she did kiss me with triumphant desire when we finished.

"I'm proud of you, you know."

I smiled against her lips. "Thanks, beautiful."

Her forehead fell against my own. "When's your next appointment?"

"Uh… Monday. I think. Monday afternoon."

"You want me here for it?"

"I think it'll be during school. But you're more than welcome to come over afterward. You know, massage my aches and pains away."

She grinned. "Oh, really now?"

Rae pressed herself against me, lowering me to the mattress. I heard books and things falling to the ground, no doubt causing a ruckus of sound below us. I grunted as her weight settled against me, but not once did I move. I wanted her on top of me. I wanted the comfort of her weight pressing me into my mattress. I slid my fingers through her hair, working it out of that small ponytail she had until it curtained us off from the rest of the world.

"Hi," she said softly.

I grinned. "Hi there."

Then, her face fell. "They're still out there, you know. The guys who ran you off the road."

I wrapped my arms around her. "I know."

"I haven't had an update from the police. Have you?"

"I haven't, no."

"Do you think they'll find the guys?"

"I'm sure they will."

Rae nuzzled her nose against mine. "I'm scared about them still being out there."

I rolled her over, hovering above her as she stared back at me. With wide eyes and full lips that called to my cock, I captured them softly. She moaned against me. Rolled her body and parted her legs, opening herself up to me. We stripped one another of our clothes. Her touch against my skin ignited something in my chest. I kissed down her neck, trying to soothe away her worries as her body tensed underneath mine. And when my lips found hers again, I whispered against them.

"The worst is behind us. I promise."

19

RAELYNN

My hands slid up his back as soft sighs fell from my lips. I parted my thighs for him, feeling his rock steady girth fall against me. I rocked slowly, not wanting to hurt him. His kisses were soft. Light. Fluttering against my skin as he ran his nose down my pulse point.

"Clint," I whispered.

He groaned. "How I've missed that sound."

He kissed down my breasts. He wrapped his mouth around my puckered peaks. My body rose for him. Bucked for him. Ignited with goosebumps that rushed along my skin. His hands caressed me softly. I felt him creeping along, tracing me with his fingertips. His lips slid down my stomach. My muscles jumped for him at every turn.

"Clint, you should be on your—"

"No."

He kissed my folds. I moaned, pressing my head

back into the pillows as his fingertips parted me. I gasped as his tongue fell between them, licking and sucking with wanton lust. I gripped my thighs around his face. He stroked softly, stoking the fire in my chest. I felt it consuming me. Like a forest fire raging through our mountains. I reached down for his hair. I gripped his tendrils. I pulled him closer to me as I rolled against his lips. His hands slid up my sides. I felt him massaging my breasts as my eyes rolled back.

And when my body popped, I trembled against the stubble on his cheeks.

"Oh—ye—Cli—yo—sh—fu—"

I couldn't speak. Couldn't catch my breath. He lapped me slowly, until my body collapsed after bowing itself out. I gasped for air as he pressed himself up. Wet kisses trailed behind his lips, leaving marks against my skin as he journeyed his way back up. His eyes found mine and he smiled down at me, glistening with my arousal against his skin.

"I want to taste."

Clapping my hand against the back of his head, I pulled him down to me and licked myself off his skin, moaning and consuming all of him I could. I felt his length pressing against my entrance. I bucked slowly, inching him deeper into my body. He growled down the back of my throat. He filled me to the brim. He stretched me and molded me, my body allowing him access to whatever he wanted.

Because I loved him.

Even if I didn't have the guts to admit it yet.

Grunts and growls fell from his lips as my hands

slid down his back. I tightened my arms around his neck, letting my knees fall off to the side. Our bodies became one. I suckled on his lower lip as his girth grew against my walls. Colors sizzled and faded in my view as we rocked and bucked, slowly climbing a precipice we'd both been craving for days.

"Rae."

"Clint."

"I've missed you. So—so much."

"All of it. I—I need—oh, Clint."

"Tell me. Tell me what you need."

I crashed our lips together, grinding my hips against his own. My toes curled as I wrapped my feet behind his calves, hoping beyond all hope I wasn't hurting him. He picked up the pace, rolling and thrusting. Moving the bed on its frame as our kisses grew sloppy. He gripped my hair and pulled my head softly off to the side. He buried his face against my neck, breathing in my scent before sinking his teeth into me.

And as that coil in my gut snapped, my jaw unhinged in silent pleasure.

"Oh—yeah—"

He growled, digging his teeth deeper as his tongue traced my pulse point. The pain and pleasure, it was all too much. My entire body wrapped around him. I pulled him down against me, forcing him to collapse. His length jumped against my walls, pouring into me as my body massaged him. Milked him. Drank him all down. I wanted all of him. Every single piece of him.

So long as he'd let me have it.

He sighed. "Oh, Rae."

Clint kissed the teeth marks he'd left behind as our bodies stayed connected. I stroked his back, feeling him quiver against me as goosebumps rushed over his skin. It made me smile, feeling them. Feeling how his body reacted to my touch. I felt him pull back, slipping from between my thighs before something gushed between my legs.

I giggled. "Uh oh."

Clint shook his head. "We'll fix it tomorrow. Just— don't move."

"Trust me, I don't plan on it."

"Good."

He snuggled down against me before falling off to the side. He grunted with pain, pulling me into his arms and away from the mess we'd created. The covers came up and settled over my bare skin as my ass sank back into his pelvis. His arm wrapped around me, holding me steadily to him as he tucked us both in. This felt right. Good. Like things should have been. I wasn't sure of much, but I was sure of one thing.

Clint belonged in my world.

"Are you okay?"

My question pierced the silence before he followed it up with a kiss between my shoulder blades.

"I'm just fine, beautiful."

I paused. "Are you sure? I didn't hurt you?"

He chuckled. "You could never hurt me."

"You know what I mean."

I turned around, gazing into his eyes. He smoothed my hair away from my forehead before kissing it softly. My eyes fluttered closed and I melted into his touch.

His arm wrapped back around me and I pressed my leg between his, seeking his warmth and his strength as the covers slipped over our heads.

"I promise, you didn't hurt me, Rae."

I smiled. "Good. Just making sure."

I lay there, gazing upon the bruising of his face. The nose brace was gone, but his eyes were still a soft black. His jaw was yellow, denoting the fading of his bruises. But it was still a painful reminder. I reached out and traced down his chest, my eyes following its contour. His lips fell against my forehead, kissing me over and over as my fingertips fluttered like feathers over the dark purple bruising of his ribs.

"Oh, Clint."

"I promise, I'm okay."

I sniffled. "My God, I'm so glad you are."

"Come here. I've got you, Rae."

I curled into him as much as he'd let me. And as I cried silent tears against his chest, I drifted off to sleep. With his fingers stroking through my hair and his lips peppering me with kisses, I gave in to him. I gave in to his warmth. His comfort. His strength. The beating of his heart lulled me to sleep. And the beating of his heart was the first thing I heard the next morning.

Before I slipped away from his grasp to go get us some coffee.

20

CLINTON

I groaned as I opened my eyes. A heavy weight felt like it was propped against me, keeping me rooted to the mattress. I reached out for Rae, expecting her to be there. Knowing damn good and well that was what I felt.

Instead, however, I felt the weight of the emptiness of the bed next to me.

"Fuck."

I sighed, lying there on my back as I stared up at the ceiling. I wished I'd woken up sooner to say goodbye to Rae. I sighed as I lay there, my arm slung over my eyes. I wanted to go back to sleep. In fact, I wanted to keep sleeping until she came back to visit. Until she came back again, so I could sit her on my lap, feel her straddle my body, and watch as she rode me off into the damn sunset.

"I need to write that down."

My hand fell off to the side, fumbling around for

my phone. And when I picked it up, I saw it was a little past nine in the morning. On a Saturday. The fuck was I up so early for? I didn't have anything to do today. So I tossed my phone onto the bed where Rae had been and rolled over, face-planting into her pillow.

Sniffing in her scent.

I dreaded the lonely weekend ahead of me. I knew Cecilia had plans, and I had no idea when the hell my father was getting back into town. He'd already defaulted on many promises. Including the one where he said he'd be back in town before I got discharged from the hospital. I snickered into the pillow, wanting nothing more than to toss that man off a fucking cliff.

He should've taken the nose-dive off the bridge.

Not me.

I closed my eyes and envisioned Rae. What she'd look like if she were with me. Her hair mussed. Knotted. Tangled. Her eyes sparkling as she stared back at me with her sleepy orbs. Her smile, lopsided from the pleasure we'd both experienced. And her body, warm and comforting against my body. I lost myself in the vision. In how things could have panned out had she stayed. I wasn't sure when she'd slipped out last night. Or this morning. But I wanted to call and make sure she'd gotten home safely.

Then I heard the door open.

I furrowed my brow as I heard Rae's soft humming filtering through the door. The smell of coffee flooded my nose, filling the room with its presence. I smiled as my bedroom door closed, and then another scent caught my nose.

Were those pastries?

"What are you still doing here?"

I went to prop myself up on my elbow just as Rae yelped. And when I shot up from bed, I saw her stumble with the coffees. The brown paper bag from underneath her arm dropped to the ground, revealing several warm danishes and pastries. She cursed under her breath as the drink carrier tilted. Some of the coffee went spilling onto my carpet as she righted herself, refusing to let the drinks fall. I watched with a grin on my face, feeling bad that I'd scared her. But also incredibly happy she was still here.

"The hell's wrong with you? I almost peed myself!"

I chuckled. "I'm sorry. I just didn't know you were still here."

"I mean, I wasn't for a bit. But I didn't want to wake you up."

I watched her dip down, scooping the paper bag up under her arm again. I grunted as I sat myself up, trying to shake the morning stiffness so I could help her. By the time I got a pillow behind my back, she was already at my side. Sitting the coffees down, rear-ranging the food, then reaching for more pillows.

"Here, lean up."

"Rae, you don't—"

"I said, lean up, you stubborn boy."

She fluffed my pillows as I did what she asked. I couldn't take my eyes off her. She had her hair piled on top of her head and she had picked her way through my drawers. She had on a shirt of mine. And a pair of sweatpants. I looked over at my dresser drawer, seeing two of them pulled out and hanging on by a thread.

"Sorry, I was tired this morning."

I shook my head. "Don't you dare be sorry. You're welcome to anything in here."

She snickered. "Thanks."

I kept running my eyes over her, because she looked fucking fantastic in my clothes. They hung off her, completely covering her form. And yet, she'd never been sexier. She'd never been more beautiful. I licked my lips as she handed my coffee to me. The black liquid still steamed from the to-go lid, and I smelled hints of rosewater and caramel.

"I know it's a bit fancy, but trust me. I tried a sample of it. It's damn delicious."

I grinned. "I trust you. What'd you get?"

Rae shrugged. "The usual. Iced caramel macchiato with an extra shot."

"I'll have to remember that."

I took a sip of the coffee and was stunned at how good it tasted. I took another sip. Then another. And soon, I was chugging the damn thing down.

Rae giggled. "Good thing I got a large."

I nodded as I continued drinking, not wanting to let go of the lid. But the coffee burned my throat. So I slowed down in order to savor the taste a bit.

"What'd you say was in this again?"

Rae smiled. "Regular caffeinated coffee with a shot of rosewater and two pumps of caramel."

I grinned. "Damn, that's good."

"There's this cute little coffee shop not too far up the road. I got Michael to drive me up there."

"Buckheads Brews?"

"That's the one."

"You know, I always thought that place was a bar until I walked in there one day. I smelled lemon bars in the damn place and got confused."

She giggled. "I don't think you're the only one to make that assumption. They had an assortment of fresh pastries on sale because they didn't get the 'pastry to filling' ratio right. I don't know what the hell that means, but I got them half off. So I got a bunch of them."

"You didn't have to do that, you know."

"I don't have to do anything. But I wanted to."

I grinned. "Thank you, Rae."

She leaned over and kissed my cheek, letting her lips linger for a little bit. I scooted over, giving her enough room to sit on the edge of my bed. She didn't take the hint. Instead, she grabbed her coffee and leapt into bed with me, taking up the spot next to me she'd had last night. I reached for a cheese danish, handing it to her before digging out a lemon one for myself.

And when I took a bite out of the damn thing, I moaned.

"Holy shit."

Rae nodded. "Right?"

"So fucking good."

"Seriously. Their cheese ones are great. But I've got, like, four apple ones in there. You'd think that's gross. But it's not when they do it."

I took another bite. "How have I not known about these things? They're incredible."

"Have you ever actually been *in* there, tough stuff?"

I cast her a look that made her snicker. Of course I'd been in that damn place. Every fucking girl at our high school had been in that damn place. Which meant just about every guy in our school had been in there at least once. Doesn't mean I'd had their food, though. Just a plain coffee while the girl I was with got some hoity-toity soy-based milk-coffee concoction. Some girl I'd hooked up with wanted to go there for a date after skipping out on class sophomore year. Just after I'd gotten my bike license, and right before I totaled my first rusted-out motorcycle. I wasn't going to tell Rae that, of course. She didn't need to know those details.

But, yes. I'd been in the damn place before.

"Got any plans for your day?" I asked.

I peeked over at Rae and watched her shrug.

"I mean, they can wait."

I paused. "What's waiting?"

"Nothing much. Just a study session with Allison."

"Is it important?"

"Not as important as this."

"Are you sure?"

She rolled her eyes. "Yes, Clint. I'm sure. I don't actually need to study with Allison. It's just tradition for us before every major test with classes we share."

"What class?"

She paused. "History."

"Oh, goodie."

"Don't worry. I'll help you through the test."

I grinned. "Skipping study sessions for little old me, huh? What's next? Skipping classes? Skipping school days?"

"In your fucking dreams, hot stuff."

"That's more like it."

I leaned over and gave her a kiss, but she turned her lips toward mine. Instead of connecting with her cheek, her lips fell to mine. And I tasted that cheese danish against her skin. She moaned against me as my tongue pierced her lips. Her jaw dropped open, allowing me inside as I reached over to cup the back of her head. I contorted my body, swallowed my groans of pain as I tasted her breakfast upon her lips.

Then I pulled back. Because my ribs were screaming at me the more I moved toward her.

I winced. "I like that cheese danish."

Rae pushed me back. "Sit up. I know you're in pain."

"Never, when you're around."

"Clint—"

"Rae, it's okay. I pro—"

"Just let me take care of you, okay?"

I heard the frustration in her voice and it gave me pause.

"Just… just let me be here for you, all right?"

I nodded. "All right."

"You're important to me. You're worth this. You're worth skipping the study session and you're worth spending time with. I know you're used to being tough. Always doing it alone. But you're not alone right now.

So, just... try to work with me, okay? It's okay to tell me when you're in pain."

"I'm just not used to it."

"Well, try to get used to it, please?"

I sighed. "I can give it my best shot."

"Here, let me fix your pillows."

I leaned forward for her again, letting her rearrange them behind me. And as she doted on me, trying her best to make me feel comfortable, I felt cared about. For once. I felt loved, for once. It'd been a long time since I'd felt things like this before. Yet she and Cecilia were practically showering me with it. I had no idea what I'd done to deserve it. To warrant it.

But I hoped one day to find a way to pay them back for it.

Rae leaned me back. "There. How's that?"

I sighed with relief. "Much better."

"Good."

I grinned. "You think I'm worth skipping your study session for?"

"Don't you start."

"You want me more than school. You want me more than school."

"Well, there are times where I want torture more than school. So take it for what it's worth."

I shrugged. "I don't know. I've heard torture can be pleasurable at times. If you do it right."

She shot me a look. "You can keep all those thoughts to yourself."

"So my hands have free rein?"

She playfully shoved me. "You're insane, you know that?"

"Insane for you, sure."

Her eyes met mine and my heart grew two times in that moment. Two times bigger than what it usually was. Rae Cleaver—the outcast nerd of our school—was slowly filling a void I had ignored for a long time. A void I'd allowed to fester for much too long. A void I'd convinced myself didn't really exist.

I love you. Just say it. Tell her how you feel.

"Rae?"

"Yes?"

My hand moved to cup her cheek. "I—"

"Yeah, Clint?"

"You mean a lot to me. You know that, right?"

She nodded. "And you know you mean a lot to me, too. Right?"

I nodded. "I do."

"So then we mean a lot to each other."

"We do, yes."

She smiled softly. "Well, then…? Good."

But for some reason, that statement didn't seem good enough. Not for everything Rae had given me. Not for everything she'd done for me. Not for everything she'd filled within me.

One day, I'll show you. I'll write it down and shout it from the rooftops.

"Just like you deserve."

Rae furrowed her brow. "What was that?"

I paused. "What?"

"You murmured something. But I didn't understand you."

"Oh. I didn't realize I'd said anything."

"Are you feeling okay?"

She pressed her hand against my forehead, making me snicker. "I feel fine, Rae."

"You'd tell me if you didn't feel okay, right?"

I brought her hand to my lips to kiss. "I would."

"Promise?"

"Promise, promise."

And as I placed a kiss to the palm of her hand, I felt her snuggle against me.

A place that almost seemed to be carved out against my body just for hers to have.

21

RAELYNN

*Raelynn*One Week Later

I huffed to myself. "Come on, where the hell is it?"

Mom poked her head in my room. "Whatcha looking for, sweetheart?"

"Nothing. Nothing. I'm fine."

"Sure you don't need any help?"

I shook my head as I rushed around my room, listening as papers fluttered everywhere. I cursed myself, catching them out of thin air before piling them into a wrinkled ball within the palm of my hand. My eyes darted around the room. I had way too many things I needed to lug to school today. I had my homework and Clint's homework. My books *and* his books. Today was an exciting day, and I needed to make sure it all went off without a hitch.

"Sweetheart, sure you don't—"

I held up my hand. "Just give me a second to recuperate. I know it's in here somewhere."

"What's in here somewhere?"

"That damn history book," I murmured.

Mom let out a soft giggle and I looked over at her.
She had her arms crossed around her chest and her
head shook itself at me. The look in her eye was skepti-
cal. But the smile on her face was telling. It made me
blush underneath her gaze. It gave me pause as to just
how much was rushing through my mind.

And on Clint's behalf, too.

"Have you checked under your bed?"

I sighed. "Nothing ever gets kicked under my bed,
Mom. I'm not twelve anymore."

She shrugged. "Sometimes the one place where I
find things are the last place I figured I'd find them."

I dropped down to my knees. "It's not going to be
under my bed. I promise you, out of all the pla—"

Mom laughed as my words stopped in my tracks. I
rolled my eyes as I reached under the bed, feeling my
fingertips fall against the hardback cover of Clint's
history textbook. I swallowed my grumbles and tried to
find the hilarity in the situation. I grinned as my mother's laughter grew to almost fiendish volumes.

"Can you keep it down up there? I've only got one
cup of coffee in me!"

Mom snickered. "Sorry, Deej!"

I rolled my eyes as I stood up. I hated that man. I
hated him with every ounce of me I had. But there
wasn't a damn thing I could do about his presence. I
stood up with the book in my hand and slipped it into

my shoulder satchel, then rifled through the papers on the bed.

"This goes with that. This goes here. Oh, that's mine. Yikes. And... where's the last page of this paper?"

I looked around the room before Mom cleared her throat.

"You mean this?"

I looked over at her and I found her clutching a sheet of paper. I walked over and saw the last little bit of typed information I needed for Clint's history paper. I took it from her with a thankful smile, then placed it with the rest of the sheets of paper. I clipped it, slipped it on top of his history book, then sandwiched it between that and his English book.

I needed to make sure I didn't accidentally turn in my homework as his.

Mom giggled. "Do you need a ride to school?"

I shook my head. "Nah, I've got it."

"Are you sure? That bag looks pretty—"

I heaved the shoulder strap over my body, grunting as I situated it. Yes, it was heavy. But I didn't want a ride to school from Mom. Because I knew what that entailed before she even said it.

"I'm fine, Mom. Really. I'll be good. Just need a bit of an earlier start."

She scoffed. "You're going to sweat through your clothes before you even get there. Come on, let us give you a ride. I can ride with you, and D.J. can drive us on his way to work."

"I'm good."

I hated the fact that Mom had officially gotten back together with D.J. It made me sick. It made me wonder if the things she'd said that night had ever been true. I wondered if she'd ever had plans to better her life. Or herself. Or her circumstance. I mean, in the back of my mind, I knew they hadn't been completely over. Someone was still paying the bills, since her applications had gone unanswered. According to her, at least. I wouldn't have been shocked one bit if they'd called for interviews and she had dodged the phone calls.

It was my mother, after all.

Mom shrugged. "Well, be careful, okay? I can tell that bag is heavy."

I nodded. "I promise I'll be careful. It's why I'm getting a bit of an earlier start. So I can take my time."

"You got any plans for after school? Maybe with this boy of yours?"

"His name's Clint. And I'm not sure."

"Did you have fun with him last weekend?"

Wow. Finally. After over a week of spending the night at Clint's place and meeting his stepmother, my own mother finally asked me about it. I tried not to let the pain and the hurt show on my face. I tried not to let it get to me too much. I mean, it had been nice, having my mother back. Having her fun banter and her attention and her love back. Not that she didn't love me. But she was a different type of mother whenever D.J. was around.

The type of mother that pretty much clocked out whenever I wasn't around.

I nodded. "We had a good time. Cecilia's really nice."

"His stepmother?"

"Mm-hmm. Very kind. She cooked this massive meal, too. Lasagna."

"Sounds like she's an amazing woman."

I heard the pain in Mom's voice. "She's amazing, just like you."

And when Mom smiled, I knew my words had at least soothed a temporary balm over whatever pain she was trying to cure with D.J. I didn't know much as a teenager, but I knew that much. I knew there was a good chance Mom had never gotten over my father leaving. Gotten over the way he abandoned us. So, being around D.J. and having D.J. always come back to her—like my father never had—sort of reassured her that she meant something to him. That she was worth something to this world.

At least, that's what the guidance counselor at my school said.

"Well, I need to get on to school."

Mom frowned. "You don't want to have some breakfast? Or some coffee with us?"

I don't want to deal with D.J., no. "Like I said, early start."

"Let me at least get you something to go. You can come down to the kitchen and I'll get you and D.J.—"

"Mom."

She paused, and I had to check myself. For whatever reason, she was pushing—hardcore—trying to get D.J. and myself into the same room. But it wouldn't happen. With all the shit happening with Clint and his schoolwork right now, I didn't have the energy to deal with my mother's abusive fucking boyfriend. I'd thrown in the towel with D.J. At least for now. If that was who my mother wanted to cuddle up with at night, then so be it. I was done putting my energy into her, trying to talk her out of this disgusting scenario.

I needed to focus my efforts on getting Clint healed and graduated.

Mom sighed. "D.J. just wants to see you, that's all."

I nodded. "Well, I don't want to see him."

"Come on, Raelynn. Just give him a chance."

"A chance?"

"Yes."

"A chance!"

"Rae, don't raise your voice like—"

I scoffed. "I've given him plenty of chances, Mom. Plenty. I gave him a chance after you came home with your first black eye. I gave him a chance after he stormed out of here one night after calling you a 'useless bitch.' I gave him a chance after he tried choking you out in the middle of the kitchen and I had to elbow him in his fucking lower back in order to get him to let go."

Mom's face hardened. "Raelynn Cleaver."

"I've given him plenty of chances. He doesn't get any more from me. I'm not you, Mom. I don't have to give him chances like you apparently feel like you need to. I don't want to have breakfast with him. I don't want to have coffee with him. I don't want a ride to school from him. And I don't want to see him. Ever."

"Raelynn!"

I shoved past my mother, feeling my satchel weighing me down. I flounced down the steps, listening as D.J.'s footsteps stormed down the hallway.

"The hell's all that ruckus in this house?"

And his question made me whip around to face him.

"You don't get to make demands in this house."

Mom paused in the middle of the steps. "Raelynn Cleaver. You shut that attitude down right now."

But I glared at D.J. "This isn't your home, this isn't your space, and that isn't your girlfriend. Because if you loved her, you wouldn't do half the things to her that you do."

"Rae! Stop!"

I took a step toward D.J. "I don't want to see you. I don't want to hear from you. And I sure as hell don't want you making demands in this house. And if my mother ever comes home with another bruise on her face? On her skin? I'm calling the damn police myself."

D.J. leveled me with a stare that could kill, but I didn't give a shit about it. I stormed out of the house, slamming the front door behind me as I made my way for the driveway. Already, I heard them fighting this morning. D.J. yelling in that house like he owned it. And Mom crying and trying to subdue him. The only good thing that might ever come from him striking Mom again is the fact that I'd live up to my promise. If Mom ever had another bruise on her skin I caught, the police would be at the house.

Getting my side of the story, despite what Mom wanted.

Sweat already trickled down the nape of my neck as I made my way for the edge of the neighborhood. I focused my mind on school. On the new week. On the excitement of the day. I smiled as Allison came into view, hopping out of Michael's car. She came rushing for me as Michael's trunk slowly eased itself open, her arms throwing themselves around me.

"Are you ready? I mean, really ready? You've probably been waiting for this for a while."

I smiled. "I'm ready for this, yes. I need to thank Michael for driving, too."

Michael leaned out his window. "You're welcome! Now, get your stuff in the back. We gotta go!"

Allison squealed as she helped me get my satchel from around my shoulder. We both grunted and groaned, heaving it into the trunk before the door closed automatically. I rushed around, watching Allison climb into the front seat. And as I slipped into the back seat, I set my eyes toward Clint's house.

Michael looked at me through the rearview mirror. "Ready?"

I nodded. "Ready, Freddy."

Allison giggled. "Let's do this."

Michael inched away from the curb and we took off down the road. We turned into Clint's neighborhood as I fed Michael directions. Down one street. Up another. A small U-turn because we took a left turn much too early. I smiled to myself as I saw Clint's house coming into view. My heart sang with delight when I saw him standing on his porch. Michael pulled into his roundabout driveway and I opened the door, watching as Clint lumbered over to the car.

It was his first day back at school, and I was ecstatic to have him there.

He smiled. "Morning, Rae."

And I smiled back. "Morning, Clint."

"Aly. Mike."

Allison rolled her window down. "Hey there, Brick. How you feeling?"

Clint paused. "Brick?"

She shrugged. "You're practically a brick wall to have survived what you did."

Michael chuckled. "She's not wrong."

Clint grinned. "Brick. I could get used to that."

Michael smiled. "All right. Hop in. Time for us to get to school."

I held out my hand. "Here, let me help."

I eased him into the car, thankful that Michael and Allison were willing to give Clint the support he needed. And the fact that they had agreed to help me almost immediately warmed my heart. It seemed as if they had accepted him. Drawn him into our little fold. I couldn't have been happier about it, too. I wanted the rest of the school year to be this way. Us, walking together to school hand in hand, with my two best friends who had come to accept Clint for who he was, what he was, and who he'd become.

Things finally felt as if they were falling into place.

I saw Michael peeking through his rearview mirror at Clint. And while I wasn't sure why, I had a feeling. I knew he was struggling to warm up to Clint. After all, Michael was the king of holding grudges. Still, I held Clint's hand tightly as we all rode to school, with Allison chattering her head off at us.

Then Michael pulled us into the back parking lot as he spoke up.

"You guys want to be dropped off at the curb?"

I looked over at Clint. "What do you want?"

He sighed. "While I don't like the idea of being catered to like that, it might help."

Michael nodded. "Say no more."

Allison turned around. "You need any help getting out?"

Clint shook his head. "You guys have done enough just picking me up. Thank you."

Michael shrugged. "Not a problem. Everyone needs help sometimes, you know?"

Clint nodded. "More than ever before, I know."

I leaned my cheek against his shoulder as Michael eased us up to the curb. I hopped out of the car, then wrapped around to Clint's side as his door opened. He was slow to get out of the car with his injuries. The bruises on his face were still a bit evident. Faded, but there. The bruise on his jawline had dissipated. His ribs still hurt him. That much I knew. But he was steadier on his hip. And his arm was finally out of that sling.

Though he still couldn't lift his arm beyond parallel with the ground.

I took his hand. "Easy does it. Take your time. We've got plenty of it."

Clint snickered. "I feel people staring."

"Fuck them. They got an issue with it, they can take it up with me."

"Oh, my hero."

I giggled and shook my head as Clint finally got himself out of the car. I wrapped my arm around his waist, feeling him inch his arm around my neck. I liked having him there. Wrapped around me. Claiming me in front of the entire school. However, I also felt him leaning against me a bit too much.

Which meant he was already tired from the moving he had to do.

"Come on, Brick. Let's get you to homeroom."

He chuckled. "I don't know if I'll get used to that kind of a nickname."

I shrugged. "Kinda suits you, though. With how big you are."

"You calling me fat, sweet cheeks?"

I grinned. "Maybe just a little."

"That's what happens when you're bedridden, I guess."

"Don't worry, I'll whip you right back into shape."

He growled softly. "That a promise, beautiful?"

And as I gazed up into his eyes, the world faded away for a split second.

"That's a definite promise, handsome."

22

CLINTON

All morning, I'd been apprehensive about going back to school. Because for once, I didn't want all the attention to be on me. I didn't want people asking me tons of questions and coming up to me wanting stories. I didn't want girls staring at me with their big doe eyes. I didn't want to tell them how I saved some girl's life by forcing drunk, bullshit assholes to chase me down. All I wanted to do was forget about everything that had happened, press the reset button, and try that entire night again.

Hell, try this entire year again so I could do right by Rae.

Dad came home for a short time this past week, making my life an absolute nightmare. I heard him and Cecilia fighting more than usual. Mostly because she kept standing up for me. Which, in my father's eyes, meant standing against him. I didn't understand that. I never would understand it. And though I was thankful for the times Rae came to visit, I hated the fact that things never quite felt like that dinner we'd shared. Just the three of us. Her, myself, and my stepmother.

Fucking hell, that man ruined everything good around him.

Through it all, though, I kept up with my physical therapy. Cecilia stayed at my side for every appointment, taking me to and from them like a parent should have. Hell, she stepped up to the plate more this past week than my father ever had in the entirety of my life! It felt great, to be honest. Having an adult in my corner for once. She cheered me on and worked me through my frustrations. She helped me stretch in the mornings, trying to work that bruised stiffness out of my muscles. After throwing down that beautiful lasagna dinner meal over a week ago, she got me back onto a strict diet. No overdoing it on the sodium, cutting back on the fatty foods, and getting rid of all the sodas in the house so I was forced to drink more water than I ever had in my entire life.

There were parts of me that didn't want to leave her care and come back to school.

But I knew I had to. Even though Rae had been a doll and come over every night she wasn't working to help me with schoolwork, it still wasn't enough. She was still doing about half of my work because I kept falling asleep. Or she kept jumping my bones. Or I kept jumping her bones.

Mmph, I want to take her home and jump her bones.

"Clint?"

Rae's voice ripped me from my trance and I found

myself still looking down at her. She had this worried look on her face. How long had I zoned out? I knew I shouldn't have taken those damn painkillers before I left the house.

I cleared my throat. "Yeah, gorgeous?"

Rae blushed. "Are you sure you're okay to be at school today?"

I nodded. "I'm sure. Yep."

"You guys need anything?"

"Clint, you okay?"

Mike and Aly's voices pulled my head over to look at them. They were still at the curb, peering out of Aly's rolled-down window. Despite the fact that I knew Mike still had issues with me, I was thankful I'd had their support this morning. I nodded at them, hoping they understood how thankful I was for their support. Even with the way I'd treated them in the past.

Rae's hand slipped to my hip.

"We can do this, Clint. Okay?"

My eyes fell back to hers. "You sure about that?"

She smiled. "You've got the three of us. You'll be good."

Aly giggled. "Yep! The four amigos."

Mike snickered. "Let's not get ahead of ourselves just yet."

I rolled my eyes. "We need a much better nickname than that."

Rae grinned. "Brick and the gang?"

Mike scoffed. "Why does he get to be the fron-trunner?"

Aly smiled brightly. "Because the three of us have to hold him up until he recuperates."

I paused. "That's… painfully accurate. Ouch. Thanks for the dose of reality."

Rae nudged me softly. "Don't worry. She's really good for that sometimes."

Mike nodded toward the school. "You two go inside. We'll meet you at Rae's locker."

And with that, he pulled away from the curb.

I walked into the school, leaning against Rae more than I wanted to. More than I wished I were. She held me against her with a firmness and a strength I'd come to admire. We walked into the school's back doors and I tried ignoring the looks. The gasps. The whispers and the attention. I hated it, which was something I never thought in a million years I'd hate. A month ago, I'd been strutting my shit. Playing up the bruises and the limping just to get the attention of the girls. And now? All I wanted to do was crawl into a hole and get away from their glances. Their whispers. Their unasked questions.

Rae kissed my chest. "Don't worry. They'll get over it."

I wasn't as hopeful about that as she sounded.

We finally got to Rae's locker and I leaned against it. I felt myself huffing for air, which was yet another thing I didn't like. Walking was still a chore, and I had no fucking clue how the hell I'd lug my books to my classes. I watched as Rae opened her locker. Her eyes scanned it quickly before they fell to her body. She groaned and rolled her eyes, then closed her locker with a bang.

My brow furrowed. "What is it?"

Aly yelled down the hallway. "She left this!"

I looked up, watching Mike and Aly walk down the hallway. And the two of them were clutching Rae's shoulder backpack thing she always had with her at school. The straps looked as if they were crying out for mercy. The bottom of the bag looked as if it were about to give way. I watched Rae as she scurried for it, allowing it to fall to the floor. She dragged it over to her locker and started sifting through things, pulling out not only her books, but mine as well.

And all I wanted to do was help her.

"Uh-uh-uh, not so fast."

Rae pressed her hand into my chest. She pushed me upright, abandoning her bag on the floor in front of her locker. She leveled me with a look as her hand slid down my torso. And when her fingertips rumbled over my ribs, my eye twitched.

Aly sighed. "We can help her. You need to rest when you can."

Mike nodded. "Trust me, the girls have it."

I bit down onto the inside of my cheek to keep from firing back. I didn't like this. Not one bit. I didn't like the sweat forming on Rae's brow. Or the soft groans falling from Aly's lips. I didn't like how hard they were working for me, because I had no idea how I'd repay them for their efforts. I mean, I could hardly bend the fuck over. How the hell was I supposed to repay their generosity to them when I was beat up like this?

I felt all eyes on me as we stood there, waiting for the morning bell to toll. We'd made it to school a little too early for my liking. Usually, I rode up on my bike just as the homeroom bell sounded. I never got here before that damn bell. And if I did, I was usually in the cafeteria, shooting the shit with Roy and the gang.

Speaking of, where the hell were those guys?

I sighed. "Thank you guys."

Rae gathered both my books and her books in her arms. "You're welcome. It's really not an issue."

Mike shrugged. "I mean, what were you going to do? Walk to school? Ride a bike?"

Aly nudged him. "Michael, be nice."

I snickered. "He is being nice."

Mike held out his hand. "See? Brick gets it."

I paused. "You guys are really gonna make that stick, aren't you?"

Aly giggled. "We really are."

Mike shrugged. "I mean, it fits. Brick walls don't cave easily. Simple as that."

I was taken aback by the compliment. Because that was what that was. A compliment. From Mike. The guy who, only a few weeks back, I'd punched directly in the face because of a comment I made about the very nice girl at his side. Thankfulness rushed through my veins. I grinned at him as I nodded my head. I reached my hand out, holding it there for him to shake.

And when Mike clapped his hand against mine, I smiled.

"Really. Thank you."

Mike nodded. "Whatever you need, dude. Just let us know."

Aly clapped her hands. "Finally! Yes. It's about time the two of you put things to rest."

Mike snickered. "I don't know what you're talking about."

I chuckled. "Not a damn clue."

The four of us stood by Rae's locker, shooting the shit and having a grand old time. I used to think that getting here before that homeroom bell was for losers and idiots. But this was a lot of fun. We stood around, making jokes and venting about classes. They put a smile on my face, and a few of my jokes put smiles on theirs. It felt nice, being around good people. Genuine people. People who didn't stand around, picking on those that walked by. People who minded their own damn business and had things to talk about other than the pussy they got over the weekend.

Fucking Roy.

Things felt different. In a good way. Laughing with Mike and Aly felt more carefree and less skeezy than it did with Roy and Marina. The past few weekends that I'd spent at home and in the hospital were actually better than the weekends I spent drinking and partying. Despite the pain and despite the hospital stay and despite the medication, I'd had more fun with Rae at my side than I did in a hot tub full of girls pouring shots down my damn throat.

Who the hell are you becoming?

Someone I wanted to become.

Aly laughed. "Oh, my gosh. Clint, you really missed it last week. Wedne—no, Thursday. Thursday morning, the principal came into his office with his robe still on. His robe, Clint."

My brow furrowed. "Why the hell did the principal come with—?"

Mike grinned. "He'd been out all day chasing down this new puppy they've gotten. His youngest let it out of the backyard, and he had to chase it down before he came into school."

Rae snickered. "Didn't have enough time to clean himself up much before he had to be in his office."

My jaw fell open. "And the man didn't just take a sick day?"

Aly shook her head. "I'm telling you, our principal is a workaholic!"

The four of us laughed at Rae's locker just before the bell tolled. The screeching sound made me wince, and Rae was right there at my side. Rubbing my chest, kissing my arm, and trying to soothe me back down onto my toes. I wasn't sure why the bell startled me as much as it had. I wasn't sure why it made my entire body ache. But having Rae there helped. Having Aly and Mike there helped.

I like having people in my life who help.

I drew in a deep breath. "What classes do you guys have first this morning?"

Mike pointed behind him. "I've got chemistry first thing. I'm all the way back that way."

Aly nodded. "I've got biology with Rae before our English class together."

Rae gasped. "That's right! You two have English together before lunch. Here, Aly. Can you take this to class for him?"

Aly held out her hand. "Of course. I wasn't sure why you didn't give it to me sooner."

I watched the two girls exchange my books and homework as people filtered around us. And for a few seconds, I didn't pay attention to the snickering. To the stares. To the whispers and the gossip fluttering around us. The only thing I paid attention to was how willing these two girls were to help me. How they coordinated my schedule, right there. In front of me. Trying to figure out ways to make this day less painful on me. Trying to figure out ways to lighten the load I had to carry.

I slowly looked up at Mike and found him grinning at me. A knowing grin. One that said, 'welcome to my world.'

Holy shit, I liked his world.

Rae sighed. "All right. Let's get you to homeroom, big guy."

Aly pointed down the hallway. "I'm going to go turn in his prior English homework. Mike, I'll see you in homeroom?"

He smiled. "I'll save you a seat."

Rae looked up at me. "You ready to go?"

And as I lost myself in her eyes, I nodded.

"I'm ready to go."

The three of them walked with me until we had to go our separate ways. Despite people talking about us, they never wavered from my side until they had to.

And it didn't take me long to understand why Rae had been friends with Mike and Aly for so many years. They were unwavering. Unfaltering. They didn't care about what those around them said. Or gossiped about. They were trustworthy. Steadfast. Willing to help at the drop of a hat.

I could get used to this.

More than I had ever gotten used to being around Roy and Marina.

23

RAELYNN

I sighed. "I wish I had homeroom with Clint."

Allison linked her arm with mine. "Well, homeroom with me will have to do."

"You know that's not what I meant."

"I know, I know. But I'm still trying to cheer you up."

"I'm just worried about him. I mean, what if he needs help?"

"He's a big boy. He'll get around on his own today."

My lips downturned. "He shouldn't have to."

Allison nodded. "I know. But it is what it is and you can't keep dwelling on things you can't change."

But I did.

All throughout homeroom, I wondered if Clint was all right. If kids were still whispering about him. Or, God forbid, picking on him. I wanted to be by his side, helping him through his classes. I wanted to be there, holding his hand and propping his arm around my shoulders. I kept imagining him lumbering down the hallways. Trying to get to his classes on time and still walking in late because he simply couldn't keep up with that kind of a pace from class to class.

At least we'd all have lunch together.

I leaned over. "Hey, Allison. Can I ask you something?"

She nodded. "What's up?"

"Is there any way you can help Clint get to lunch?"

"Oh, I already told him I'd help him."

I paused. "Wait, you did?"

"Well, yeah. We've got class together before our lunch break. Why wouldn't I?"

I smiled, leaning toward her to give her a hug. I wrapped my arms around her, thankful that my two best friends were finally opening up to Clint being around. I mean, I knew he'd been an ass. But I saw a change in him. A softer demeanor. A desire to do better for himself. It warmed my heart that I had Allison's support. It warmed my heart that she was willing to reach out and help Clint in such a manner.

I kissed her cheek. "I really appreciate it."

She rubbed my back. "Don't worry. Michael and I got this. We're here to help. Okay?"

"Okay. Yeah."

The bell tolled, signaling our first transition to class. Allison and I set off for our first period. Biology. Science, first thing in the fucking morning. Like, really? Who the hell made that schedule? Who in the world decided that biology at eight-thirty in the morning was a wonderful idea for anyone?

Then I felt Allison tapping me on the shoulder.

"Don't look now, but look at our two guys."

She pointed, and my heart warmed at the sight. I gazed down the hallway, watching as Michael walked alongside Clint. I smiled at them, watching Michael carry Clint's books. He had slowed his walking pace to stay by Clint's side, and kept him engaged in conversation. Hell, I even saw Michael reach out and steady his hand against Clint's shoulder when he stumbled over his own two feet in the hallway.

I smiled as my heart melted into a steaming puddle of thankfulness.

"Told you," Allison whispered.

I rolled my eyes as she linked her arm with mine. It was time for our morning torture session with one of the most boring teachers in this high school. I swear, his voice never wavered from its one monotone pitch. He wore the same five outfits every week. Every day, of every week. Like those outfits were specifically designated for those particular days of the week, and no other days.

I sighed. "Ready for the purple vest?"

Allison snickered. "You think he'd switch it up at some point in time, right?"

A small commotion at the end of the hallway ensued, and it caused us to pause in the doorway of the classroom. I looked down the hallway, squinting, as I tried to figure out what was going on. I saw Clint against the wall. At least, I thought it was Clint.

When Michael came into view, I knew that had to be Clint.

I watched Michael place his hand on someone's chest. Backing them away from Clint. I didn't know what was going on, but it looked bad. I started down the hallway.

Until Allison pulled me back.

"They've got it."

I scoffed. "Something's wrong. I have to get to Clint real—"

"You're going to be late for class."

I whipped around. "I don't care if I'm late for class, Allison."

Kids started yelling and I turned back around. I saw Michael shoving a kid down the hallway before teachers began intervening. Only they didn't go after Michael and Clint. They went after the kid that had been pushed behind the corner. I didn't know what was going on. But what I saw warmed my heart even further. I saw my best friend wrap Clint's arm around his shoulder and help him into class.

Before running out of the room and sprinting down the stairs to his own.

Allison sighed. "Well, that's something I didn't think I'd ever see."

I smiled softly. "Right?"

"Do you think Michael will ask me to prom?"

I did a double-take. "Say what now?"

"Prom, Rae. Keep up. Do you think he'll ask me?"

"I mean—I—I don't—do you—do you want him to?"

She nodded. "Yes."

My eyebrows rose. Mostly because I'd never heard Allison be so blunt before.

"Well, then I'm sure he will."

"Girls."

The teacher's voice caught our ears and pulled us into the classroom. He held the door open for us and we made our way to the back. Where we always took our seats. I kept peeking over at Allison, trying to read her face. As we cracked our books open and focused on the lecture that would surely put us all to sleep, I wondered what was going through her head.

I didn't have to wonder long. Because once our teacher turned his back, she leaned toward me.

"Do you think I should drop hints?"

I kept my eyes on the teacher. "Yes."

"What kind? I'm not good with this kind of stuff."

We kept our voices low. Trying our hardest to make sure our conversation didn't interrupt the lecture. Or catch our teacher's attention.

"I mean, just start talking about things. You know, like prom dress shopping, or the fact that you don't have a date yet. Michael's smart. He'll eventually catch on."

Allison sighed. "I really hope so."

I grinned. "You really want this, don't you?"

She shrugged. "Yeah. I do."

"It's nice, seeing you admit it."

She looked over at me. "I don't really know when I started feeling this way, you know."

"I mean, sometimes you don't."

The girl in front of me turned around, giving me a mean-ass look. But I simply glared back at her. She needed to shut the hell up with that face of hers. Allison and I were having a very important conversation. My best friend of all these years was finally admitting that she wanted to be more than friends with Michael.

This was a monumental moment.

Allison held back her giggling. "He's been really sweet lately, you know. We've been spending a lot of time together."

I smiled brightly. "I feel a story coming on."

The girl in front of me whipped around. "Are you two serious?"

And even though our conversation had gone unnoticed, her harshly-whispered outburst caught our teacher's attention.

"Ashley. Turn around and pay attention, please."

She tossed me another glare, but I simply smiled at her. I wiggled my fingers at her, waving goodbye as she turned around in her seat. She slumped down, crossing her arms over her chest. And as our boring-ass teacher struck up his pointless lecture again, Allison pointed to her notebook.

I nodded my head.

I sat there, waiting for her note to be scrawled out. And while she wrote, I thought about how normal this all felt. Allison and I always talked away biology. Science was easy for me. Always had been. So long as I read the chapters, I'd be okay. Not once did I ever have to take notes in my science courses all throughout school. It just… clicked for me. Things made sense in the science world. Hypotheses and testing to figure something out? That resonated with me in an ethereal sort of way.

Hey, if video game design didn't work out for me, maybe I had a career in some science field somewhere.

Allison tapped my shoulder before passing me a note. And when I unraveled it, the smile on my face grew wide. My eyes flittered across the words, warming my soul and making me happier than I'd been in a long time.

Allison was totally smitten with Michael.

He's just been over at the house a lot. And my parents really like him. He gets along with my dad. Mom even lets us stay in the basement together. He'll come over and we'll watch movies. Or talk. Or do school work together. And a few days ago? He took my hand for the first time. His hand is so warm, Rae! I really hope he asks me to prom.

The great thing about writing notes back and forth was that it looked as if I were taking notes. All I had to do was look up every once in a while, nod at our teacher, then I was good to go to keep writing. I used my chicken scratch to write out what I wanted to say as quickly as possible. I erased a few words and tried writing them clearer, just to make sure Allison could actually read it. Because apparently, doodling and having a mind for graphic design didn't translate to good handwriting.

Allison, that's so awesome! I mean, I know Michael likes you. I see it in how he looks at you and wants to be around you and stuff. Trust me, if you drop those hints and make comments from time to time about how you don't have a date to prom? He'll pick up on the hints and ask. I mean, this is Michael we're talking about. Once he knows there's a good thing coming his way, he charges head-on to get it. Remember the deal he had with his parents about his car?

That had been a doozy of a school year. As I passed the note to Allison, the memory pulled me back. The three of us had taken driver's ed at the same time. Same after-school class. Same teacher. We even tripled up to take the same driving test together with our teacher in order to get some experience. And Michael wouldn't stop talking about the deal he'd made with his parents. If he passed his test the first time in the DMV with no questions missed on the written test and no points docked on the driving portion, they'd buy him his first car. But if he missed anything, he'd have to do what most kids did—ask permission to use their parents' car.

I mean, I'm sure they were banking on Michael getting at least one thing wrong. I mean, even the slightest thing! But when he aced that written test while we were all in the DMV, I grinned. And when he came back from that driving portion without a scratch on his record, I threw my head back in laughter.

A week later, his parents had anted up. They'd bought him the SUV he drives now, and he was damn proud of that car. That's Michael, though. That's always been his personality. When Michael wanted something he knew could be his, he went full-steam ahead in order to get it.

All Allison had to do was make it known that she wanted to be his.

"Pop quiz, everyone!"

Just as Allison passed her note back to me, the class groaned. I looked at her and quickly tucked the note away in my back pocket as our teacher passed out the worksheets. I saw the soft panic on Allison's face. But she didn't have to worry. During times like this, I let her cheat off my test. We had a code and everything down for it. And not once had we ever gotten caught.

But she didn't look over at me once during the quiz.

The bell to switch classes rang and we all rushed the teacher's desk. I tossed my pop quiz at him and waited for Allison, who was the last to get out of her chair. She had a confident smile on her face and a skip in her step as she handed our teacher her quiz. Then she came over and linked her arm with mine.

"That wasn't nearly as hard as I figured it would be. It was a recap quiz."

I smiled. "Ready to get going?"

"Let's see if we can catch Clint and Michael down the hallway where we saw them. I can help Clint into English, if he needs it."

"Thank you so much, Allison."

"What? We have the next class together."

"Can you just let me thank you without brushing it off and making me feel weird about it?"

She sighed. "I'm sorry. I just… every time you thank us, it reminds me that—at one time—you thought we might not help. And it makes me sad."

I shrugged. "Because at one time, I knew you guys wouldn't have. I'm really glad you've come around to him."

"He's changed a lot, you know. I already see it in him."

I nodded. "I see it, too."

"You think it'll stay that way once he's healed?"

"I don't know, Allison. I guess only time will tell with that one."

As Allison pulled away from my side to go help Clint out of his class, I pondered on that question. I thought about it as I made my way for my own class. I watched Allison walk off with Clint, but it didn't warm my heart like usual.

Would he stay this way after he was all healed?

Or would he go back to Roy and his gaggle of goons once he could hold his own again?

24

CLINTON

I groaned. "Thanks again, Aly. I really appreciate it."

She helped me into my seat. "Really, it's not a problem at all. I'm glad I can help."

"You wouldn't be willing to help an old man to lunch, too, would you?"

"Already planned on it. Don't worry."

She sat next to me, offering a kind smile in the process. It felt weird. One, because she usually sat at the front of the classroom. And two, because the smile she gave me was genuinely kind. Not the snide or berating kind of smiles I'd gotten used to with her. She set my books on top of my desk before situating her own, and I wondered what she was thinking. What was going on in her head? Was she helping me because she wanted to? Or because Rae kept putting her up to it?

Why did I want it to be the former?

"Oh. Great."

Aly's voice caught my attention and I looked over at her. As I followed her gaze, I saw what she was looking at. Roy and Marina had strolled into class, taking up their regular seats not too far away from us. Aly grimaced as she looked toward them, easing herself back into her seat.

I just hoped the pair didn't make a scene in the middle of class or something.

My eyes stared up at the clock, watching the minutes tick up to the top of the hour. And with every second that passed by, our English teacher didn't come into the room. Where the hell was that woman? Why was she so late this morning?

"You feel as bad as you look, dude?"

I saw Aly's head whip over toward me as I bit down onto the inside of my cheek. Roy's voice echoed in my ear as he leaned over, trying to close the space between us. I rolled my shoulders back, ignoring the pain in my collarbone. I slowly rolled my head around, trying to loosen myself up. All I had to do was ignore them. *Don't engage.* Because the second I engaged them, we were in trouble.

I let the comment roll off my back.

But I shouldn't have answered.

"I'm healing just fine. Thanks."

Roy scooted his desk a bit closer. "You got physical therapy or some shit you're doing?"

Had it not been for the grin on his girlfriend's face, I would've actually thought he cared.

"Yep. Three times a week right now. For the next few weeks."

Roy nodded. "Uh huh. Right. So you'll be back in shape soon enough?"

I licked my lips. "That's the plan."

"That's a shame. Really."

Aly scoffed. "Put a sock in it, Roy."

I slowly panned my gaze over to him, taking in the fire in his eyes. I shouldn't have asked, but he had me baited. Right there on his fucking hook.

"What's a shame?"

Roy snickered. "I mean, you getting back into shape. It's been nice not having you around."

Marina giggled. "Too bad that cliff was only twenty feet high."

I heard part of the class gasp at her comment. It was the top of the hour and the damn teacher still wasn't in the room. Where the fuck was she, anyway? I stared Roy down, trying my hardest to be the bigger man. There was no need for me to talk down to a woman. I certainly didn't want to become my father. I didn't want to let my anger take hold of me like it did him. That was Roy's bitch, so it was Roy's issue to handle.

My eyes held Roy's. "Yeah. Too bad, I guess."

Roy grinned. "I knew you were a depressed little shit."

Aly piped up. "That's enough, Roy."

Marina giggled. "Should've done us all a favor and finished what that bridge started."

Aly flew out of her chair. "The two of you are

relentless. Can't you hear yourselves? Cut it the heck out."

Roy's eyebrows rose. "Wow. Strong language coming from you, Miss Priss."

I held my hand up, signaling for Aly to stop. "The two of you can talk to me. There's no need to involve her."

Marina scoffed. "Fucking around with her, too? Rae not enough for you anymore?"

I pointed my finger at her. "You keep my girl's name out of your mouth. It's not my fault you two have debased yourselves to absolutely nothing."

Roy smiled devilishly. "You mean, like you used to be?"

Marina frowned. "What, you think you're better than us now?"

"You think you've outgrown us?"

"Somehow leveled up in life?"

"You think this'll make Daddy love you more?"

"Or stop beating up on you? I've heard the stories. Roy tells me everything. Are you that open with Rae?"

"Does she know everything?"

"Or does she only know your cock size?"

"If you can still get it up, of course."

"Hey, asswipes!"

Aly's voice pierced through their banter and caught the attention of the entire class. My eyes widened as the curse fell from her lips, and I turned to face her. She had her fists clenched. She ground her teeth together. Her eyes bounced between Roy and Marina, her body vibrating in fear.

I leaned forward. "Aly, it's all right."

She leveled me with a quick look before turning her attention back to them.

"The only shame in this room is you two. The only people in this room who should throw themselves off anything are the pair of you. This entire school's sick of your shit. You hear me? Absolutely sick of it. Sick of you, Roy, for the bullshit you pull in the cafeteria. Trying to act like you're big stuff when all you want is for good ol' Mommy to pay you some attention. And you, Marina. Everyone's sick and tired of coming around corners and catching you flirting with other guys when we all know you're still sucking Roy's—"

"Aly," I said curtly.

Her eyes flickered to me before she sighed. "All of us know that the only reason you two are still together is because nobody else can stand to hang out with either of you or listen to your asinine stories about getting prematurely drunk at parties before going off and doing God-knows-what to one another. So, shut the fuck up. Face forward. And leave Clint the hell alone with your shit."

The entire class fell silent. I sure as hell didn't know what to say. I'd never heard Aly curse. Much less that much in one fell swoop. I slowly panned my gaze over to Roy and Marina. Their eyes bounced between us as I gave them a punctuated head nod. Letting them know I agreed with everything that had just flown out of Aly's mouth.

With a few grumbles, they scooted back into their

place. Faced the front of the classroom as everyone began whispering.

About them.

Not about me.

Aly sighed a soft sigh before sitting back down in her seat. I slowly turned my attention back to her, feeling a shocked smile cross my lips. She flipped her books open as our teacher finally made her presence known ten minutes after class was supposed to start. Aly leaned over, flipping open my own book to the page we needed to be on.

Then she looked up at me.

"What?"

I shook my head. "Thank you, Aly."

She shrugged. "We're all tired of their stuff."

"Oh, now you say 'stuff.'"

She smiled at me, and it caused me to chuckle. We muffled our laughter as the teacher started her lecture, rushing us through our homework so we could get to 'the good stuff,' as she called it. And while I loved my English class—mostly—this book we were reading could go kick rocks. It was the first book in all of high school I'd been forced to read that I didn't enjoy one damn bit.

Catch-22 could suck my—

"I really don't like this book."

Aly's murmur caught my ear and it made me grin.

"Me, neither. Don't worry."

She sighed. "Switching the points of view the entire time between, like, seventeen different characters is just a bit much."

I snickered. "Can we put that on Amazon somewhere? I feel like we should warn the masses."

"Is there something you'd like to share with the class, Clint?"

The teacher called me out and everyone turned to face me. Aly started giggling, hiding her face with her notebook as a grin trickled across my cheeks. I liked this. I liked talking with her in class. I had no idea how the fuck I'd ever stayed friends with the likes of Roy and Marina. But, I didn't see myself ever trading what I had now for what I'd had in the past.

The teacher cleared her throat. "Clint?"

I licked my lips. "I was just telling Aly here that we should write up a review on Amazon, warning people about the painful point of view changes in the book."

The teacher nodded. "What don't you like about them?"

I shrugged. "For one, it's distracting. By the time you come back around to a character's story, you have to flip back to their last chapter to see where their story left off. It's tedious."

Roy sniggered. "He's actually reading the book, for fuck's sake."

Marina murmured. "Guess loser pussy really changes you."

The teacher diverted her attention. "Roy. Marina. Anything to add?"

And when they shook their heads, Aly snickered.

"What's that for, bitch?"

Marina blurted out the statement and the teacher's jaw dropped open.

"Marina. Up here. Now."

She stood up. "No. I want to know why this goody-two-shoes thinks she can judge us just because we don't like reading these shit books."

Roy grabbed his girlfriend's arm. "Just get up to the front of the class."

"Hell, no! I'm tired of Allison and her judgmental glances. I'm tired of them thinking they're better than us. Just because the rest of us Sparknote this shit doesn't mean it makes her any better that she actually reads the books. And Clint, for that matter. Fucking loser after that fall of his. You're no better than—"

"Detention! Both of you! For the rest of the week!"

The teacher's exclamation caught our ears. Her words caused Aly to panic.

"Wait, who?"

The teacher crooked her finger. "Roy. Marina. Up here, now. And if you so much as make another peep, I'll move to have you both suspended from school. Until further notice."

Roy slammed out of his desk, scooting it across the floor. He jumped at a couple students staring him down, who all jerked back from him. I shook my head, watching as the dynamic duo made their way to the front of the class. Marina kept staring Aly down. Like she was about to do something drastic. I reached my hand out, placing it on Aly's desk. Marking my territory and letting them know that if they messed with her, they messed with me, too.

Then, watching as Marina and Roy shook their heads at me, I saw Aly turn her attention my way as well. I peeked over at her, watching as a sly grin crossed her face. A grin that said 'I got you.' A grin that said 'I'm on your side.'

And for once, I understood what it felt like to have a friend.

25

RAELYNN

*Raelynn*Three Weeks Later

I sat on the couch, waiting endlessly for Mom and D.J. to get out of the damn place. The two of them were going out for a date night. Which ultimately meant they'd be out until the break of dawn before they stumbled back in. Drunk, horny, and ready to make all sorts of noises until they finally passed out around breakfast time. It had been the same routine for the past couple of weeks, and it made me sick.

This time, however, I had a few plans in store for myself to keep my mind off things.

"So, how's your friend?"

D.J.'s voice filled the room and I tried my hardest not to roll my eyes. I was ready for them to leave. I wanted them to get out. Not because I didn't want to be around my mother, but because I was done entertaining D.J. I had no desire to get to know him. No passion to get close to him again. I didn't care about accepting him into some sort of fold or making him feel part of the family.

I just wanted him out of my space.

"Rae?"

I sighed. "Yeah?"

"Did you hear me?"

"I did."

"Well, is your friend doing all right?"

I shrugged. "He's fine."

"That's good."

"Yep."

"So, how's school?"

"It's school, I guess."

"What have you been up to lately? Anything fun with your friends? What are their names. Um… Mac and Dani?"

I rolled my eyes. "Michael and Allison."

"Right, right. How are things with them?"

"They're good."

"That's good."

I gazed out the window, wondering when Mom would get downstairs. I knew she wanted me to keep D.J. occupied because 'it upset him whenever he had to wait around' for her. Wow. What a fucking winner, Mom. But I didn't want to fight with her on it. She'd obviously made her choice, and in a few months I'd be graduated and out of here. Getting a place with Allison close to UCLA and rooming with my best friend ever.

And hopefully, finding myself a job or something not too long after that.

D.J. sighed. "You know how much longer your mom's going to be?"

I shrugged. "As long as it takes for her to feel confident walking down those stairs."

"We're going to be late."

"Then push back the reservations."

"We don't have reservations."

"Then there's no need for you to hop down her throat about it."

I whipped my head over, shooting D.J. a look. And as he rolled his eyes at me, I scoffed. I got up from the couch and left the room, refusing to be near him one second longer. Mom could take all the fucking time in the world she wanted to get ready. That was her right. And he had no right to get upset with her when all she wanted to do was look pretty for him.

Besides, I had to start getting ready myself.

Mom poked her head out. "That you, Rae?"

I walked down the hallway. "Yep."

She put her earrings in. "I thought you were talking with D.J. for me."

"Yeah, well. I'm done talking."

I walked into my bedroom and closed the door. I didn't want Mom talking me into going back down there. And not a minute later, D.J. was yelling up the stairs. Like it was his damn house.

"You coming, Lu? We don't have all night!"

"Come on. I'm sure you look fine."

"The restaurant won't have space for us if we don't leave now!"

"Lu!"

I almost opened my door and told him to shut the hell up. But I heard Mom finally call out for him. Telling him she was coming. I walked over to my window, listening as the two of them bickered downstairs. And as they left through the front door, I watched them walk to D.J.'s car. He looked up at me and paused. Right by his door. I pointed my fingers to my eyes before pointing back at him. Letting him know I was watching him. Always.

And after he shook his head at me, the two of them dipped into his car.

I scrambled out of my bedroom after that. I had to power clean some things. The kitchen sink was full of dishes, courtesy of the asshole that had just left. I wanted to vacuum the living room floor. Clint and I had a movie night on the books. One where we'd order pizza, curl up underneath some blankets, and watch movies until we passed out on the couch. Or upstairs in my bedroom. I grinned at the thought. Holy hell, Mom would shit bricks if Clint came down the stairs tomorrow morning.

Then again, she and D.J. would be snoring too loud to hear us doing anything in the morning, anyway.

I scrubbed at the dishes before rinsing them off in the sink. I stacked them neatly in the dish holder, letting them drip-dry on the counter. I pulled the vacuum out of the closet and struck it up, chastising myself for getting so sweaty. I had less than an hour to pull everything off. Especially since Clint was already halfway through his physical therapy appointment.

"Come on. You gotta get a shower still."

I ran the vacuum over the carpet as quickly as I could. Spot-treating it, really. Just to make it look a bit more decent. I shoved it into the closet and kicked the cord underneath the door, hoping it didn't come springing back out at the most inopportune moment. I ran up the steps, taking them two by two. Wanting nothing more than to barge into the bathroom and take the hottest shower alive.

But I settled for a cooler shower. Cold enough to get me to stop sweating without chilling me to the damn bone.

Out I hopped, ten minutes later, with a towel wrapped around my body. I rushed into my mother's bathroom, digging out her blow dryer. I didn't want my hair dripping wet for Clint once he got here. Especially if he wanted to play with it.

Oh, I loved it when he played with my hair.

I flipped my head over and felt the heat blast against my neck. I didn't know how to turn the heat down on the blow dryer, though. Was that even a function? So my neck began sweating. And my face. By the time my hair was dry, the rest of me was wet again. From the damn hair dryer being much too hot.

"Fuck."

I toweled myself off as I walked into my bedroom. I looked at the clock, groaning as my eyes read the time. Shit. It was already six o'clock. He was getting out of his appointment now, which meant he only had to cross town to get here.

"Gotta hurry, Rae," I murmured to myself as I rushed around with my fan on full blast. Trying to stop the sweating as I worked up yet another one. I pulled on some clothes and ran a brush through my hair. I fanned my face, trying to get the redness to stop pooling in my cheeks. I lay down on my bed, spread eagle, letting my damn crotch and my armpits air out.

I was so fucking nervous to have Clint over, it almost made me sick.

Why he insisted he come over after his last physical therapy appointment I wasn't sure. But who was I to say no? I wanted to spend time with him. I wanted to celebrate this moment with him. His first round of PT was over. And after a check-up tomorrow afternoon at the hospital, we'd know whether or not he needed another round. With every passing day for the past three weeks, he'd gotten stronger. He needed less and less help to get to classes. His bruises had faded into small, yellow patches of skin and his limping completely ceased.

Watching him heal had been an incredible journey.

But feeling how close we had become had been even better.

My phone ringing on my bedside table caught my ear. I reached over for the phone, hoping and praying it wasn't Clint. Because I knew there was the slimmest chance that he'd be too tired to come over. I slapped my hand over my phone and pulled it up to my face. I saw Allison's name and smiled. Just who I wanted to talk to. She'd know how to calm my nerves down.

Until Allison blurted out what she wanted to say.

"Michael asked me to go to a movie tonight!"

I paused, my jaw falling open. "He did what?"

"Yes. Yes. I'm sorry. I wanted to call and see how you were doing and all because I know Clint's coming over but… Michael asked me out!"

"Ah!"

I squealed on the phone with her as I jumped up from my bed. I bounced around, shaking my hair out and pumping my fist in the air. Finally. Fucking finally! Michael had grown a pair of balls and asked Allison out on a date. I flopped back down onto the bed, my lungs panting softly for air as my hair splayed out along the comforter.

I smiled. "Oh, my gosh. I'm so fucking happy for you."

Allison giggled. "You think it's a date, right? This is a date?"

I paused. "Of course it's a damn date!"

"Because, you know, he didn't specifically use the word 'date.' I mean, he said, 'Do you want to go to a movie with me tonight?' Not 'Do you want to go on a date with me tonight?'"

"Allison."

"I know. I know. I just—I really don't want to read anymore into this than I should."

I grinned. "He's asked you out on a date. I promise you."

"So I'm not crazy? You know, getting dressed up and doing makeup and borrowing Mom's jewelry?"

I giggled. "Not crazy at all. I want you to have fun tonight. But make it easy for him to make a move on you during the movie."

"Wait, what?"

"Uh, yeah."

"What kind of move? You think he might…?"

I snickered as I sat up in bed, listening to Allison whisper the word. Like it was so dirty.

"Kiss me?"

I rolled my eyes. "You're seventeen years old, Allison. Pipe up."

She sighed. "What do I do if he tries to kiss me? Or hold my hand?"

"Do you want to kiss him or hold his hand?"

"I mean, maybe?"

"Allison."

She sighed. "Maybe a little bit."

I smiled. "You mean a lot a bit?"

"Shut up."

I laughed softly. "If he makes a move and you want it, then let it happen. You know how Michael is. If he wants something, he'll initiate it. And if you're not ready, tell him that. But, don't sit there with your arms crossed over your chest or some shit like that. Just be open. Be you, because that's all he wants."

She giggled. "I can do that."

"Promise?"

"Yep. I promise."

"Good. Now, I have to go. I still need to put myself

together before Clint gets here. I expect a call in the morning telling me all about this movie!"

"If we watch it."

I gasped. "Allison!"

She laughed heartily into the phone. "Love you, mean it!"

My jaw fell open in shock as she hung up the phone. Did my little Allison just make a comment about not actually watching a movie with a guy? Holy hell, my little girl was becoming all grown up.

"Way to go, girl." I smiled to myself as I tossed the phone back onto my bedside table. Then I walked over to my mirror and ran my fingers through my hair, trying to tame some of the frizz. My cheeks were still red from rushing around, but the sweating had stopped. I made my way back into my mother's bathroom and found some of her body spray, so I decided to take some liberties.

And those liberties led into other trials. Other experiments. Other curiosities.

Soon, I smelled like something called 'cotton blossom' and looked like a damn clown. I turned on the hot water, splashing it in my face and trying to get it all off. Some of the makeup didn't actually come off. The mascara didn't run. The blush didn't budge. I gawked in the mirror as I scrubbed at my face, putting as much hand soap on my skin as I could manage.

Then, I looked down at the makeup I'd tried and groaned.

"Holy fuck, it's waterproof."

I searched around in the drawers for something to

take this shit off. And through it all, I lost track of time. I finally found some makeup remover and doused it on a washcloth, hoping it was enough. I wiped it over my face and the makeup magically came off. Like a key slipped into just the right door. I breathed a sigh of relief as I scraped the putty off my face. Layer by layer, cursing myself for being so damn stupid.

Then, with my face redder and puffier than ever, a knock came at the door downstairs.

Just. Fuck.

26

CLINTON

"So, do you want to go ahead and do the evaluation? Or do it tomorrow?"

I paused, wiping the sweat off my brow. "I mean, if we can knock that shit out now, sure."

The therapist chuckled. "All right. Well, go ahead and stand up for me. I'm going to run you through a series of tests."

"You mean, more torture."

He grinned. "If you need a breather—"

I held up my hand. "No, no. I got it. Just... let me finish my water."

I'd be damned if I'd let this fucking accident get the best of me. I'd been going at this physical therapy hard. Harder than ever before. I did all these exercises when I wasn't in my therapy classes. Two, sometimes three times a fucking day. I refused to let it beat me. I refused to be crippled for the rest of my life. I refused to never feel the rumbling of a bike between my legs again. Or feel the wind wrapping around my body as I cruised down the highway.

I mean, Dad and Cecilia weren't on board for something like that yet. But I was trying.

"All right, Doc. Hit me with it."

My therapist laughed. "Hold your arms out. I'm going to press down on them, and you fight back."

I grinned. "You mean I can punch you in the face?"

"Not that kind of fighting back."

"Be more specific next time."

We laughed and bantered through the test. And while I still wasn't happy with how much work it took to get through those damn exercises, I proved a lot. I had most of my range of motion back in my arms. My collarbone was strong. All the bruises had healed up, leaving me with only the emotional and mental scarring of that night. My muscles felt better than they had in weeks. My ribcage no longer hurt. My back had straightened itself out and those vertebrae had slipped right back into place.

For once, I felt like myself again.

"All right, Doc. Give it to me straight. How did I do?"

I slumped down into my chair after the evaluation was over. Cecilia stood in the corner, clapping her hands softly and cheering me on. My therapist handed me another bottle of water, watching me as I cracked it open with ease.

And a smile slid across his face.

"You want my personal or professional opinion?"

I took a swig. "Why not both?"

He sat back. "Sounds good enough. Well, personally? You're doing fantastic. You're strong. You're stable. It's obvious you're not in any sizable amount of pain anymore. And the strength you've gotten back in your body is outstanding for only a month of in-and-out-patient therapy."

"So, what's your professional opinion?"

"In my professional opinion, you're clear to make a full recovery."

I leapt out of my chair, sending the water flying into the air. My therapist launched out of his, clapping me on the back as I hugged him tightly. I buried my face into the crook of his neck. I hopped around as Cecilia rejoiced in the corner. She came up and hugged me, pulling me away from my therapist. I picked her up and swung her around, still feeling the smallest twinge in my ribcage. But not much.

Not compared to what I'd gotten used to.

The therapist laughed. "Let's get you a follow-up appointment on the books for three months out. You know, just to check on you and make sure you're doing okay. I'll take the liberty of cancelling your appointment with the hospital tomorrow."

I set Cecilia down. "Thank you. So much. I really, really appreciate it."

"Not a problem, man. Come on. Let's get you checked out and I'll give you a formal list of exercises to keep up twice a day. Every day."

I felt like I'd been saying that a lot lately. That I was appreciative of people's efforts. But it was the truth.

Cecilia, for sticking by me day in and day out with all this shit. For my therapist and the cursing he put up with to get me to this point. For Rae, and Mike, and Aly. Their support in school and huffing around my books when they didn't have to.

Rae, especially. For helping me keep my head above water with my grades.

I really have to thank her tonight.

Cecilia walked with me to the check-out desk. "What kinds of issues should we keep an eye out for?"

I snickered. "Already losing faith in me?"

My therapist grinned. "Honestly? I don't think there will be any trouble. He's strong. And he's only been getting stronger. But keep an eye out for the usual things. Unexplainable bruising around rehabilitation sights. Any sort of a fever spike. Redness, tenderness, or being swollen in these areas. Also, backsliding. If, for some reason, he backslides in pain or mobility, come back and see me immediately."

Cecilia nodded. "I'll make sure to keep an eye out."

I got myself checked out with my appointment. Scheduled just before we broke for Christmas break. I offered my arm to Cecilia, walking her out to her car instead of the other way around. It felt nice, escorting my stepmother to the car. For weeks, she'd been the one escorting me. Holding tightly to my waist in an attempt to get me to the car safely. And while I'd been appreciative of everyone's help over the past few weeks, it felt nice to help myself again.

Even if Dad wasn't here to witness any of it.

"So how are you feeling?"

I smiled at her question. "I'm feeling great. Really."

"Good. You still got plans with Rae tonight?"

I nodded. "At her place, yeah. Is it still okay if you drive me over there?"

"I mean, I'm certainly not going to make you walk."

"I'd drive myself if there was another car here for me to use. But for some reason, Dad decided to park his at the airport this time around."

She sighed. "I know exactly why your father did it."

I snickered. "Well, I was going to play dumb, but…"

The two of us had a small laugh at his expense, but it was a tense sort of laughter. I knew convincing the two of them to let me have another bike would be almost impossible. That was definitely a purchase I'd have to save up for on my own down the road. After I graduated and got out from underneath my father's hawk-like eye. But having a regular car didn't seem completely unreasonable.

Until Dad randomly started outright refusing me access to his.

It wasn't as if I'd driven it much. I preferred my bike, mostly because I didn't have to ask his permission to use it. But there were a few occasions where I'd needed to use his car because my bike was in the shop or something. And he'd never been hesitant to give me his keys.

Now, though, he was actively keeping his car away

from me. Getting it out from underneath my claws. Like hiding his keys. Or locking it down in the extra garage we had around back.

Or driving it to the fucking airport instead of having Cecilia take him so he could park his car in long-term parking.

My stepmom sighed. "I'm working with him on it. But you know how your father is."

I nodded. "I know. I know how he is. I know it'll take some time to convince him that I'll need a set of wheels again."

"You know he won't go for the bike, though. And neither do I."

"Trust me, I wasn't even dreaming of asking you guys about it."

She cranked up the car. "Good. Because I didn't want to fight with you about it."

I snickered. "I don't think we could fight if we wanted to."

"You think?"

And when I looked over at her, I shook my head. "Nope. I know."

She smiled at me as she backed the car out. Then we made our way out of the parking lot. She started heading toward home, getting out on the main roads and getting hooked up on every stoplight. It was frustrating, to say the least. I was ready to see Rae. Ready to hold her in my arms. Ready to give her the good news.

Ready to bend down and kiss her lips without it hurting so damn much.

"Well, let me work on your father a bit more about getting you a car. I think I know a sweet spot that'll work."

I chuckled. "Don't do anything you don't want to. That's all I'm saying."

She slapped my knee playfully. "Hey, now. I don't know what kind of woman you take me to be, but I can class it up when I want to."

"Which is why I still don't understand how you fell for Dad."

She sighed. "There is a side to your father you don't see much. A kind, romantic, and very caring side of him."

"Yeah, well. Let him know that sometimes it should come out to play with his son, too."

"What? You want him to send you two dozen white roses and some dark chocolates?"

I burst out laughing. "You're an absolute mess."

She giggled. "A mess that's trying to get you some wheels so you can have your independence back."

"Thank you for that, though. Seriously. I know I wouldn't even be able to have that conversation with Dad without him biting my head off."

"Well, I think you should have your freedom back. Especially now that this police investigation is winding down. It's becoming clearer and clearer to everyone involved that you weren't responsible for what happened. That should be enough to earn you your independence back."

I smiled. "Thanks."

"I mean, just look at it from a practical point of

view. You shouldn't be relying on others to get around. You're eighteen years old. You're months away from graduating. And soon, you'll be off doing your own thing. You'll need a car to coordinate the life you want. Especially since your bike was completely totaled in the crash. There's no reason in this world why we can't take that insurance money and put a down payment on a car for you. It makes no sense."

"Take a left here."

"Got it."

"Cecilia?"

"Yeah?"

I placed my hand on her knee. "Thank you for being here for me."

She eased herself to a stop in the middle of the road. The middle of the dark, dank, smelly road that led us all the way to Rae's house. Lamp lights flickered in the distance, casting an eerie glow over the whole neighborhood. And as Cecilia's hand fell against mine, she squeezed it softly.

"You're welcome, Clint."

I sighed. "I just… not having Dad around for any of this hurt. Knowing how much he blamed me for all this hurt. Probably more than the physical pain I was in."

"I'm so sorry, Clint."

I shook my head. "No reason for you to be sorry. It is what it is. But I'm lucky I had you. I'm lucky you were on my side. Thank you for that, Cecilia. I'm glad this has given us a chance to get to know one another."

She blinked back tears as she brought my hand to

her lips. She kissed it softly, leaving behind traces of her chapstick. She sniffled and I reached over toward her, wrapping her up in the most awkward hug I'd ever experienced.

It still felt wonderful, though. Feeling her hold me like that.

"I'm glad, too, Clint. I'm glad we got to spend some time together."

I snickered. "And you make an awesome as hell milkshake."

She giggled softly. "I'll make sure to make them more often for you."

I pulled back and watched her wipe at her tears. She settled into her seat, then I pointed out which house was Rae's. She eased us up to the driveway, dropping me off at the curb. But, before I got out, I leaned over and gave her a quick peck on the cheek.

"Thanks again."

She smiled. "Anytime, Clint. Now, go see your girl. I'm sure she's excited to see you."

And the woman didn't have to tell me twice.

27

RAELYNN

*S**hit. You look like a blown-up bobblehead, Rae.*
The knock at the door startled me, causing me to toss myself out of my mother's bathroom. I scrambled for the steps, ready to throw myself into Clint's arms and drag him inside. My heart leapt into my throat. I heard a car driving away from the house as high beams filtered through the windows. Shadows pivoted along the walls, beckoning me further toward the front door as I jumped down the steps.

"Coming!"

Me and my red face are, at least.

With water droplets speckling the front of my shirt, I fluffed my hair back one last time, then unlocked the door. I threw it open, staring up into the eyes of the boy I'd come to adore. And the second his eyes laid themselves on me, he stepped forward.

"Holy fuck, I've missed you."

He breathed the words against my lips before he

wrapped me in his arms. He picked me up against him, pulling me to my tiptoes as I gasped in shock. My arms slid around his neck. He barreled into my house, cloaking my back and pulling me close to him. His tongue filled my mouth. His essence overcame me. The smell of his cologne wafted up my nostrils, curling my toes and making me tremble against him.

He kept walking until my back was pinned against a wall. Any wall. I didn't give a shit which wall it was. He kicked his leg out, shutting the door closed with a crash as the world fell away.

And I took the time to melt into his kiss.

"Oh," I moaned down the back of his throat. He dipped down, gripping my thighs as he picked me clear up off my feet. My head fell off to the side as the kiss deepened, our tongues doing battle for the upper hand. I sucked on his lower lip and raked my teeth across his tongue. He fisted my hair, pulling my head off to the side as he dragged his warm, wet lips down my neck.

I gasped with desire in my bones.

Not once did he comment on how red my face was. Not once did he realize its puffiness. He kissed me. Devoured me. Ground his hips against me as he pinned me to the wall with his strength. I was taken aback by it all. By the way he effortlessly picked me up. I groaned as he pulled my shirt off to the side, sinking his teeth into my shoulder.

And when his face came back to meet mine, he cupped my cheek, causing me to smile as I drank him all in.

I giggled. "I take it things went well?"

He kissed me softly. "Better than 'well.'"

"Well. I suppose that's… good."

I grinned at him as he snickered. I laughed softly as he pressed a kiss to the tip of my nose. But when he captured my lips again, I sighed. Groaned. Rolled against him as I felt his cock pulse to life. The kiss was long. Sensual. His tongue lingered and his taste filled my mouth. My hands meandered into his hair, twirling up into its curls. He'd let it grow out a bit. Just enough for the ends to start flipping upward. Curling in on themselves and giving me just enough to hang on to.

I adored it.

"So are you going to tell me the good news, then?"

Clint paused. "Oh. Yeah. I should do that."

I snickered. "You really should, handsome."

He pulled back, seating me against the wall with his hips as his hands found mine. He threaded our fingers together. I placed my hands above my head. He pinned me to the damn wall, his eyes falling to my breasts. The way he licked his lips made me cast out all desire for our movie night. Replacing it with another desire.

"Clint?"

He shook his head. "My God, you're breathtaking."

I blushed. "You seem much better."

He smiled. "Because I am. They've cleared me, and expect me to make a full recovery."

"Wait, what?"

He nodded. "My therapist even cancelled my

appointment with the hospital tomorrow. I don't have to see anyone for another three months."

"Wait, what!?"

He chuckled. "I'm free as a bird, and stronger than I've been in weeks."

"Clint! Holy shit!"

I bucked against him, freeing myself enough to wrap myself around his body. I hugged him close, burying my face into the crook of his neck. And as he held me tightly, our laughter filled the room. Tears of happiness rushed my eyes. Finally, this damn nightmare was over. Clint had been healed. He'd recuperated. And it seemed as if things were finally swaying back in our favor.

I kissed his neck. "I'm so happy for you."

"Mm, keep doing that and I'll show you just how happy you make me."

I kissed his skin again. "That a promise?"

Softly, deftly, I planted kisses against his skin. He pulled me away from the wall, carrying me into the living room as he made his way for the couch. I kissed up his pulse point, nibbling against his earlobe as I let my hands wander underneath the collar of his shirt, feeling his muscles rolling underneath that taut skin of his. He held me closely, his hands cupping my thighs tightly. He was back. My Clint. The old Clint. The strong, dexterous, confident Clint.

A new lease on life.

"You're mine."

The growl that left his lips made my eyes roll back. He dropped me to the couch, shedding his jacket and his shirt before falling to my body. I slid my hands down his back, memorizing the way his muscles rippled. My fingertips rumbled over their edges and fell into their divots. It was as if his body had been carved just for me. I molded to him, filling his empty spots as my legs spread for him. His tongue invaded my mouth. Pushed its way through as his hands shoved my shirt up. Ready, and waiting, to feel me.

"I. Need. You. Rae."

His kisses punctuated his words as he helped me lean up. Off came my shirt. And with a snap of his fingers, off came my bra. He groaned as it slid down my arms, casting itself off to the side like magic. I heard him toe his boots off as he laid me back down, the cushions catching my soft descent as his hands roamed my body. I arched and rolled against him. His lips kissed down my neck, causing goosebumps along my arms. The valley of my breasts welcomed his lips. My nipples stood up and applauded him as he journeyed his way down. I moaned for him. Groaned out his name. Bucked against him as the heat between my legs grew to searing temperatures.

"Clint, please. Now."

Off came my pants. My panties. My socks. My body, bared for him. Ready for his carnal taking. I watched his eyes roam over me. He stood up, hovering over me as his lean, chiseled abs came into view. The rings around them called to my eyes. My fingertips burned with a need to touch them. Clint grabbed my ankles, pulling my legs around until my back sat against the couch cushions.

Then he dropped to his knees.

"Clint, you don't—fuck!"

He hummed between my legs as he nibbled my thighs. He bit down into them, tasting them and raking his teeth across my dollops of excess. I spread myself for him, wanting nothing more than for him to devour me. And as I ran my hands through his hair, he kissed closer to where I wanted him. Lapped his tongue over where I needed him. Teased me relentlessly. Until I was a panting, sweating mess.

"I can't. Clint, you have t—oh!"

"Trust me, I'll get there, gorgeous."

His tongue sank into me and my eyes screwed shut. With every lick, I bucked against him. With every massage of his hands against my thighs, I rocked steadily against his lips. I shook uncontrollably, my legs giving way over his shoulders. My heels pressed into his muscles. I felt the whole of his body pulsating for my pleasure, and mine alone. My body ebbed endlessly, surging with electricity as it short-circuited my mind. All I knew was Clint. All I felt was Clint. All I smelled —and all I wanted to taste—was Clint.

"Yes. Yes. So clo—Cli—I—you—right there. Right there. Right there. Don't stop. Don't stop. Don't —stooo-ah!"

My body contracted as he threw me over the edge. His tongue pressed deeply, releasing me to the wolves as I plummeted through the stars. The world around me tilted. I felt things shifting and twirling in on themselves. My body contorted, trying to get away from the pleasurable assault as Clint fixed his grip around my legs. He pulled me closer, even as I tried backing away. Sweat dripped down the nape of my neck as my hands curled tightly into his hair. Nails raked across his scalp. His growls rattled my ribcage. I bucked wildly, losing all control of my body as he catapulted me to the heavens.

And as I crash-landed back against the couch, he rushed up my body.

"Now, I can take what I want."

His words made me weak in my knees as his lips fell against mine. I tasted myself on him, and it shut the rest of my body down. I was his, forever. For as long as he wanted. I'd weather any issue. Any trial. Any tribulation, just to keep him at my side. I had to have him now. There was no stopping for a movie. The only thing that mattered was being with Clint, in this moment.

"You're perfect, you know that?"

I whispered the words so softly I wasn't sure he'd heard me. But when he pulled back and gazed into my eyes, I knew. I knew he'd heard. He grinned down at me with that insolent little smirk of his, but his eyes twinkled like wildfire. He looked happy. Proud. Content. Satisfied. All the things he deserved to be.

And I wanted to make sure he experienced nothing else.

I helped him get his pants off. His boxers. His socks. Then, when the two of us were bared for one another, he slipped between my legs. I felt him press into me, our eyes never wavering. My jaw unhinged as grunts fell from his lips. But he didn't falter. He sank into me, my body swallowing him whole. I clung to him, my legs locking and my hands curling into the meat of his back. We fell to the couch cushions as he began pumping into me. In and out. With such a rhythmic pattern it left me breathless.

"Clint. Oh, yes. I've missed this. I've missed you. I'm so—so happy for—"

"Fucking hell, Rae. You're marvelous."

Our kisses grew sloppy. Our movements grew desperate. The couch moved with our efforts, scraping along the carpet as our bodies collided. The world faded away. Time and space had no existence between us. There was only me, Clint, and the loving look in his eye as he plunged deeper into my body.

Robbing both of us of our words.

He hooked his arms behind my legs, folding me in half. My jaw unhinged in silent pleasure, and I felt that coil tightening in my gut. He drove faster. Harder. Imprinting my body into the couch as our tongues intertwined. I swallowed his growls, matching them with my whimpers. My moans. My sighs of ecstasy. My heart beat for him. My body shook for him. I needed him, more than I'd ever needed anyone in my entire life. Tears of happiness sprang to my eyes as that coil tightened. As his body raked against my swollen nub. As his girth pressed against the whole of me, muting my world with the fire he pushed through my veins.

"Rae. Holy shit. Rae. I'm so close. I just—Rae. I need—"

"Oh, yes!"

My back arched and I fell over the edge. My back

locked out and my jaw unhinged as unearthly sounds left my lips. He pounded relentlessly into me, snapping his hips against mine. The sounds of skin slapping skin filled my living room, drowning out the rest of the world around us. I felt him pulse once. Twice. Three times, before it happened.

He collapsed against me, our bodies spent against one another as evidence of our debauchery pooled between my legs. And as I laid there, watching the ceiling twist and turn, it became official.

Clint didn't know it yet, but I'd officially made love to him.

Because there was no other boy in this world for me, if not him.

28

CLINTON

I collapsed against her, completely spent as my body unleashed inside hers. I had no more strength left in me. After physical therapy. After recuperation. After fighting for weeks against my own body, it had finally worked in my favor. I promised myself that when I was finally strong again, I'd pick her up. Take her the way she deserved, and make love to her in ways she'd never experienced before.

Because, unbeknownst to her, I was making love to her.

I wonder if she feels the same way.

My face fell to the crook of her neck. Her arms wrapped sloppily around me as her pulsing pushed me out of her body. I lay there between her legs, soaking her in and memorizing everything about her. From the way her breasts felt against my chest to the way her heat cloaked my pelvis. The way my back burned with her raking nail marks and the way that sensation made me smile.

Even the way she clung to my hair. It made me want to keep growing it out. Because if that was something she liked, I sure as hell wasn't taking it from her.

She sighed. "Got a movie in mind you wanna watch?"

I snickered. "Pretty sure we just created our own."

"This is the part where I'd swat at you if I wasn't so drained."

"And that's the part where I'd catch your hand if you actually had the energy."

"I blame you for taking that energy away."

I grinned. "I'll gladly take that blame any day."

I kissed her skin as the two of us recuperated. Then, reluctantly, I peeled myself away from her body. I didn't know how long her mother would be gone. And the last thing I wanted us to do was get caught butt-ass naked on her mother's fucking couch. I chuckled as I slipped onto the floor, falling against my back. Rae giggled as she rolled off, softly falling into my arms.

"Come here, beautiful."

She kissed my shoulder. "I love it when you call me that."

She fell off to my side, her leg tossed between mine. Her arm lazily sat around my waist and I felt her cheek pressed against my arm. Finally, for the first time in weeks, I could hold her like I wanted. Without pain. Without fear. And without needing to shift. I slid my fingers through her hair, working out the knots we'd already created. I stared at the ceiling, keeping an ear out for any cars coming down the road.

And as Rae pulled a blanket over us, she gazed up into my face.

"What are you thinking about?"

Her voice snapped me from my trance. "What was that?"

"You had something on your mind. What were you thinking about?"

I paused. Mostly, because I wasn't sure if I should tell her. I mean, it wasn't really a good topic of conversation after what we'd just done. But, now that I didn't have physical therapy and rehabilitation occupying my mind, I found other things occupying it.

"You know you can tell me, Clint."

I nodded. "I know."

She kissed my jawline. "What's got you so distracted?"

I sighed, lowering my voice to a whisper. "I thought I was going to die, Rae."

She moved away from my side and I reached out for her. I didn't want her to move. Hell, I didn't even want to bring up the conversation. I didn't want to lie to her, though, either. I shot up like lightning, swallowing back a small groan. While the pain in my ribcage was mostly gone, it had its moments. Just like my physical therapist said it would. Rae held the blanket against her body as she covered her beauty from me. I reached out for her, pulling her back into me as I re-situated us. My back was against the couch while we sat on the floor, facing a blank television screen. One that should have been playing a movie, had we taken the time to actually indulge that whim.

Her cheek leaned against my shoulder. "You almost did."

I nodded. "You know, when I was bleeding out at the bottom of that hill, the only thing that kept me going was your voice."

"What?"

"Yeah. I think, even before I heard your voice, my body knew you were there. My heart did. And had it not been for you, that river would've dragged me off and I would've been done for."

She pressed deeply into me. "I wasn't going to let that happen. Not by a fucking long shot."

"I know. I wouldn't have pulled through had you not been there, Rae. Looking back on it now, I knew it was Mike calling out for you. I heard him. I heard him telling you to stop. And had you listened, I wouldn't be here."

"Michael was just trying t—"

I shook my head. "I'm not blaming him for anything. He was worried about you. And rightfully so. Just—thank you. For coming after me anyway."

"You're more than welcome, Clint."

"And thank you for coming to visit me, despite the dickhead my father can be. I'm glad that didn't keep you away, because I'm not sure I could've pulled through in that place had it not been for you."

She kissed my cheek. "Sure you would have. You're a fighter."

"Is it possible for a fighter to be tired of fighting, though?"

She cupped my cheek, turning my face toward hers. "Of course it's possible. But that doesn't mean a fighter loses his passion. It simply means he rests. This is your resting time, Clint. It's time for you to lean on those you can trust. But it doesn't mean you stop fighting. Not until you reach the top of wherever you want to be. And I'll be right there, fighting along with you. Every step of the way. Until you have everything you want out of your life."

I paused. "How the hell did I luck up with someone like you?"

She grinned. "You're good at sex."

I snickered before my lips found hers again. She giggled against my mouth as my tongue parted her lips. I cupped the nape of her neck. I held her to me as she moved against my body. I felt her straddle my lap, climbing against my body until she pressed against me once more. I slid my fingers through her hair, holding her tightly to me. And as her hands slid down my chest, they settled against my heart.

My rapidly-beating heart.

"Rae?"

"Yes, Clint?"

"There's something I need to tell you."

She pulled back, our eyes meeting while she studied me. My thumb stroked over her cheek as her fingertips danced along the outlines of my chest. The words were on the tip of my tongue. Sitting right there, percolating just for her. All I had to do was find the courage to say them. And I figured after almost dying, it'd be an easy thing to do.

But, it wasn't.

"Clint? What's wrong?"

I shook my head. "Nothing. I just—"

A flash of lights streamed through the living room windows and I'd never moved so fast in all my life. Rae rushed around, gathering her clothes as I stayed on the floor. I reached for my boxers, pulling them up so quickly I got my damn balls caught up in them. I moved my clothes to a corner, watching as Rae rushed into the kitchen. Never in my life had I gotten dressed so quickly. I didn't know I had that kind of speed built into me. I pulled my shirt over my head as the light faded down the road, not bothering to pull into the driveway.

And as Rae threw the front door open, she giggled breathlessly.

"Holy shit, that's the neighbors."

I panted. "So not your mom?"

She shook her head. "Not even a little bit."

She looked at me and the two of us threw our heads back in laughter. She closed the front door, then locked it to make sure we had enough time to piece ourselves together. Just in case the next time was her mother. I held my arms out for her and she fell into them, her body trembling from the adrenaline rush.

"I just knew it was them."

I chuckled. "Me too, sweetness. Me, too."

"So, want to actually watch that movie now?"

I kissed the top of her head. "Whatever you want to do."

We settled onto the couch and flipped through her television channels. There weren't many. At least, not as many as my father had on his package. And while it seemed like a simple thing, it illuminated a stark contrast between our worlds. Eventually, we settled on some sci-fi thriller. Rae clung to me as aliens did some things on screen I was only half-paying attention to. Because my mind kept ripping me back to the accident. Back to that embankment, to the moment my head slipped under water.

And the tug against my jacket as Rae pulled me out.

"Shit!"

"Fucking hell, warn a girl next time."

"Oh, come on. You're smarter than that. Be smarter than that."

"She's got heels on. She's not smarter than that."

I quirked an eyebrow. "What's wrong with heels?"

She shrugged. "I don't know. But the dumb girls in movies like these always wear heels. It's the stereotype."

"Odd."

"Right? You should change that in your writings. You know, make a new trend for women in pop culture, or something like that."

"Wow. I completely forgot I'd told you about my writing."

"Don't worry. I won't take offense this time."

She smiled up at me, and I felt my heart warm. It

always felt warm with her. Whenever I was in her presence. I rubbed my hand up and down her arm, dancing my eyes between hers. She really was a beauty. A little button nose with wild hair framing her face. Deep pools of amber brown that gladly dragged me along their current. That was a river I'd happily drown myself in. The river of freckles that smattered themselves across her nose and her cheeks. The river of creaminess that dripped against her skin, accenting the dark features she possessed.

Rae snickered. "What are you staring at?"

The girl I love. "The most beautiful girl in the world."

The front door ripping open pulled us from our universe, and Rae immediately hopped back. I shot myself over to the other end of the couch, trying to look as natural as possible. With my legs spread and my hands settled against my thighs, I hooked my eyes to the television. I heard Rae panting softly, and the second her mother's eyes darted between the two of us, I knew we were caught.

"Oh. I'm, uh… you must be Clint."

I nodded. "Yes, ma'am."

She walked toward me. "Pleasure to meet you. How are you feeling?"

I shook her hand. "I'm feeling much better, thank you."

"I didn't know you were coming over, I'm sorry."

"It was kind of a last minute thing. My last therapy session ended and I guess I just wanted to see Rae. I hope that's okay?"

She smiled. "You're welcome here any—"

"Aren't you even gonna help me with these fucking food bags?"

A man's tinny voice resounded through the house as Rae's mother ripped her hand away from mine. I stole a glance at Rae, watching as her face fell. She shot me a look that I think was supposed to apologize. But it happened so quickly I almost didn't catch it.

"D.J., it's only two bags. Get over it."

Ah. The infamous D.J. The exact man I didn't want to meet.

Just great.

I watched a spindly man walk through the door, carrying two food bags with him. There was an insignia of a restaurant emblazoned on them, but I didn't catch it. The first thing I caught was the angry look in D.J.'s eye. The argument seated on the tip of his tongue. The second thing I caught was how hard he stared me down before flickering his gaze over to Rae.

"This your friend?" he asked.

Rae nodded. "This is Clint."

He huffed. "Should be more space between you two."

Her mother balked. "Excuse me?"

Rae snickered. "You're not my father. You certainly don't get to dictate what's too close. Especially when you're in a house that isn't yours."

"Seems like your mother needs to teach you manners."

I cleared my throat. "Or, you need to simply learn your place."

D.J. dropped the bags. "What did you say to me?"

I stayed seated on the couch, keeping my cool. "I said, maybe you need to learn your place."

D.J. lunged at me, but Rae's mother stopped him from going any further. I, on the other hand, didn't even flinch. I was used to men like him. He reminded me a lot of my father. I heard both Rae and her mother murmuring, though I didn't take the time to figure out what they were saying.

Especially after Rae took my hand and pulled me up from the couch.

"You need to cool down."

"I'm gonna go get a beer."

"Yeah, you do that."

"Come on, Clint. Let's go upstairs."

"That boy shouldn't be taking her up anywhere."

"This is my house. You can it and get in there."

"I really hate that man."

"Rae, give me a second."

Voices swirled around me as Rae tugged me toward the stairs. She led me up them, her hand vibrating as it held mine tightly. I saw how tense her shoulders were, how angry she'd become. I took one last peek around the corner, glancing into the kitchen. Long enough to see that D.J. dickhead crack open a can of beer. He and Rae's mother were already arguing again. Lowly. And to themselves. Part of me wanted to stay behind to make sure he treated that woman with respect. But the other part of me gave in to Rae's tugging and pulling.

"Come on. We can hang out up here and not be disturbed."

I followed her all the way down the hallway.

Despite my inherent worry for her mother's safety.

29

RAELYNN

I pulled Clint into my bedroom and slammed the door closed. I leaned against it, watching as he took a seat on my bed. D.J.'s voice boomed up the stairs. "Don't you be slammin' doors in this house!" And when he did, I heard my mother start cursing him out.

"You bastard. Don't you dare talk to my daughter that way!"

"You're the one who told me she needed more structure. And apparently, manners!"

"Well, you sure as hell aren't the one to teach her about those. You barely have them yourself!"

"And now I see where she gets her wonderful tone. You think she's gonna end up a fucking doormat like her damn mother!?"

My lower lip trembled as I tried blocking it out. I felt something strong wrap around me, pulling me against something steady. I gripped the leather I felt against my skin and drew in a quivering breath. I buried myself against him, trying to mute the fighting as he walked me over to the bed.

"It's okay. I'm right here. Focus on my voice, Rae. I've got you."

I drew in a shuddered breath. "Fucking D.J."

"Let it out. Whatever you want to say, I'm here for you. I'm not going anywhere."

"He's such a fucking maniac. All the damn time! Especially the last time around. He used to not give a shit about what I did. He never used to think he owned this house until he just got back with my mother. I don't know what the fuck she told him, but I can't stand it."

He rubbed my back. "There we go. There it is. Let it all out."

He sat back down on my bed, pulling me into his lap. And I freely went along with him. It felt marvelous, having someone here with me. Not being alone while I listened to Mom and D.J. go back and forth at one another downstairs. Clint leaned back against my bed, drawing me deeper into him as I fell against his body. The bed bounced. But I stayed right there with him. Snuggling into him and wrapping myself around him, until our limbs were tangled up so tightly I wasn't sure where I ended and he began.

Clint kissed my forehead. "Is it always like this when he's around?"

I nodded slowly. "Practically. He's an absolute dick-hole, too. Hits her. Uses her. And thinks he can get away with it because he pays some bills. I was so proud of my mother for putting in applications. For finally kicking him out and standing up for herself. I believed her, Clint. Really, truly believed her that it was over. That this nightmare of a man—"

"I want you to get one thing straight, Rae. That idiot down there? That's not a man."

"I know. I know."

"No, I don't think you do. Look at me."

I slowly panned my eyes to meet his. "Yeah?"

He gripped my chin. "D.J. isn't a man. He's a child, masquerading in the body of a man. He's got no clue what it means to be strong. To fight. To enjoy what he's got in front of him. The only thing he knows to do is take. Drain. And take advantage when he can. He's no better than my father. In fact, I'd easily put them in the same field together. They're one and the same. Understand this, Rae. He's not a man."

I sighed. "Why can't Mom leave him?"

"I don't know, Rae. Sometimes, women are raised to believe they don't have any other options. Or maybe she's got a hole of hurt she's trying to fill that she doesn't know how to fill any other way. What I want you to know is that D.J. isn't a man. And even if he was, what he's saying down there should have no bearing on who you are, or what you do with your life. Ever."

"He's just an absolute asshole. He charges in here and starts demanding shit from people like he owns the fucking place. I can't stand it. I told him the next time Mom came home with bruises on her skin, I'd be calling the damn police myself."

He grinned. "Good for you. I hope you keep your word on that."

"I plan on it."

"And Rae?"

I sighed. "Yeah, Clint?"

"At any point in time, you can call me. I know I don't have wheels right now, but my stepmom would have no issues coming to pick you up. Anytime, day or night. You call, and I'm here."

I smiled softly. "Thank you."

He kissed my forehead. "It's the least I can do for what you've done for me."

My eyes fluttered closed and I melted into him. I let the sound of his kisses drown out the sound of D.J. and Mom fighting. I curled into him, letting him hold me. I cried softly against him, allowing myself to be weak with him. Part of me still felt stupid. But the rest of me was thankful to have Clint there. It felt nice, having him support me like this. Having him weigh in on this issue and talk some real, solid sense into me.

Because some days, I wasn't capable of doing it myself.

I felt something vibrate against the bed and figured it was my phone. Until I peered over Clint's body and saw my phone still sitting on my bedside table. I furrowed my brow as the vibrations happened again. Only this time, Clint sat up. Taking me with him before his arms moved away from me.

"That's my phone."

I nodded. "Get it. It might be Cecilia."

He looked at me. "Are you sure?"

"Why wouldn't I be?"

"I don't want to interrupt what we've got going on right now. I mean, she's probably just calling to see when to pick me up. I can easily call her back."

I placed my hand on his knee. "Clint, pick up the phone. I won't take offense. It's fine, okay?"

"Are you sure?"

I cupped his cheek. "I promise. Thank you for listening to me. And for your reassurance."

He turned his face, kissing my palm. "Anytime, Rae. Anytime you need."

He pulled his phone out from his back pocket before his eyes widened. He picked it up in a hurry, and I wondered what was going on. Who was on the other line? It didn't sound like Cecilia when he picked it up. I scooted closer to him, trying to take stock of what the man's voice on the other end of the line was saying.

But, I couldn't understand a word coming from Clint's phone.

"Uh huh. Yes. I understand. Really? You found them? I—thank—I can't—thank you, Officer. Yes. Yes, I can. Just let me know what time and I'll be there. No, no. I'm good. I'll have a ride. My stepmom, yeah. I'll make sure of it. Yep. Eleven?"

He looked over at me like he was searching for something. All I could do, though, was shrug.

I mouthed to him. "Who is it?"

And when he mouthed back 'the police,' my jaw dropped open.

"Yes, Officer. Just—let me ask someone something really quickly. Uh huh. Hold on."

Then, he put his hand over the speaker of his phone. "They want me to come in at eleven in the morning tomorrow."

My eyes widened. "Did they find those boys? Did they catch them?"

He nodded. "That's what they're saying. They want me to come down to the station tomorrow and try to I.D. them."

"Holy shit, Clint. You have to go. You have to do this. Those boys deserve every ounce of justice the system can bring down on their fucking heads."

"Cecilia's probably going to take me."

I nodded. "Do you think she'd let me come along? You know, to help I.D. them, or something?"

He breathed with relief. "I'm glad you offered, because I was struggling with the words to ask."

"I'll be there, Clint. Just confirm with them the time. Okay?"

And with a nod, he returned to his phone call. "Officer? Yes, hey. I'm back. Sorry about that. Uh, eleven tomorrow in the morning works just fine. I'll be coming with my stepmother and the girl that was with me that night. Yes, the girl that found me. Uh huh. Yeah, she got a glimpse of them, too. A good one. Yep. I'll ask her if she can. But, either way, I'll I.D. them and answer your questions. Uh huh. I'm sure she will, too. Yep. I'll make sure she's prepared. Again, thank you so much."

He hung up the phone and tucked it away in his

back pocket. I clamored on top of him, the argument raging downstairs already falling to the back of my mind. A massive smile crossed my face as Clint's hands fell to my hips. Holding me steady in his lap. Our foreheads fell together. I giggled as I touched his nose with mine. I slid my hand through his hair, silently wondering if he'd keep growing it out. Because it felt nice in between the slats of my fingers.

Clint sighed. "Thank you for coming with me in the morning."

I nodded. "Of course. I wouldn't have it any other way."

"They said they might want you to try and I.D. the guys if you got a good look at them."

"I'll never forget their faces."

"And they might have some questions for you. You know, to wrap things up and make sure all their letters are dotted and crossed."

I nodded. "If your stepmom can pick me up, we're good."

"I know she will. She likes you."

"Really?"

He snickered. "Yeah. She calls you 'my girl' already."

I shrugged. "I mean, I kind of am your girl."

He grinned. "I suppose, kind of. Sure."

I gasped, feigning shock. "Why, Clint. I never! How dare you betray me in such a way?"

"I have betrayed thee in no such fashion!"

I burst out in giggles and covered his face with kisses. His back fell to the mattress, and I went right along with him. I followed his every move as I peppered him with my lips. Kissing his cheeks. His forehead. His neck. His shoulders. He rolled me over, pinning me beneath his comforting weight. And as the argument finally died down below us, I smiled up into Clint's face.

"You're not going to get rid of me any time soon. So deal with it."

He kissed the tip of my nose. "Wouldn't dream of it, gorgeous."

"Plus, I'm ready to see those assholes get what's coming to them."

He chuckled. "And the truth really comes out."

"Hey, I can be supportive and vindictive at the same time. Girls are great multi-taskers."

"So, does that mean you can kiss. And. Hold. A. Conversation?"

He punctuated his words with fluttering kisses to my lips. Pulling me deeper into his atmosphere and refusing to let me go.

I giggled "Mm. I. Think. So."

He kissed me deeply. "Or, we could just do that."

And as I rolled him over, straddling his hips once more, I figured we could do a little more than that.

30

CLINTON

I saw Rae sitting on the front porch as we pulled up to her house. I sat in the front seat with Cecilia, but the second I caught a glimpse of Rae's face, I booked it to the back seat. I got out and slipped inside, leaning over to open Rae's door. And when she dropped down next to me, I saw the blank stare on her face. The way her lips were softly downturned. She had bags underneath her eyes and a tremble to her hand as she gripped the excess fabric of her jeans.

I reached over, settling my hand on top of hers. "You okay?"

But all she did was shrug.

"You guys ready to go?"

I nodded at Cecilia's question, then felt her ease us out of the driveway. I wanted to press the questions. I wanted to pull out of her what was wrong. But I didn't want to do it in front of my stepmother. Rae wasn't okay, though. And I had a feeling it had something to do with last night.

I watched as Rae gazed out the window. She watched the world pass us by as she sank heavier and heavier into the leather seats of the car. She didn't speak. Not one fucking word. And I desperately wanted to ask her what the hell happened after I left last night. I called Cecilia to come get me around midnight, and D.J. was still there. Her mother and D.J. had still been downstairs, going back and forth at one another. It was like they never stopped. She'd say one thing and he'd clap back. He'd say something wrong and she'd chew him out for it. It made me sick, leaving Rae in that kind of environment last night. I almost had a mind to ask Cecilia if she could come back with us.

But I figured that might've been crossing a line with Rae's mom.

Had D.J. done something to her? Said something to her? Because if he had, he was done. If he'd touched her, or berated her, or said anything to her that wasn't a compliment or asking her how she was, that asshole was dead meat. I didn't care that he was decades older than me. I didn't care that Rae's mother would probably hate me for it. The only thing I cared about right now was Rae's well-being.

And her being wasn't well at all.

Calm down, Clint. Focus.

I drew in deep breaths as I held Rae's hand. She didn't move. Didn't budge. She kept her eyes trained out the window and she didn't move her hand. She didn't flip it over so I could lace our fingers together. She didn't scoot closer to me so we could cuddle. She just leaned against the door. Heavily. Like she wanted to burst out and run away.

"All right, you two. We're here."

I softly squeezed Rae's hand. "Ready to get out?"

Rae ripped her hand away from mine and pressed out of the car. And after catching Cecilia's worried stare in the rearview mirror, I quickly followed behind her. The deal was for my stepmom to wait in the parking lot for us so we could make the quickest getaway possible. That, and I didn't want her worrying over my shoulder while I answered questions and did a lineup. If anything, I wanted to be there for Rae. I wanted to support her and help her through this. And I wasn't sure I'd be able to do that with my stepmother looming over my shoulder.

"Rae. Rae. Stop. You're walking—stop!"

I gripped her arm and spun her around just outside the precinct doors.

She sighed. "What?"

I furrowed my brow. "You haven't said a damn thing all morning. What's going on?"

"I just want to get this over with."

"You want to try not lying to me this time?"

She bit down on her lower lip. "Can we talk about it after we get this over with?"

I nodded. "I'll take that."

I slipped my hand into hers and away we went. We walked into the police station and checked in with the front desk. And I felt her holding my hand tighter than ever before. I slipped my arm around her as an officer came out, ushering us back into a room. There was a table with a photo album of pictures. A harsh light beamed down onto the laminated pages. I looked over at Rae before we walked over, my eyes fluttering over the pictures in front of us.

And before the officer could even tell us what the fuck was happening, I saw it.

Rae nodded. "That's the car."

The officer stepped up to the table. "Can you point to it?"

I pressed down onto the picture. "That one. That's the car that ran me off the road."

The officer nodded. "And you're sure of this?"

Rae snapped her eyes up. "I'll never forget what that car looked like."

I shook my head. "Neither will I. That's the car. Both of us are sure."

The officer grinned. "All right. Follow me. Time for the lineup before we ask you both some questions."

Rae clung to me as we were ushered into another room. Beside us was the officer who greeted us in the first room. And on the other side of us was a man who looked like a detective. We stood in front of a window that peered into a room, with something that looked like a height chart plastered onto the back wall.

I snickered. "Wow. It really does look like the TV shows."

And when Rae let out the softest giggle, it spread a wide smile across my face.

There she is.

The detective turned to us. "All right. It's simple. Some men will file in, and you two will point out the guys you recognize."

Rae finally spoke. "How many men are there going to be?"

The detective shook his head. "I'm not at liberty to discuss that. All you two have to do is point out the four boys from that night. Okay?"

I nodded. "Got it."

The first line of guys filed in, and I recognized none of them. I looked down at Rae to see if she had any opinions, but she shook her head, too. None of them looked familiar and I felt my stomach drop. Until another line of guys filtered in.

Rae perked up. "The one on the far right."

The officer nodded. "Number?"

I licked my lips. "Number One. Definitely. He was the one calling the shots that night. The one driving."

Rae scoffed. "He's the one that kept making the sexual jeers at me all night. He's one of those boys."

The detective sighed. "Any other ones look familiar?"

And when we both shook our heads, they sent the guys away.

We looked at five lines of guys before pointing out the four boys that had attacked us that night. I was confident in every single one we picked out. Rae was right there with me, too. Backing me up and even explaining what their roles had been. The leader. The driver. The one feeding everyone else opened beers. She even explained my relation to two of them, outlining the fight that had taken place at school. Her memory was fucking dead-on, and it was impressive.

But I knew it'd lead to a lot of uncomfortable questions with the officer later.

Anger radiated off her. With every line of guys that trudged in, she squeezed my hand harder. Her face grew redder. Seeing their faces brought back memories I wanted to forget. But Rae looked like she could practically kill over them. I smoothed my thumb over her knuckles as I pulled her close, trying to calm her down as much as I could.

Then, as we were ushered into a room for questioning, Rae turned around.

"What happens now?"

The detective cleared his throat. "Well, there are some questions the police will want to ask. All you have to do is answer them as honestly as you can. If you don't remember, say you don't. And whatever you do, don't lie. They'll write down your testimony, you'll sign it, and that'll be admitted into evidence when these boys go on trial. If they go on trial."

Rae bristled. "What do you mean 'if'?"

I sighed. "I have to press charges."

She paused. "Wait, you haven't done that already?"

The officer slipped into the room. "We haven't gotten to that point yet. But once you answer my questions, we can go over his options."

The detective nodded. "You're in good hands. Just answer the questions honestly, then we can go over what to charge these boys with. If you want to press them."

Rae scoffed. "Of course he's pressing charges. Right?"

She looked up at me, searching for an answer. But I didn't know what to say.

"Right. Clint?"

I sucked air through my teeth. "What would I even charge them with?"

The officer put a hand on my shoulder. "Once we get your signed testimony, we'll get you linked up with a lawyer. Because you're going to want to talk to one, kid."

Rae looked up at me. "You'll talk to one at least, right?"

I nodded. "Of course. Yeah."

But, deep down, I wasn't sure if I wanted to.

I mean, yeah. I'd almost died. But I'd had a hand in how this played out, too. The fight on the football field. And I didn't have the cleanest record with the police department in the first place. They'd broken up way too many parties I'd attended over the years. I'd gotten myself into plenty of trouble, speeding around on my bike and defacing public property with spray paint because I'd been an asshole as a freshman. Did a guy like me really stand a chance in court with something like this?

I wasn't sure. And Rae didn't like that.

"You have to press charges, Clint."

I sighed. "Let's get these questions answered first. One step at a time, okay?"

"Why in the world wouldn't you?"

The officer interrupted us. "If the two of you would take a seat, we don't have a lot of time."

The detective nodded. "Go on. I'll be in the hallway once you're done."

"Clint?"

The helplessness in Rae's voice punched me in the gut. I led her over to the table, trying my best to rip her away from the topic of conversation. My mind swirled with too many things, and it made it hard to concentrate. One step at a time. All I wanted to do was take it one step at a time. And after this sworn testimony or whatever the hell it was came to a close, we could discuss the next steps. Talk about what came after this.

Preferably with Cecilia.

I sat at the table. "Thanks for having me over for dinner. I really appreciate it."

Allison's mom smiled at me. "You know you're always welcome, Rae. Anytime."

Allison's father nodded. "Especially after the day you had yesterday."

I peeked over at Allison. "My day."

My best friend nodded. "I told them about you and Clint heading to the police station. I hope that's okay."

I nodded slowly. "Yeah, yeah. That's fine."

Her mom slid the biscuits to me. "You know if you want to talk about it, we're here."

Her dad spooned me up some mashed potatoes. "Do you know if he's going to press charges at all?"

Allison scoffed. "I think he should, at least. Those boys need to get what's coming to them."

My eyebrows rose. "Wow. Harsh language coming from you."

Her mom murmured. "Well, it's true. The whole town is abuzz with it. Apparently, they almost killed him. Doesn't matter their age, they deserve to pay for their actions."

Her father grunted in approval. "And maybe their parents will learn a thing or two about actually keeping tabs on their kids from now on."

I didn't want to talk about it. Especially with her parents. But it was nice to know they were on my side. Especially since it took so much to convince Clint to press charges. I still didn't know why. I still didn't know why it had taken a lengthy conversation in the back of his stepmother's car in order to convince him to press charges against these assholes. I mean, they'd done so much to us that, apparently, I had a right to press charges as well.

I promised Clint that if I didn't press charges, he would.

Allison's mom filled my lemonade up and her father kept spooning food onto my plate. I loved coming over to eat with them. More because I enjoyed the family dynamic. They treated me like their own daughter, wanting to know about my life and giving me advice. Her father always stuffed me full of food, too. Which was outstanding, because he was an incredible cook.

I hummed. "This meatloaf is fantastic, Mr. Denver."

He smiled. "I'm glad you like it. I tried something a bit different with the spices and everything. Wasn't sure how it would turn out."

Allison's mom smiled. "It's great, honey. Really."

Allison piped up. "Does this mean Mom cooked dessert?"

I grinned. "Oh, was there a tag-team situation in the kitchen tonight?"

Her mom giggled. "I got the cobbler in the oven a bit late. So, dessert won't be for another hour or so. But, yes. There's cobbler in the oven cooking and fresh vanilla ice cream in the freezer."

I groaned. "You guys spoil me way too much."

Her dad chuckled. "And we'll make sure to send you home with some leftovers for you and your mom later on in the week."

I stuffed myself stupid before we were excused from the table. Which resulted in Allison and me lumbering up the stairs. I always ate too much whenever I came over for dinner. It just happened that way. We fell onto her bed and stared up at her ceiling fan, watching it go around and around and around. And as her door slowly shut itself because once the air conditioning kicked on, she rolled toward me.

"All right, Rae. Are we talking about the police station first, or my date?"

My eyes bulged. "Holy shit, your date!"

"Don't tell me you forgot."

"I didn't forget. I just… temporarily forgot it existed?"

She pursed her lips. "I'll forgive you this time, but only because I love you."

I lobbed my head over to see her. "How was the movie?"

"It. Was. Phenomenal! I met him there and he had the tickets and snacks already bought. Got my favorite, too. A small Dr. Pepper with those little crunch bite things, as well as some popcorn for us to split."

"Sounds like your kind of movie night."

"And guess what?"

I paused. "What?"

Allison scooted up to my ear. "He held my hand during the movie."

My jaw dropped open. "Allison! You scandalous little thing, you."

She playfully swatted at me. "Hey, now. Not all of us can have the hoppin' sex life you have."

"And it is hoppin'."

She giggled. "You're insane, you know that?"

I rolled over onto my stomach. "Okay, tell me. How did he do it, how far into the movie did he do it, and did you like it?"

"Okay. So, we weren't that far into the movie. I mean, maybe fifteen minutes before he tried. And he tried three times before he succeeded."

"Why? Did you keep pulling away or something?"

Her face flushed red. "I kept reaching for popcorn and things without paying attention to what he was doing."

"Allison!"

"I know! I know! It was terrible. I felt awful. But he did succeed."

"So… did you like it?"

She sighed. "I mean, it was a bit awkward at first.

I've known Michael for years. It kind of felt like I was holding my brother's hand or something at first?"

"That's not good."

"No, no. It didn't feel like that the entire time. I think maybe he was nervous because he tried twice before and I moved and all that stuff. But once I relaxed into it and kind of leaned against him, it felt nice. You know, not completely awkward."

I nodded. "You think you'd do it again? Holding his hand?"

She paused. "I think I definitely would."

The two of us squealed together before we buried our faces into pillows. I was happy for her because I knew how much she wanted this. I knew how long she'd been crushing on Michael, and it was nice that the two of them were finally opening up that door between them. A door that practically everyone had seen, but no one was willing to admit existed.

Then Allison sighed. "All right. Your turn."

I groaned. "Do I have to?"

"Why don't we start with Clint pressing charges. You said he was?"

I nodded, tilting my head to the side. "Yeah, he is."

"How do you feel about that?"

I shrugged. "I don't like the fact that it took him so long to make that decision."

"What do you mean?"

"The entire police thing was just a mess. I mean, we picked out the car, picked those boys out of a lineup, then answered a barrage of questions that ended up being some written testimony we had to sign."

"Sounds pretty standard, actually."

I shrugged. "We talked in the back of his step-mom's car about the pros and cons of pressing charges. Pros and cons, Allison. Like he was planning to move into a home. Or changing up his wardrobe. Or choosing what college to apply for."

"Really?"

"Yeah. It was frustrating as hell, too. Apparently, I had the option to press charges, and when I blurted out that I'd be pressing charges, Clint changed his tune. Said if I didn't press charges, he promised he would."

"So he didn't really make the decision to press them."

"Nope. He did it so I wouldn't. And I still don't know why."

She furrowed her brow. "That's insane. He was severely injured."

I shrugged. "I know. Trust me, I get it. It boggles my mind, too. I'm just glad he's pressing them, one way or another. He needs to. Those boys need to rot."

"Do you know when he's talking to a lawyer?"

"Tomorrow, actually. After school. To see what steps he needs to take next."

"Do you know what they're going to charge those boys with?"

I sighed. "I don't have a clue."

"Do you want my opinion?"

"I'd love anything you've got for me right now."

Allison sat up. "Okay. Objectively speaking, here's

what you've got. They approached you in the parking lot, right?"

"Right."

"And they said all this stuff to you before Clint distracted them, right?"

"Uh huh."

"Then, Clint drove off and they followed him. Pursued him, right?"

I nodded. "Yep."

"And even though Clint tried shaking them, they kept following him. Until they ran him off the road."

I swallowed hard. "Yeah."

"In my eyes? The only thing Clint has accountability for is getting their focus off you. That was his fault, and it had good intentions. Good motives. Everything else was spurred on by those boys. From pulling up to you guys in the first place to chasing him down, no matter what. To me? The charge should be attempted murder."

And after a brief pause, I nodded.

"You make a very good point about that."

Allison scoffed. "There's no point about it. Drunk or not, those boys knew what they were doing. If they had enough sense to keep in control of that car long enough to be able to ram Clint over the edge of that bridge, then they had enough sense to choose not to."

I grinned. "You sure you don't want to be a lawyer or something?"

She giggled. "Nah. I'm just really good at arguing. Dad hates it."

"Let me guess. You get it from your mother."

"We've chased Dad out of the house a few times. No joke."

The two of us fell apart in laughter, and it felt good to be laughing again. Especially with the whirlwind this weekend had been. Between listening to D.J. and my mother literally fight all Friday night to the police trip with Clint Saturday morning, I was exhausted. Deep in my bones. I was frustrated, I felt numb to the world, and all I wanted to do was crawl underneath a rock and stay there.

Yet, somehow, Allison had me laughing.

"You two ready for dessert?"

Her mother's voice filtered up the stairs and we scrambled off the bed. We raced back down the stairs, flopping onto the couch as her mother divvied out massive bowls of cobbler and ice cream. We all sat together, with Allison and me between her parents while we watched a movie and ate our fill. I laughed with them. I sniffled with them. We watched the sweetest little comedy that had us all roaring with laughter and holding back tears.

But all too soon, it was time to go.

"Here, there's plenty of leftovers. Take some to your mother."

"And some cobbler, too. We'll never eat all this I made."

"Want some lemonade?"

"I could pack some of this ice cream on ice for the trip back."

I snickered, holding the bags full of tupperware. "I

promise, you guys, this is more than enough. Thank you. I really appreciate it."

After handing me one last bag of food, Allison got the keys to the car from her father. She drove me home, and I sat there for a second gathering the mental energy to walk into the house. I didn't see D.J.'s car, which was a massive relief. But something in the pit of my gut told me I was still walking into something bad.

Allison put her hand on my shoulder. "You okay?"

I nodded. "Yeah. I'm good. See you tomorrow morning?"

"See you then."

I pressed out of the car and made my way for the front door. And when I found it unlocked, my stomach dropped. Mom always locked the door. Even when she was home. Which meant someone had left and she hadn't bothered to lock it. The second I heard her sniffling, I knew. I knew exactly what had happened tonight.

"Rae? Is that you?"

I closed the door behind me. "Yeah, Mom. I'm home."

"What's that smell?""

"Cobbler and dinner from the Denvers' house."

"Can you bring it into the kitchen, please?"

I sighed as I made my way down the hallway. Shadows flashed across the walls as Allison backed out of the driveway, and I wanted nothing more than to chase her down. My home had become a living hell, and I didn't want to be here anymore. Especially when I saw my mother wiping at her eyes.

Because of fucking D.J.

"You hungry?"

She shook her head. "Just put it in the fridge."

I did as she asked, then walked over and put a hand on her shoulder. I squeezed it softly as I gazed blankly at the wall, wondering if it would ever stop. If my mother would ever notice her worth. If she'd ever pull herself out of this hole and move on with her life.

"I'm sorry for whatever he did to you tonight."

Then, without letting her explain, I showed myself off to my room.

32

CLINTON

I sat in the lawyer's office, hating the fact that my father was here. I knew this would happen, too. I told Cecilia not to tell him. I told her to just keep it between us. I didn't need Dad coming to this damn meeting with me. Cecilia would've been fine. Hell, I could've done this damn meeting myself! I mean, it took me a little bit to grasp the fact that I was about to press charges on four boys who tried killing me. But, all I had to do was digest that fact. Digest the—the realness of it all.

And of course, the second Cecilia updated my father, he was on the first plane ride home.

"Did we have to do this today? This couldn't have waited?"

Cecilia scoffed. "Howard, you didn't have to come. I told you I had this under control."

Dad shook his head. "The only thing you would've

done is rack up a larger bill than necessary asking tons of unnecessary questions."

"So, you're only here to moderate your funds. Is that it? You don't care that we're here to prosecute the boys who almost killed our son?"

Dad paused. "You mean *my* son, Cece?"

I kept myself poised in my chair, even though I wanted to melt into a puddle on the floor. The second the lawyer's door opened, though, Dad shut his fucking face. Guess he'd learned his lesson with the doctor in the hospital. I peered over at Cecilia, watching as she crossed her leg over her knee, trying to keep her composure as much as possible, even though I saw the anger in her eyes.

Thank fuck, I'm sitting beside her.

"Afternoon. My name is Omar Littenberg."

The lawyer held his hand out for Dad and he stood to shake it. Cecilia stayed seated, but she shook his hand in kind. I stood, staring the man in the face with a grateful smile. And as I shook his hand, he held mine just a little longer than necessary.

Had he heard what had happened from the hallway?

Fuck. "It's really nice to meet you. Thank you for seeing us on such short notice."

He dropped my hand. "Of course. When I caught word of what happened from the police station, I immediately cleared my schedule."

Cecilia smiled. "You came highly recommended by the detective over there."

Dad scoffed. "I'll be the judge of whether or not you take my son's case."

Omar sat down. "Actually, you have no legal voice in this room."

Dad paused. "Excuse me?"

I sighed. "I'm eighteen, Dad. He doesn't need your consent. Only mine."

"Well, if he wants his check paid, he'll make sure he has my consent."

Cecilia hissed. "Howard, stop it. We're here for our son."

"My son."

I sighed. "Yes, you came recommended by the detective at the police station. He said something about you taking on these kinds of cases before?"

Omar nodded. "Mm-hmm. I specialize in juvie cases. Because they are usually presented to the court and judged in a much different fashion. You might be of legal age, but the boys who ran you down aren't. They're still seventeen, so their court proceedings will happen in a different light."

"Fair enough. So how much do you know about what happened?"

"I know as much as I need to know. Let me rattle it off and see if I've got it right."

Dad sighed. "Can we speed this up a bit?"

Omar darted his eyes over to my father. "This first meeting is free of charge. That's usually how it works with most lawyers."

Cecilia humped. "Now, will you hush?"

"Don't you talk to me that way."

"I'll talk to you however I want if it means you'll sit down and support your son for once."

I sat there with my eyes closed, waiting for them to stop bickering. And when Omar cleared his throat, I opened my eyes.

"The gist of it is you were approached by these boys, they chased you off, you tried to outrun them, and they ran you off the road and over a bridge. Correct?"

I nodded. "That's the gist of it, yes."

"Anything else you want me to know?"

I felt my father's eyes burrowing into me and I felt sick to my stomach. I wanted to tell the lawyer why they'd chased me off. I wanted to tell him I was defending the girl with me. Rae. And I saw he was waiting for me to bring her up. Cecilia reached over and took my hand, squeezing it for reassurance.

But I saw the look in my father's eye. Even from the corner of my own. If I didn't speed this up, there would be hell to pay.

He probably has a plane to get back to soon.

"Um, nothing I want to add for now. I'm really just looking for what we'd charge them with. I don't know how that all works."

Omar nodded. "Fair enough. I know this is probably pretty overwhelming. So I'll make it easy for you. Should you choose me for your case, I'd try the boys for attempted murder."

Cecilia gasped. "Murder?"

Dad scoffed. "They didn't try to kill my son. Come on."

Omar shot him a look. "I'm speaking with your son. I'd appreciate it if you didn't interject."

The two of them stared off with one another before the lawyer's attention fell back to me.

"They intentionally went after you. They intentionally ran you off the road. I've seen the crime photos. I've read the reports. The theories. And from the looks of the scene, you got off your bike and tried making a break for the woods. Didn't you?"

I felt my face pale as Cecilia squeezed my hand tighter.

"Is that true, honey?"

Dad murmured under his breath, but I didn't catch it.

"Uh, yeah. That's—that's true. You can see that from the pictures?"

Omar nodded. "Clear as day. Your bike is mangled in one place, but you went over the railing in another. There are separate sets of tire skid marks. Same tires, different areas. They intentionally pushed you over that railing. That's as much attempted murder as anything I've ever come across."

Holy shit. "Well, I appreciate your bluntness and honesty. Thank you."

"Mr. Clarke, these kids are lucky you're still breathing. Otherwise, they'd be staring down the barrel of a very unfortunate future. If it makes you feel any better, I can go easy on them. Suggest juvie for a spell, as well as a specialized schooling atmosphere and court-mandated therapy in exchange for no jail time and having their record expunged."

I paused. "I'm not sure if that makes me feel any better."

Cecilia butted in. "You have to do something, Clint. They really did a number on you. Even if you simply sue them for the hospital bills or something—"

Dad snickered. "Yeah. Pay me back some of that money."

"Howard!"

I rolled my eyes. "Please excuse him."

"Did you just excuse me for someone else?"

I looked over at my father. "I did. Because you're acting absolutely insane right now and I'm tired of it."

His eyes lit up with fire as he stood up from his chair. His eyes panned toward the lawyer as he buttoned his suit coat. Cecilia got up quickly and followed him out of the room, trying to talk some sense into him. And as the door closed behind them, I cleared my throat.

"I'm really sorry for that."

Omar shook his head. "Not your fault, Mr. Clarke."

I sighed. "So, if I wanted to press charges, what would we do?"

"We'd gather evidence and serve each of their families with a formal subpoena. The boys are being held right now, so there will be a bail hearing. In which case, I'll call for no bail since the charges are attempting to take your life from you. I'll pose that they're a threat for now, then suggest they be moved to a juvie facility where they can continue their studies while keeping you safe. Then a court date is set and we work on presenting the facts."

I nodded. "How long will this take?"

"I have a few questions."

Dad came barging back into the room and the lawyer shot out of his chair.

"Sir, you'll keep your voice down and keep it kosher. Or I'll have you removed from the premises."

Dad walked around the desk, standing toe to toe with the man. "My son needs to focus on his studies. Not fussing over putting four boys in prison."

"They tried killing your son."

"And he probably provoked them! Look, I know my son better than you. Better than anyone. He's a troublemaker, just like they are."

Cecilia yelped. "Howard! Stop it!"

"No! I'm done with you hopping all over my back and acting like my son is some wounded puppy. You said it yourself, Mr. Whatever Your Last Name Is, he's a legal adult. He doesn't conduct himself like one, though. Every single issue I've ever had with this boy has been brought on by prior actions. Did he tell you two of the boys that approached him that night had gotten into a fight with him earlier in the week?"

Omar shook his head. "No. But I read that in the report."

I stood up. "How do you know that, Dad?"

He glared at me. "Because I keep tabs on you. Everything you do. You got into a fight with two of those boys, didn't you? On the football field, at school. You stormed up to them and started wailing on them.

For no reason. And you don't see them pressing charges on you, do you?"

Cecilia stepped to the forefront. "Are you saying Clint deserved to be run off the road?"

Dad rolled his eyes. "Hell, no! What I'm saying is that they came back for revenge. Like every single seventeen-year-old boy does when he's been wronged. My son isn't innocent in any of this. And the last thing he needs to be doing is batting off criminal charges of his own when he should be focusing on clawing himself out of high school. Because believe you me, his grades are barely there, at best."

I flopped back down into my chair. I didn't know what else to do. What else to say. I didn't have any more fight left in me, and I didn't care. I stared at the wall, listening as my father unleashed. He went on a damn rampage as my stepmother tried to calm him down. And all the while, the lawyer stood his ground. Took everything in. Listened to him with a nod of his head.

I just wanted to go home.

No, not home.

I wanted to go see Rae.

"Mr. Clarke?"

Omar's voice ripped me from my trance. "Yeah?"

Dad hissed. "You mean, 'yes, sir.'"

I nodded slowly. "I'm sorry. Yes, sir?"

"It sounds like your family has some things you need to discuss. Pros and cons, and all that."

Dad huffed. "You're damn right we do."

Omar pointed his finger. "One more outburst out

of you and you're hauled away in handcuffs. Do you hear me?"

Cecilia stepped closer to him. "Howard, I'm begging you. Stop it."

He shrugged her off. "I'd like to see you try."

Omar shrugged. "Fair enough."

He pressed a button underneath his desk and two massive men appeared in the doorway. My eyes bulged as Cecilia stepped toward me, and I wrapped my arm around her shoulder. She gasped and squealed. We watched as Dad struggled against the two massive brutes. It felt like an out-of-body experience, watching him struggle like that. Watching him fight against them until they dragged him out of the office.

Then one of them reached over and closed the door.

"You aren't going to throw him in jail, are you?"

Cecilia's voice sounded frantic. But part of me hoped the lawyer did. I looked over just in time to see Omar shake his head, though. Which disappointed me a bit.

"No. He'll just be removed outside until he can calm down. But this meeting won't take much longer. I know you still have some things to mull over and discuss."

Cecilia nodded. "We do, but you've been very helpful. Thank you so much."

I watched the lawyer reach into his desk. He pulled out a small card, then scribbled something across the back. He didn't hand it to my stepmother, though. He handed it directly to me. I took the card from him and he shook my hand. But he held my gaze with a fervor that magnetized me to my spot.

"When you have a decision, you call me, okay? But, if you need anything—ever—reach out. I'm here to help. Always."

And as I read between the lines of his unspoken offering, I pocketed his card.

A warning much like the one the doctor in the hospital gave me.

33

RAELYNN

Michael smiled. "You look nice today, Allison."
I watched my best friend blush. "Thanks, Michael. You don't look half bad yourself."

"Is that a new shirt? I don't think I've seen it before."

"Nah, it's just been a while since I've worn it."

"Well, you should wear it more often. It really suits you. That color and everything."

I watched the way Allison smiled up at Michael. I saw the way he gazed down at her. I snickered to myself in the backseat, but the two of them didn't seem to hear me. Like we'd done for a while now, the three of us were in front of Clint's house. Picking him up for school. Even though he got stronger by the second, he still didn't have a set of wheels to get himself to and from campus. And by his words, he'd rather 'drop off that damn bridge again than ride a bus.'

Needless to say, he only cracked that joke once before I got on him about it.

I saw Michael go for Allison's hand again and I silently cheered him on. Allison was terrible about moving while Michael was making a move on her. I'd watched her do it twice this morning. I felt so bad for the guy! Because I knew she wasn't doing it on purpose. And when he finally got her hand within his, I mentally tossed my hands into the air. I didn't want to make a big deal out of it because I didn't want them to feel self conscious. Allison had always been easily embarrassed, and if Michael thought—for one second —he had embarrassed her, he'd stop everything he was doing immediately.

And none of us wanted that.

I watched their fingers intertwine before my gaze wandered out the window. I watched their reflection as the two of them talked softly amongst themselves. I liked the two of them together. They were cute. In my eyes, they were made for one another. But that kind of shit was also subjective. I tried to give them all the privacy I could afford. You know, with me being in the backseat and things like that.

Come on, Clint. We're gonna be late.

I pulled my phone out and looked at the time. We'd pulled into his driveway ten minutes ago, and part of me was growing worried. Had he hurt himself again? Was something wrong? I looked around at the windows upstairs, clocking his bedroom window. I didn't see the curtains fluttering. Nor did I see shadows passing by.

The light was on, but no one was walking around. So he was obviously up.

Maybe I should send him another text.

I sent off my third text that morning, reminding him that we were outside. And if we didn't get a move on, we'd be late for class. I peeked back over at Michael and Allison, watching as they continued to smile and talk and gaze into one another's eyes. Allison had curled up into the passenger seat of the car, turning herself to face him completely. And Michael? Well, he was leaning well over the arm of his seat. Getting as close to Allison as he could before she pulled away from him.

Such an adorable couple.

A movement out from the corner of my eye caught my attention and I whipped my head back toward the window. My heart sang with delight as Clint walked out, his bag slung over his shoulder. But something was off about his movements. His eyes were downcast. He lumbered slower than usual. He wasn't walking with the same sort of confidence I usually saw in him, and I wondered what had happened.

Is his father home?

Michael cleared his throat. "Is Clint okay?"

Allison sighed. "So I'm not the only one that noticed. Good."

I shook my head. "I don't know. Don't say anything, okay?"

Michael nodded. "I had no intentions of it. He's been through enough lately. If he wants to talk, we're here."

Allison backed him up. "Uh huh. And if he doesn't want to talk, we're still going to be here."

I threw open the car door. "Thanks, guys. I really appreciate it."

I helped Clint into the car beside me, and not once did he look at me. He closed the door and flopped down next to me, sitting his bag between his legs. I ran my hand up and down this thigh and squeezed his knee softly, trying to get him to look at me. But even from behind his sunglasses, I saw him staring blankly out the window.

With his head turned away from me.

"Morning."

I said it as softly and evenly as I could. So the worry wasn't prevalent in my voice. But all he did was nod.

Michael looked at him in the rearview mirror. "How'd you sleep?"

Clint shrugged. "As good as I could."

Allison giggled. "I know how those nights are sometimes. Melatonin always helps me. I mean, I know it's technically to help kids and all that. But it helps me, too. Especially if I'm worried about a test. Are you worried ab... out a... test?"

The more Allison peered back at us, the more I shook my head. Too much. She was talking and saying way too much. Her nerves were getting the best of her, and Clint would sense that. She apologized with her eyes before turning back around, the car slowly bobbing and weaving as Michael drove us all to school.

And the entire time, Clint was silent.

On the one hand, I wanted to push it. I wanted to know what the fuck was going on. But I didn't want to do it in front of Michael and Allison. Because I knew that would make Clint very uncomfortable. So I kept massaging his knee and his thigh until Michael dropped us off. He pulled up to the back doors of the school and let us out, then went to go park the car with Allison. I had a feeling we wouldn't see them again this morning. So I pulled Clint off to the side. Into the shadows of the side of the school.

Where no one could see—or hear—us talk.

"Hey, are you okay?"

Clint shrugged. "I'm as good as I can be."

I snickered. "Which is apparently not very good. I know something's wrong. Do you want to talk about it?"

Clint dropped his bag. "Just—that shit with the lawyer yesterday."

I nodded. "What happened?"

He leaned against the brick wall of the school. "Dad's back in town."

"Oh, no."

"Oh, yeah. I told Cecilia time and time again not to tell Dad about the fucking lawyer. And of course, she didn't listen. She's awesome, but she never fucking listens. It's like she thinks Dad's actually gonna be this decent-as-fuck person one of these days. Then she gets shocked and hurt and scared when he loses his shit. She's been married to him for four years! The fuck is she thinking!?"

I placed my hands against his chest. "Deep breaths. Come on, take them with me. There we go."

I walked Clint through some even breathing. He was shaking against my hands, and I needed him to settle down. That explained everything. With his father back in town, shit always popped off. I smoothed my hands over his torso, trying to relax him. I watched him sink heavier and heavier into the brick wall as a cloud hovered over his head. His arms fell to his sides. He wrapped me up in his embrace and pulled me close. He kissed my forehead, sending electricity surging through my body as I closed my eyes. Tucked my head underneath his chin. And reveled in the way he stroked my back.

Clint sighed. "Dad doesn't want me pressing charges."

I scoffed. "Of. Fucking. Course."

"He still thinks I had something to do with it. And he's been keeping up with the police reports because he knew about the football field fight."

I sighed. "Shit."

"Yeah. To him, that's proof enough that I apparently deserved what I got. Because, to him, those seventeen-year old boys were just 'being boys and doing what boys do.'"

I pulled away a bit. "Did he actually say that?"

Clint nodded. "Right there in the fucking lawyer's office. I was so embarrassed I wanted to melt into the goddamn floor."

I gazed up into his eyes. "Clint? Your father's a piece of trash."

"Don't I know it."

"Clint, you need to press charges. They could have killed you. They almost did. Who the fuck does your dad think he is?"

He gave me a wary smile. "It's okay, Rae. There's no need for you to get worked up. I'll figure this all out. Especially once Cecilia can stop updating my dad every second of every fucking day."

"She just loves your dad. I get it. I mean, I don't know how she loves your dad. But she does."

He paused. "You get it?"

I felt my cheeks flush and I looked away from him. Fucking hell, I'd almost given myself away. Well, I'd practically given myself away, was more like it. Clint chuckled and pulled me back to him, placing a kiss to the top of my head. And as he rubbed my back with his large, strong hands, I felt my eyes fall closed.

"You keep doing that, I'm gonna fall asleep."

He kissed my head again. "My only wish is that we were in a bed somewhere so I could fall asleep with you."

I wrapped my arms around him. "Sore this morning?"

"A bit."

"Did you take your pain medication? Any of it?"

"Half a pill. It takes the edge off without making me loopy."

"Good. I wouldn't want you to be in too much pain today."

"Look at you, worrying about me like a good woman does."

I giggled. "Of course I'm going to worry about you. I care for you. I care about what happens to you. Unlike your fucking father, who I'd like to toss into a raging inferno."

He snickered. "Tell me how you really feel."

I kissed his chest. "Please don't let him make this decision for you. I'm here if you need to talk, but if you want my honest opinion, you have to press charges on these boys. They flagrantly came at you. They deserve what they're getting."

Clint nodded. "Okay."

The word was so soft. So timid. So... unlike Clint. It made me want to wring his father's fucking neck. I tilted my head back and stood on my tiptoes, placing a kiss against his lips. He paused for a split second before cupping my cheek. I felt his tongue sliding across my lips. I willfully opened up for him, wrapping my arms around his neck. And as our tongues fell together, the school bell rang in the background.

I groaned. "Fuck."

He chuckled. "Come on, beautiful. Let's get you to class before you experience what life is like on the other side of being on time."

"Does it have more kisses? Because I'd gladly experience it if it had more kisses."

"You're a mess, you know that?"

"A mess for you, Clint."

He gazed into my eyes before capturing my lips one last time. And then he picked me up off my feet. He tossed me over his shoulder, causing me to laugh out loud as he picked up his backpack. He spanked my ass cheeks, over and over. Until we got around the corner of the school.

Then he carried me inside, heading straight for my locker as laughter poured from my lips.

34

CLINTON

I watched Mike and Aly at lunch as I sat beside Rae. She leaned against me, falling between my legs and resting her weight against my chest. I'd missed holding her like this. I'd missed taking the whole of her against me and supporting her. As I wrapped my arms around her body, threading our fingers together, she pressed herself into me as close as she could get.

Thank fuck for that half a pain pill.

"So, Clint. How were classes this morning?"

Mike's voice ripped me from my trance and I nodded.

"Eh, they weren't too bad. English is getting interesting again, though. Now that we're finally onto another book."

Aly rolled her eyes. "Right? Catch-22 was the biggest drag alive. I still can't believe I forced myself to read that thing."

302 | REBEL HART

I snickered. "I didn't at all. I did the SparkNotes version and prayed a bit for the test."

"And let me guess, you still passed it."

I shrugged. "I mean, I felt confident about it today. Why? You hate me for it?"

"Hey, everyone's got their subject. Mine just isn't English."

Rae snickered. "Which is actually a shocker, since you love to read your textbooks."

Aly stuck her tongue out at Rae and it made me laugh. Mike, too. His eyes connected with mine and I nodded toward him, trying to get him to wrap his arm around the damn girl. I mean, Aly had practically leaned herself against him. Every chance she got, she tried touching him in some way. Her hand on his forearm whenever she was laughing at a joke of his. She paid attention intently every time he said something. She was throwing off signals more than any girl had ever thrown signals at me. And Mike seemed completely oblivious to it.

So I jiggled my arm at him before pulling Rae closer. Hoping he got the fucking point.

Aly looked over at him and blushed. *She* got the point. But Mike? He looked like he was about to puke. The poor kid had probably never put his arm around a girl before in his young adult life. I grinned as I watched Aly scoot closer to him, trying to make it as easy on him as possible.

And when he finally wrapped his arm around her, she placed her head against his shoulder.

"Hi there, Michael."

He grinned. "Hey there, Allison."

Rae giggled. "Awwww, how *cuuuuuute!*"

All of us started laughing, which caused Michael to pull Allison closer. She wrapped her arm around his waist, holding him while he held her. It was cute, really. The two of them made a fantastic couple. They looked the part. Talked the part. Thought in the same way, and had much of the same goals. I'd learned that over the multiple car rides we'd all had together over to the school. They talked about college. Career goals. Moving out and getting places of their own. They had the same sorts of ambitions with life, and in some ways I envied them.

You know, their ability to have options.

"You know, this day feels like it's crept by like a slug."

Rae's voice pulled me from my trance and I kissed the top of her head.

"I don't know. It's flown by for me," I said.

Mike shook his head. "Nope. I'm with Rae on this one. It's crept by painfully slow."

Aly shrugged. "I don't really care, to be honest."

Rae giggled. "If you could live here, you probably would."

"Hey, now. Hey. Just because I enjoy school doesn't mean I want to live here. I mean, cafeteria food for all three meals? I would rather d—"

She caught herself and everyone whipped their eyes over to me. Aly went to apologize, but I simply shook my head at her. This was exactly what I didn't want. I didn't want people tiptoeing around me. I didn't want people feeling they had to mute themselves in order to preserve my feelings. I didn't want things to change that drastically, simply because I wanted to try and keep things as normal as they could be. I wanted Rae leaning against me, I wanted my two new friends to joke around and poke fun at me, and I wanted to get through this school year with some sort of a future away from this place intact.

Aly stumbled over her words. "Clint—I'm —I'm so—"

I held up my hand. "Really, it's okay. This is exactly what I didn't want to happen. I don't want you guys feeling like you can't crack jokes or poke fun at things or generally have a laugh. I almost died. It happened. But it didn't kill me. It's going to take more than that. Okay?"

Aly nodded softly. "Okay."

Mike saluted me. "Loud and clear, General."

I snickered. "Rae. You good?"

She sighed. "Yeah, I'm okay. Just—don't like thinking about it."

I pulled her close. "I know you don't. I know."

Aly piped up. "So, what are you going to do now that you've identified the guys and whatnot?"

I paused. "What?"

Rae cringed. "I kind of told her about the trip to the police department."

Mike furrowed his brow. "Police department? Everything okay?"

I waved my hand in the air. "Yeah, yeah, things are good. Just had to identify the guys from that night. Pick out the car. Answer a few more questions. Shit like that."

Mike nodded. "How'd that go?"

I shrugged. "I mean, it came and it went. Rae was there to back me up on things. It was nice, having her there for support."

She tucked her head underneath my chin. "I'll go with you anytime, anywhere, if you need my support."

"Thanks, beautiful."

Aly sighed. "Awww, how cute."

Mike chuckled. "Now you know how Rae felt a few minutes ago."

I smiled as Mike pulled her closer, tucking her underneath his arm. I felt them staring at me, and I knew what they really wanted to know. I looked down at Rae, finding her eyes. I saw her shaking her head softly, silently telling me I didn't have to talk about it if I didn't want to. And while this isn't a conversation I wanted to have with many people, this was a conversation I could tolerate with Mike and Aly.

Which was more than I could have ever said for Roy and the gang.

"I mean, I had a talk with a lawyer yes——"

Rae interrupted me. "Seriously. If you don't want to talk about it, you don't have to."

Mike nodded. "That's true. If it's too much or something——"

I held my hand up. "You guys. It's fine. I promise, if I didn't want to talk about something, I wouldn't. Plain and simple. No matter how you guys felt about the matter."

Aly grinned. "I have my ways, trust me."

Mike nodded. "She really does. It's irritating, but endearing at the same time."

Aly shrugged. "All I heard was 'endearing.'"

Rae laughed. "Like the genuine woman she is."

We all had a laugh at that one before their eyes came back to me again. The laughter died down and the mood turned somber. I knew they wanted to know because they cared. Not because they wanted to exploit a weakness. But that was new to me. People genuinely caring instead of merely wanting to poke fun at some sort of a weakness I had within me.

It took me a second to get my feet underneath me for the story.

"Well, uh, I had an appointment after school yesterday with a lawyer. My stepmom went with me. And Dad. He was… well, he was himself."

Aly furrowed her brow. "What does that mean?"

Mike's face fell into stone. "What did he do to you?"

I shrugged. "What doesn't he do to me? Look, my father's a hard man. Always has been. And, if I'm being honest, he thinks that part of this whole issue is my fault."

Aly balked. "He thinks you being pushed over that bridge by a car is somehow your fault?"

I nodded. "That's how my dad is. I've always given him a hard time. Shit like that. So, in his eyes—once he found out about the fight on the football field— immediately I had as much of a hand in this as those other guys did."

Mike paused. "Football field fight?"

Rae sighed. "Two of the guys that night were from that fight."

Mike's lips downturned. "What the fuck?"

Aly gasped. "Michael!"

"What? I mean, seriously. Come on. Your dad can't actually think any of this was your fault. They almost killed you. They were drunk, from what I could gather from that night. They should be rotting away in jail. Or juvie. Or something."

I shrugged. "My father pretty much showed his ass in that office. Said things like I needed to be focusing on school instead of chasing down four guys I'd provoked."

Aly's jaw dropped open. "What!?"

"He also said I'd been a problem child my whole life. Essentially tried to paint me as some bad boy trying to get the one-up on someone before they got the one-up on me. He told the lawyer that he didn't see those boys pressing assault charges on me when I started the fight. So why should I press attempted murder charges on them simply because they were seeking out revenge like most young boys do?"

Mike's face turned red. "Is it always like this with your father?"

I sighed. "I mean, let's just say I've talked a big game in the past with bruises I've come to school with."

"Oh, Clint."

Aly reached across the table and offered her hand to me. And when I took it, I felt like I had a genuine friend in her. An ally, so to speak. It felt good, opening up to them. Leaning on them during a time like this. And before I knew it, my mouth ran away from me. I told them everything. When the hitting with my father started. The parties I went to on the weekends to get away from it all. The reasons why I came to school and bullied other people around. How I enjoyed it when my father was off on his trips and shit like that. I couldn't get my damn mouth to stop running until it had all come pouring out. And when I was done, Aly wiped tears away from her eyes while Mike placed his hand on my forearm.

"Clint, we're in your corner, man. You need to know that when I tell you this. Okay?"

I nodded. "Hit me with it."

Mike sighed. "You can't let these assholes off the hook. I'm serious. They deserve everything coming at them, and you can't let them get away with it. We're in your corner. The three of us. Backing you up if you need it. And if you need a place to come crash sometime, I'm sure my parents wouldn't mind one damn bit if you came and crashed at my place."

"I thought you hated my guts, Mike."

He shrugged. "I did."

"So… what's changed?"

He grinned. "You put your neck on the line for our girl. And that means more than anything that's happened in the past."

And when his eyes met Rae's, she snuggled against me. I wrapped my arms around her body and mindlessly kissed the top of her head as Mike pulled his hand away. I felt accepted by them. Loved by them. Respected by them in ways I'd never felt with anyone else in my life. For the first time, I understood what it meant to have genuine friends. I understood what it felt like to trust someone. I planted my nose into Rae's hair and breathed deeply as Mike pulled Aly closer into his side.

Then, Aly spoke up.

"So, who wants to come to my study party this weekend for midterms?"

And collectively, the three of us groaned together.

35

RAELYNN

"So, ready for the study party this weekend?"

Clint's voice sounded in my ear as I turned around, standing next to his locker. I leaned against it, watching as he placed his hand just beyond my shoulder. He was back. I loved it when he did this sort of thing. Cornered me and gazed down into my eyes with that knowing grin on his face. I licked my lips as my hand reached out for him. I slid my fingers along his chest. I let them settle against his heartbeat, reminding myself once more that he was still breathing. Still alive.

And that this wasn't a dream.

"You, Clint Clarke, want to go to a study session this weekend."

He shrugged. "Might be fun to watch Mike weirdly try to mack on Aly again."

I nodded. "Oh, oh. Gotcha. So, not about studying at all."

"Just about the drama. And the laughter. Nothing else. You know how it goes."

I winked. "I definitely know how it goes."

"But also maybe a bit of studying."

I quirked an eyebrow. "Actual studying?"

"Hey, that homework you aced for me has set a dangerous precedent I have to keep up with now."

I giggled. "Come here, you idiot."

I gripped his shirt and pulled him down to me, crashing our lips together. As the last of the school bells tolled, signaling the end of the day and the departing of the busses, the ringing swallowed the world around us. My tongue found his, rushing goosebumps along my body. I felt students running by us, trying to get to their rides home before it was too late. Clint fell against me, pinning me to his locker. His hands fell to my hips as I slipped my arms around his neck. I giggled against him. His warmth surrounded me. And as he pulled me closer to him, his arms engulfed my back.

Making me feel safe, and reminding me of just how far he'd come with his recuperation.

"You know, that crash might actually be the best thing that's ever happened to my academic career."

I snickered against his lips. "You just like the fact that I did your homework."

He cupped my cheeks. "I mean, I'm also showing up to classes. Paying attention. Generally not being an ass."

I paused. "Maybe a little bit of an ass."

"Oh, now you're just asking to get punished."

"That obvious, huh?"

I smiled before I captured his lips again. His hands cradled my cheeks softly as the rest of the student body slowly trickled beyond us. I slid my hands through his hair, enjoying how he'd grown it out. The stubble on his jawline tickled my skin, sending shivers up and down my spine.

And as I groaned softly down the back of his throat, he broke the kiss. Nuzzled our noses together. Pressed his forehead against mine.

"Maybe we could go somewhere more private so I can dole out the punishment accordingly."

I giggled. "Only if you admit I had a little bit to do with how well school's going for you."

He paused, gazing into my eyes. "Don't you ever get it twisted. Rae. You're the sole reason why I'm doing so well."

I felt my heart skip a beat with his words. "Come on. Let's go back to my place."

"Your mom's not there?"

I shook my head. "Nope. Went out with D.J. last night, which means she won't be home for a day or two."

"I'm sorry, Rae."

"It is what it is. I mean, she made her choice. I can't do anything to change her mind about that choice. She'll just have to deal with his shit, I guess."

"Do you want to talk about it?"

I shook my head. "Nope. But, I can think of other things I want to do."

I winked at him and that impudent little grin of his stretched across his face. I helped him exchange his books for the ones he needed out of his locker. Then, together, we started for the school doors. Our hands laced together as we started for my house. We walked across the school lawn as the summer sun beat down against our shoulders. His hand wiggled away from mine before he threaded his arm around my waist, pulling me close to him.

Then he kissed the top of my head. "I could do this after school every day, you know."

I grinned. "Come back to my place and punish me?"

He snickered. "Spending time with you, you numbskull. But, also yes, now that I think about it."

I swatted his chest. "You're relentless, you know that?"

"And you're gorgeous. Not my fault I can't stop staring at you."

"I'm pretty sure that is the billboard definition of a 'personal problem.'"

"You don't hate it, though. Do you?"

"Now hold on a second there, buddy. I never said anything about not enjoying it. You're just not going to blame that horny teenage mind of yours on me."

He chuckled. "You're a bit to blame. But in all the best ways."

I smiled. "Just know you aren't the only one that feels that way."

He growled playfully as he pulled me closer into his body. I worked my hand into his back pocket, feeling his strength rolling around against my palm. I leaned my head against his chest as we turned down my street, and the dirty, dingy smell of the place almost passed me by. I sighed with contentment as we made our way for the house. I saw it looming in the distance, like a darkly-smeared stain on a light blue canvas. Thunder rumbled in the distance, despite the sun hanging high in the sky. And as we walked all the way up to my porch, my mind began churning with all sorts of thoughts.

All sorts of nasty, wanton thoughts.

"Do you have to work tonight?"

Clint's voice caused me to focus. "Uh, no. I'm not on the schedule for a couple of days."

"I've noticed you haven't been working much lately."

I shrugged. "I think the manager is hesitant to schedule me. You know, since I was his main closer."

He paused. "Ah."

"It's fine, though. Really. Just means I get to spend more time with you."

"But I know you want the hours."

I reached for my keys. "I mean, I do. Yes. I need the money. But I've been saving money for a couple years now. I just have to shift around a few things and not spend so much of my money at once, and I'll be okay. You know, still on track for things."

"What kind of things?"

I slid the key into the lock. "You know, plans for after school."

"We've never really talked about those, you know."

I paused. "We haven't, actually."

"Want to talk about them now?"

I shrugged as I opened the door. "I mean, they aren't much. I want to move out and get a place with Allison. That'll probably put me near UCLA, since that's where she's headed for her architecture degree. I'll live off my savings for, hopefully, five months while I find a job. Then I can start saving money to go to a community college or something like that."

"What do you want to study?"

We walked inside. "Graphic design of some sort. You know, do something with all this doodling I do on a regular basis."

"Doodling?"

I nodded. "Yep. I enjoy drawing. Have we not talked about this?"

"Not enough for it to ingrain itself into my memory."

Huh. Odd. "Well, we can talk about it now, if you'd like."

I closed the door behind us and went to turn the lock. And as I did, I felt Clint's hands fall to my hips. His lips pressed against the shell of my ear, causing me to press back against him. Our bags dropped to the floor. My head fell back against his chest. I sighed as his hands traveled my body, massaging my excess and caressing my clothed breasts.

"How long have you been drawing?"

His voice was low. Rumbling. Sensuous. I moaned softly as he nibbled my ear, making my knees quake underneath me. He slowly walked me forward, pinning the front of my body to the door. He kissed down my neck, making me gasp as he pulled the collar of my T-shirt off to the side.

"Clint."

"Answer the question, Rae."

Then he spanked my ass softly, causing me to jump.

"Oh. I, uh… um… for as long as—I don't know. I just always have."

He nodded. "Kind of like my writing."

"Uh huh."

His fingers slid into the loops of my jeans. "Can you get a graphic design degree at a community college?"

He pulled me back into his rock hard girth and I moaned against the door.

"I don't—I don't know. I—I'm sure there are certificat—oh, Clint."

"Focus, Rae. I'm trying to get to know you better."

I groaned. "You're trying to torture me."

He chuckled. "Same difference."

"I don't—have it all quite planned. I guess I just—shit, Clint."

"You guess you just what, beautiful?"

His hands slipped underneath my shirt. "You can't do this to me. You're just—"

He bit into my shoulder with a growl. "Just what?"

I whipped around, no longer able to contain myself. My back fell against the door as I cupped his cheeks, pulling his lips to mine. But he stopped just mere centimeters from my lips. I felt his hands fisting my shirt. Ready to draw it over my head. My eyes found his and I saw a fire behind them. A fire I hadn't seen in weeks. I breathed the air he afforded me. I nuzzled my nose against his. And as his eyes closed, I heard emotion fill his voice.

"Whatever you want to do with your life, I'll always support it."

I love you. "Thank you, Clint."

His eyes opened. "I'm serious."

I love you. "I know."

"Wherever you go and whatever you do, I'll be cheering you on. From wherever I am."

I love you so much. "Thank you, handsome."

"And when I'm done with this beautiful body of yours, I want to talk through what your plans are. So we can get you progressing down a road you want to be on."

I love you to the moon and back. "Sounds good to me."

Our lips fell together and his hands gripped behind my thighs. He hoisted me against him, pinning me to the front door as his tongue fell down the back of my throat. He pulled me away, effortlessly carrying me up the steps and to my bedroom. I reached out with my hand to slam the door closed. I sucked on his lower lip as growls bubbled up his throat. My back fell to the mattress as he freed my hands from around his neck. He threaded our fingers together and pinned them above my head. He kissed down my cheek. My neck. My clothed chest and my stomach. I rocked against him as my thighs heated, waiting for him to strip me of my clothes.

And it took us no time to get one another naked.

He filled me with his girth and rocked against my body. He tossed my legs over his shoulders and pounded into me. My jaw unhinged, crying out in ecstasy as he took what he wanted. With me freely giving it to him. I gripped his hair and raked my nails down his back. I felt myself pouring onto him, coating him in my mark. Our pants filled the room. Our kisses grew sloppy as my legs slipped off his shoulders. He pulled out and flipped me around, raising my hips in the air. Contorting my body in all the ways he wanted before filling me.

Again.

And again.

And again.

"Fucking hell, Rae. Shit, I've missed this."

"Clint. Clint. Don't stop. Please, holy hell, don't stop."

"Never. I'll never stop. Rae. I'm close. Rae!"

"Clint! Fuck!"

His hands slid down my spine. I felt him shaking against my ass cheeks. His length grew within me, pulsing and throbbing and aching for release. I gripped my bed sheets as he pinned my cheek to the mattress, wrapping his hand within my tendrils. And as I lost myself in his frantic movements, my body popped. My pelvis erupted. Electricity blinded my vision as my jaw unhinged in silent pleasure. Freezing my movements as my body clamped down around his.

"That's it, Rae. Holy fuck."

His growls raised goosebumps all over my body. The things he made me feel were outstanding. He collapsed against my body, shaking as he filled me to the brim. My pulsing pushed him out. His lips pressed sloppy kisses against the marks he left on my shoulder. I released the bed sheets from my grip, sliding my hand through his hair as he pressed his face into the crook of my neck.

I love you.

I love you, Clint.

Just say it, Rae. Say the words.

He panted for air. "You're amazing, you know that?"

I love you. "So are you, Clint."

"I just want to be like this forever."

I love you. "I don't blame you one bit."

"You mean that?"

I fucking love the hell out of you. "Every word of it."

And just as he pressed his lips to the shell of my ear, my phone rang from my jeans piled on the floor, causing me to groan as the all-too-familiar ringtone burst the moment the two of us had created.

"Fuck."

Clint paused. "Who's calling, beautiful?"

"Work."

36

CLINTON

I kissed her lips. "I promise you, I'll make it home okay."

Rae sighed. "Are you sure? Because I'm sure if I called Michael—"

"Leave Mike to his own devices. If I know boys like I know them, he's probably with Aly enjoying his time. Plus, my house isn't far from here."

"I could call them back and tell them—"

My face fell. "You'll do no such thing. They need you at work and I know you need the hours. Get ready. I'll walk home, okay?"

"I really don't feel good about this, Clint. You aren't fully recuperated. You've just been cleared to heal outside of the therapist's office. It might be too long—"

I pressed my lips against hers, sealing her words off with yet another kiss. I wrapped my arms around the girl I'd just made love to, pulling her as closely to me as

I could get. Her lips smashed against mine. Our teeth clattered together. She made me feel as if I were on cloud nine, floating among the stars threatening to cover the whole of Los Angeles. I knew she was worried about me. I was, too. My stamina was still on the mend, and there was a good chance I'd have to stop for a breather or two on my walk home.

But I wasn't going to let that hold me back.

"Go. To. Work. Rae."

I punctuated the words with kisses before my hands slipped to her hips. She sighed as her forehead fell against mine. I felt her fingertips curling into my chest. My heart beat against her skin. Against her hands as they tried keeping me rooted. I knew she didn't want to go to work. They had interrupted us at a terrible time. And truth be told, I wanted to hop back into bed and hold her. I wanted to leap back into her arms, pull her against me, and fuck her into that mattress until the words poured effortlessly from both of our mouths.

I knew she needed the hours, though. Especially if she wanted to save to move out after graduation.

Rae sighed. "At least let me know when you get home safely. Okay?"

I nodded. "Of course. This'll give me time to stretch my legs. Work on my stamina. Allow me to clear my head for a bit before getting into the house."

"Is your dad still there?"

I paused. "Yeah. He's still home."

"Are you going to be okay?"

It made me sick she even had to ask. "I'll be fine, Rae. I know how to stand my ground with him."

"I don't know about this."

I cupped her cheeks. "Look. It's a twenty-minute walk. It's not even six o'clock. You'll hear from me before you get ready and leave for work in the first place. I promise."

And after a pause, she nodded. "Okay. Let's get you out of here, then."

"Atta girl."

She walked me to the front door before pulling me in for one more kiss. She fisted my shirt, wrapping it around her hand before pulling me down to her lips. I growled down the back of her throat and cloaked her in my arms. I loved it when she took control like that. When she thought she had the upper hand. I whipped her around, backing her into the wall in front of the door as my knee pressed between her thighs.

The glorious thighs I'd just relished with my lips.

Rae giggled. "We're both going to be late if you don't stop."

I grinned. "I'm not the one that initiated that kiss, beautiful."

"I guess I'll take the blame for it. But just this once."

"Just this once, indeed."

I chuckled, then captured her lips one last time. I kissed the tip of her nose, both of her cheeks, then planted one on her forehead. And after pep-talking myself in my head, I finally pulled away. I left her house, walking myself up the street and out of view before I stopped to catch my breath.

And for the first time in a long time, I admired the world around me.

I noticed the flowers lining the sidewalks as I walked by them. I noticed the cracks in the concrete where the land below it was slowly winning the war. I gazed up into the light blue sky, slowly cracking against the colors of a sunset teeming on the horizon. Things I'd never noticed while zooming around on my motorcycle. A world I had yet to experience because of the fast-paced, angry life I'd led up until this point. The breeze blew against my face, drying the beads of sweat on my brow as they formed.

It felt different than the breeze on my bike.

It felt comforting. Soothing. Not like the talons that clawed at my leather-jacketed back while speeding through town. I mean, yes. I missed my bike. But there was something about the world around me that couldn't be appreciated while on it. Like the rabbits hopping around in people's front yards. Or the laughter of young kids growing up down the off-shoot roads I passed to get to my own. The grass was green. I mean, incredibly green. A vibrant green that reminded me of those darkened neon signs in antique shops around the city.

I smiled at the life around me as I turned down the road I lived on.

I had a lot of good things going for me now. I had a great girl in my corner. I had new friends I felt I could trust. Who supported me and weren't dragging me down and encouraging me to be an absolute asshole. I had a stepmother who wanted a relationship with me. I had teachers who were helping me get through homework and missed tests so I could still graduate. Hell, even the principal of the school smiled at me every once in a while, instead of frowning my way with disapproval and frustration in his eyes.

I felt good about life, for once.

I stopped for one last breather a couple of blocks away from my house. I watched it looming in the distance, sparkling underneath the harshness of the sun. Sweat dripped down my back as I sighed. I watched the off-colored white glisten against the deep red shutters of the house. During the entirety of my childhood, I remembered that house in three distinct ways. Three different sets of colors that all popped more than the houses around it. Maybe it was the fresh coats of paint put on it every year that kept the house lively. Maybe it was the fact that it was the biggest house on the block. Or, maybe, it was the fact that we had the only house with a wrap-around porch as well as a wrought iron front gate that was barely utilized.

Either way, it stood out.

I picked up the pace. I went from standing still to walking. To speed walking. To jogging. I burst into a sprint, pumping air through my lungs and feeling them expand into my back. I felt the last pangs from my ribcage fall free, releasing the last of the pressure in my gut. I smiled at the sensation. At how free my body felt. I rushed up the driveway and leapt onto the porch, relishing the sweat that dripped off my brow. Down my nose. Drenching my neck and the collar of my T-shirt.

I felt alive, for the first time in my life.

And I wanted things to stay that way.

"Stop it, Howard! This has gone far enough!"

"Who the fuck do you think you are, yelling at me like that? Shut the hell up and listen, like you were always so good at!"

"Oh, is that why you married me? Because I kept my mouth shut and looked pretty for you?"

"The hell else are you good for? I whisk you away on all these vacations and it's not like you put out anymore!"

"You're an absolute asshole, you know that?"

Immediately, the blood drained from my face. How I could have ever convinced myself that things were getting better I had no idea. I heard my father yelling at Cecilia. I mean, just roaring at the top of his lungs. The only shocker was that she was yelling back. For the first time—well—ever . I stood on the porch, wondering if I should continue my walk. Maybe I could walk far enough to get to that coffee shop. The one where Rae got me that insanely good coffee and all those pastries.

I turned my back to the front door, readying myself to walk away. Until I heard something crash.

"Howard! Stop!"

I burst through the door, charging my sweaty ass down the hallway. I followed the sounds of my father screaming at her. Cursing at her. Calling her every single name in the godforsaken book. I grimaced at some of the shit that came out of his face. What kind of man talked to a woman that way?

A coward, that's who.

"Howard, you're hurting me. Please."

"Yeah? Well, maybe you know now how much it hurts me for you to be such a money-sucking cocktease, Cecilia."

"Howard!"

"Dad!" I yelled at him as I burst through the double doors into the kitchen. I saw him standing there, leaning over Cecilia with his hand tightly wrapped around her forearm. She leaned away from him, trying to wiggle away. And the fear in her eyes widened them as she whipped her head over to look at me.

"Clint."

I nodded. "Cecilia."

Dad glowered. "Get out."

I shook my head. "Not on your life. Let her go."

Dad slowly panned his gaze toward me, pinning me with a glare. He tightened his grip around Cecilia's wrist, causing her to squeal. She tried yanking away from him again, but he pulled her closer, almost causing her to lose her balance. I took a step closer to him, slowly reaching for the wooden spoon on the kitchen island.

And as he watched my movements, he chuckled.

"Go to your room, son."

Instead, however, I curled my hand tighter around that damn wooden spoon.

Because he sure as hell wasn't ripping another good woman from my life.

37

RAELYNN

"Welcome to Grady's Groceries. How was your shopping trip?"

"Yes, the milk aisle has changed to accommodate more items. It's over here, all the way down along the wall."

"Yes, sir. I'll make sure your coupon is acknowledged."

"We do take competitor's coupons! Because we pride ourselves on having the best prices in-store."

"I'm sorry, we stopped carrying that kind of ice cream when their ingredients were proven to be genetically modified. But I can help you find some other wonderful choices."

I put on the best face I could, even though I wasn't happy with being at work. I wanted to spend more time with Clint. I still wanted to be at home, in bed, curled up next to him. His bruises had finally faded into nothingness and I caught a glimpse of the strong, brutal boy I remembered from school. From before all this happened. His touch seemed gentler, but his movements were still powerful. Still reminiscent of the fighter I knew was still deep down within him.

I wanted to experience more of him. Especially now that he had a new lease on life.

I couldn't deny the change I'd seen in him over the past few weeks. How toned down his reputation at school had become. How much he hung around me and Michael and Allison, as opposed to going back to Roy and Marina and the rest of those dickweeds. He paid more attention in classes. Didn't crack jokes or cause a ruckus. The subdued nature that came over him during recuperation seemed to be trickling into his regular life, and I liked it. Not that I didn't like him before. But he gave off the idea that he might want to pull away from all that bullying bullshit. The poking fun at people and making people's lives a nightmare.

The thought made me smile.

"And here I thought work didn't make anyone happy."

Michael's voice ripped me from my trance. "What in the world are you doing here?"

He smiled. "Can't I come by and see my best friend while she's stuck at work?"

"How did you know I had to work tonight?"

"The distressful text you sent Allison."

I grinned. "So you were with her when I sent that text."

He shrugged. "Yeah, we've been spending some time together."

"Uh huh. And what kind of time are you spending with her?"

"Not the kind of time you and Clint are spending with one another, I'm sure."

I snickered. "Hardy har har."

"The deli still got those ham and turkey sandwiches?"

"And I know for a fact they just restocked your favorite energy drink in the vending machine outside."

"Oh. Yes. When do you take your break?"

I paused. "Give me twenty minutes, and I can probably take ten. But not more than that."

"Fair enough. I'll go ahead and get my food and annoy you until you take your break."

"Thanks."

He winked. "Anytime, Rae."

"Don't let Clint catch you winking at me. He just might slug you for it."

"I'd have a few words to say to him before he did something like that."

"Wait. Like what?"

Michael shrugged. "Like, 'Thank you for almost dying because it convinced me to kick things into gear with Allison.'"

"Maybe don't put it like that."

He chuckled. "Not exactly like that, no. But in some respects, I do owe me and Allison to what happened to him. As morbid as it sounds."

"So, there's a 'you and Allison' now?"

"I mean, not officially. But I guess being there with you that night and seeing what happened with Clint.

What he did for you and what you were willing to do for him. It made me realize what I wanted, you know? I mean, with Allison. No offense."

I shrugged. "None taken. You're not my type anyway."

"I don't look very good in leather."

"I mean, you might be able to pull off leather assless chaps."

"Don't go giving Allison any ideas now."

I giggled. "You know damn good and well she'd die if you ever did that to her."

"It's one of the things I adore about her."

I had to pause Michael's story in order to check out a few customers. But they quickly dwindled down. He got his sandwich and his energy drink. And I was thankful for the soda he purchased for me. I clocked out for my ten-minute break, meandering outside to sit with Michael. We sat on a bench and watched the sun cast colors across the sky while the summer breeze slowly cooled us down.

I took a sip of my soda. "So, tell me what you adore about Allison."

Michael almost choked on his sandwich. "What?"

"That's where we left off a little bit ago. You said Allison's lack of a sexual appetite was one of the many things you adore about her."

"Not lack of a sex—Rae. Come on. You know what I meant."

I giggled. "I'm giving you a hard time. I knew what you meant."

"I mean, I just—it's Allison, you know? She's intelligent and cute. So, so cute. She's got goals and ambitions, and she likes my jokes. Her hands are as soft as they look, too."

I grinned. "Her hands, huh?"

He rolled his eyes. "Get your mind out of the gutter."

"What? I've held Allison's hands a lot over the years. I know what they feel like."

"Uh huh. I'm sure that's what you meant."

I threw my head back, laughing. "That's exactly what I meant."

"You're a terrible liar."

"Doesn't mean I can't try."

"You know I just—I keep thinking back to that night. Looking over the bridge and seeing Clint sprawled out. You know? And I just—I kept thinking about this crush I've got on Allison. Like, the fuck am I holding back for? What am I waiting for? It's not like she's going to approach me. She's certainly not that kind of girl. And what if I get pushed over a bridge tomorrow? Or the next day? Am I really going to go out like that? With Allison not knowing how much I like her? She deserves better than that shit."

I nodded. "She does."

Michael paused. "I'm thinking of asking her to prom."

I rolled my eyes. "After that entire diatribe, you're only thinking about asking her?"

"Cut me some slack. I've already asked her to the movie and she invites me over every chance she gets. Give me at least some credit."

I snickered. "All right. But only a little bit of credit."

"You think she'd go with me if I asked?"

"I swear, the two of you. You're gonna kill me, you know that?"

"What do you mean?"

I took another sip of my drink. "Do you know how long she's been asking me when you're going to ask her to prom?"

"Wait, what?"

I nodded. "Yep. I keep telling her to drop hints or just outright ask you herself. But every time I suggest that, she acts like I've slapped her across the face. I'm telling you, Michael. If you ask her, she's going to say yes. She's practically jumping out of her skin waiting for you to ask."

He snickered. "Wow. Well, that makes me feel good."

"I'm serious. You have to ask her. Our nights are going to be miserable if you don't. She'd be so happy if you asked. Hell, she'd probably say yes before you could get the damn question out."

He laughed. "Well, since we're on this same track, you think Clint will ask you to prom?"

"Yeah, I'm sure we'll go together. I mean, it's not like he has to ask. We're officially together, I suppose."

"You suppose? After everything you've been through?"

I felt myself blush. "Okay, yes. We are officially together. So, yeah. We're going to prom together."

"You still don't sound too sure of that. Is everything going okay with his recuperation?"

I shrugged. "I mean, he's always struggling with his dad. Which I'm sure is affecting his recuperation efforts. But he's okay. Far as I can tell."

"I'd like to get his dad in a room for a few minutes."

I scoffed. "Wouldn't we all."

"So, how are the two of you? You know, now that he's on the mend?"

I felt myself blush deeper. "I guess we're good."

"You guess, huh?"

"You're a dick, you know that?"

He chuckled. "Maybe a bit. Can I ask you something, though?"

"Of course. I mean, you have to spit it out soon because I only have one more minute, but—"

"Do you love him?"

The question didn't catch me as off-guard as I figured it would. In fact, it was easy to answer. I bit down onto the inside of my cheek as I turned to face Michael. And with a nod of my head, I answered his question.

"Yeah. I really think I do."

Michael grinned. "Then, you should tell him. I don't know much about Clint, but I'd like to think I know him better after these past few weeks. The lunches we've shared and helping him to class. He strikes me as the kind of guy who won't believe something is real unless you say the words. So say them."

I paused. "What if he doesn't feel the same way?"

"I can tell you, from the bottom of my heart, that's not true. Not one bit."

"But, there's a chance. Right?"

He sighed. "Rae, if that boy doesn't love you after all you two have been through and after all you've done for him, he sure as hell isn't worth any more of your efforts."

I nodded slowly. "True."

"Tell him, Rae. Tell him, like I'm going to tell Allison she's going to prom with me."

"Whoa, now. I didn't realize we were talking on that sort of a level now."

He nudged me with his shoulder. "You really are patronizing sometimes. You know that?"

I giggled. "It's why you love me."

He wrapped his arm around me, pulling me close to him. "Always and forever, girl. I'll always have your back."

"Even if I screw around with your mortal enemy and somehow make you guys friends?"

He paused. "I mean, maybe."

The two of us laughed, but his words hit home. Michael was right. If I wanted Clint to know I loved him, I had to spit it out. And there was a good chance he wouldn't do it first. Not because he didn't want to. But because he'd been through enough. He'd taken enough first steps to last someone a lifetime. It was damn time someone took the reins from him and let him rest a little bit. I didn't want to wait a second longer to tell him how I felt. Even if it blew up in my face. Even if he broke my heart. Even if I completely regretted the decision. At least I'd know. I'd know where we stood, and he'd know he was capable—and worthy—of being loved.

And I wanted to be the person to finally give that to him.

38

CLINTON

I gripped the wooden spoon, pulling it to my side. "No."

He growled at me. "No?"

I shook my head. "No. I'm not going anywhere. And I suggest you let Cecilia go."

As I stood there, staring at the fear in her eyes, I felt the entire room shift underneath my feet. My father's anger filled the space, pushing it outward and upward and downward. But, I steadied myself. I looked him straight in his eyes and held his stare. Held my ground. Held that wooden spoon in my hand, just in case that man decided to charge me.

This stopped today.

I mean, fucking hell. I was a fighter everywhere in my life except my own damn home. The fuck was that about? No more. I was done being pushed around by my father. I was done feeling weak. I'd just fought for my life, and now I felt like the time had come for me to fight for my freedom. To fight for peace. To fight for the sanity of this household and to buck up against my father.

And I was done allowing Cecilia to suffer the same angry wrath I had all my life. She deserved better. That woman had been there for me every step of the way through this shit. I wouldn't let my father hurt her. I wouldn't let him mangle her. I wouldn't let him taint her the way he'd tainted me down through the years. Because if he didn't have any issues putting his hands on her right now, that meant it had happened in the past.

Something that boiled my blood.

Dad's eye twitched. "What? You think you're a big man now?"

Cecilia tried wrenching away from him, but it didn't work. He tightened his grip further against her skin, causing her to cry out. I took a step forward, flipping the spoon in my hand. I caught it, feeling the weight of the damn thing settling against my palm. And as Dad's eyes flickered down to it, something else crossed my mind.

It wasn't simply Cecilia that deserved better.

I did, too.

"The fuck are you smiling about? Put that damn thing down and get out of here."

My father's voice ripped me from my trance and I felt my lips curling up. Further. Wider. Until my teeth gleamed at him and happiness flooded my veins. I deserved better. For the first time in my life, I felt like I deserved something more than this. Something more than Dad. Something more than the life he'd given me. Something more than the emptiness of his money. I looked at Cecilia and winked, letting her know that the two of us were getting out of this. No matter what I had to do.

Then, finally, Dad dropped her arm. "The fuck are you smiling about, son?"

I snickered. "I'm not your son."

His eyebrows rose. "Pretty sure I knocked up your mother with you. So, yeah. That makes you my son."

"Takes a lot more than sperm to make you a father, Dad."

He started walking toward me and Cecilia reached out for him. Telling him to stop. Telling him that she'd get me to go upstairs. He turned around, pushing her back toward the kitchen counter as she stumbled on her feet. And as she caught herself against the counter, she cried out. Her voice filled with panic, horror, and anger.

"He's just recovered, Howard! Stop it!"

I didn't flinch. As my father stalked toward me, I looked him straight in his eyes. I wouldn't let him control this house anymore. I wouldn't let him control my life, or my happiness, or my worth. I kept Cecilia in the corner of my eye, checking to make sure she was all right. And after she got back up onto her feet, I narrowed my eyes at my father.

"The fuck are you looking at, Clinton?"

I sighed. "I'm not afraid of you anymore, Dad. I don't know why you're so angry. I don't know why you hate me so much. But I'm done trying to figure it out.

I'm done trying to figure you out. This has to stop, and it stops now. And if you don't want it to stop, I'll call people who will help me stop it. For my sake, and Cecilia's."

He put his finger in my face. "You leave my wife to me."

"Not a chance in hell."

He paused. "What did you just say?"

I stepped up to the plate, mere inches from my father's face. One on one, without a care in the world as to what he did after this. Because if he beat me to a bloody pulp, I'd take both the doctor and the lawyer up on their offers. So long as they helped Cecilia out in the process. My smile settled into a grin. A snarky grin I'd learned from him over the years. His nostrils flared with anger. His eyes bulged with revenge. I smelled the stench of alcohol on his breath and shook my head.

Pathetic. "I said, not a chance in hell, Dad."

Before I knew it, my father's hands pressed into my chest. The wooden spoon went clattering to the ground as my hands came up in defense. Cecilia screamed in the background, and the whole world fell black. Black at night. Black, like the color of my soul. Well, the color my soul had been. Rae changed a great deal of that. Cecilia changed a great deal of that. And in that moment, I wondered if Rae would be proud of me. Proud of me standing up to my father. Proud of me holding my ground. Proud of me fighting for my own happiness and safety within the walls of my father's mansion.

And I decided she would be. If she knew what was

happening right now, she'd be proud. Possibly screaming at me like Cecilia currently was. But she'd be proud after the fact.

Not today, Dad. You're done with this shit today.

The only thing I processed was the smell of alcohol. The only thing I felt was my father's storm unleashing against me. He held so much anger within him. He had such fury in his fists. The only thing I saw were his angry eyes coming at me as I shoved him in his chest, listening as Cecilia screamed in the background.

"Stop it! I'm calling the police if you don't cut it out right now!"

Her voice faded away. Fell into the background as I moved and ducked my father. Whatever this storm brewed from, I wasn't going to be my father's punching bag any longer. If he wanted a fight, a fight is what he'd get. And I'd make sure to repay him for every fist that ever connected with my face. I'd repay him for every bruise he ever wrung around my neck. I'd repay him for every knee to my stomach and every elbow to my back and every time he pinned me against my fucking bedroom wall to teach me a lesson about being late for school.

Because damn it, we all deserved better.

Even my father.

"Stop! Please!"

"You're a selfish little brat, you know that?"

"Howard, no!"

Drunken fists flew around in the air and I dodged every single one of them, until a couple connected with my ribs, causing me to grunt out. But the only thing saving me was the fact that my father was completely smashed. He teetered on his feet, giving me a chance to get away from him. I slunk around him in the kitchen, moving away from him and watching as he stumbled into the kitchen counters. I gripped my step-mother by the upper arms and moved her out of harm's way, ripping open the kitchen door and pushed her into the dining room just as my father came up behind me.

And when he fisted my shirt, he ripped me away from my stepmother.

Away from the woman I'd defend tonight.

"Get back here and fight me like a damn man."

Cecilia cried out. "Howard! Stop! No!"

I scoffed. "Just getting the innocent out of the way before I teach you a lesson with your own medicine."

And as Dad slung me across the kitchen, forcing me to the ground, I heard him come for me. I felt his footsteps growing closer. I scrambled off the floor, readying myself for a fight just as his hands connected with my chest again.

Barreling me back into the garage door.

"No! Clint!"

I grunted as my back slammed into the doorknob. "Fuck."

Dad chuckled. "You want to play tough guy, not a problem. Because by the time I'm done with you, you'll know why I'm the father and you're the son."

I snarled. "In your fucking dreams, you psychotic abusive fuck."

He tossed me to the ground and I used the momentum to slide myself underneath the kitchen table. I heard Dad pulling at chairs and filling the kitchen with his growls. With his curses. With his anger. I scrambled up to my feet on the other side, then leapt onto the table itself. He looked up at me, his eyes wild and unfocused, filled with the alcohol he'd been drinking as I leapt above him, landing on the kitchen island.

Cecilia gasped. "Clint! Be careful!"

And as I hopped back down onto the floor, I scooped the wooden spoon back up, grinning at my father before he charged me once more.

"Look out!"

39

RAELYNN

I wiped down my register as I planned it all out in my head. Tonight, I'd tell Clint exactly how I felt. Tonight, I'd wrap him up in my arms, plant a kiss straight against his lips, and shout from the rooftops how much I loved him. I smiled as I thought about it. I couldn't wait to get my arms around his body again. My movements grew furious as I cleaned everything down as quickly as I could, closing up the grocery store for the second time since the incident.

My manager had been hesitant to schedule me to close after everything that took place.

"Ready to go?"

I jumped at the sound of Michael's voice. I whipped my head up, watching him as he stood at the edge of my register. Not a soul came in or left the grocery store, and I wondered how long he'd been standing there.

I furrowed my brow. "You're back?"

He snickered. "I never really left."

"You left after your break. I saw you get in your car."

"Yeah, well. I went to visit with Allison for a bit. Then I came back. Been standing here for about twenty minutes watching you clean and murmur to yourself."

I paused. "I was murmuring?"

He grinned. "Yep. And it's a good plan, what you've got going."

"Shit, you heard?"

He shrugged. "I mean, you were murmuring. And you did kind of explain to me that you were going to do it anyway. Good thing I'm here to drive you, right?"

"Then, why do I get the feeling you're not just here to drive me to Clint's?"

"What? Can't I come visit my best friend while she's working?"

I grinned. "You overprotective little thing, you. You're worried about me."

He rolled his eyes. "Look, it freaked me out, what happened to you and Clint that night. Okay? So sue me if you don't like it. But if you're closing down this grocery store again, I'd like to be here to make sure you get to wherever you need to be safely enough. You know, until Clint's back to doing that for you."

I smiled. "Thank you, Michael."

"I love you, Rae. Let me know when you're ready to go, and I'll get you over to Clint's."

I reached over the cash register and hugged his neck. Then I finished up what I needed to do. I cashed out my till and took it over to my manager's office. And I found him staring at the parking lot cameras. I cleared my throat, pulling him from his trance as he jumped in his seat. He whipped his head around with widened eyes, and my gut dropped for him.

Looked like Clint and I weren't the only ones affected by what happened.

I passed off my till and clocked out. Then Michael and I headed to his car. I felt the eyes of my manager on us the entire way. He stood at the windows of the grocery store, watching us until we got to the car and got in. I even saw him watching us in my rearview mirror as we drove off.

Making our way for Clint's house.

Michael had a smirk on his face for the entire ride. And as we listened to his bullshit classical music, I found my inner peace. I found my inner strength. I rehearsed the things I wanted to say to him as we made our way for his house. I felt myself filling with hope. Excitement. Anxiousness. But not the bad kind. The good kind.

Because I knew this meant taking another step for Clint and me.

A step I felt we'd both been ready for.

"You want to rehearse?"

I peeked over at Michael. "What?"

He snickered. "Rehearse. You know, what you're going to say to him tonight."

I shrugged. "Nah. I'm good. I usually wing it with stuff like this."

"You're going to wing it when it comes to telling Clint how you feel for the very first time>"

"I mean, I usually wing it with my English speeches and I do just fine with those."

He paused. "You didn't plan out that speech you gave last year?"

I shook my head. "Nope."

"That massive speech you gave on *1984* sort of applying today."

"Are you not hearing me right? Clean out your ears, Michael."

He chuckled. "Holy shit, you're amazing. You know that?"

I smiled. "And I hope that's one of Clint's many reactions tonight."

"If it isn't, I'll kick his ass for you."

"Michael!"

"What? Come on, Rae. I see how happy he makes you. I see how much this boy means to you. And if he doesn't love you or if he hurts you or if I even suspect he's manipulating you or leading you on in any way? He's got it coming to him. Because you're my friend, Rae. My best of friends. And we have to stick together."

I reached over, taking his hand. "I love you so much."

He smirked. "Love you, too, Rae. Now, you ready?"

"As ready as I'll ever be."

"Good. Because we're here."

I drew in a deep breath as we pulled into Clint's

driveway, stopping just shy of the porch. Michael squeezed my hand for reassurance, and I leaned over to kiss his cheek softly. I wanted him to know how thankful I was for his friendship. How thankful I was for accepting Clint into our fold. And as I hugged him tightly, I pressed my lips against his ear.

"Thank you. For everything."

He nodded. "I'll hang around for a bit, just in the slightest case this goes haywire. All right?"

"You won't have to, but thank you anyway. Give it about ten minutes, then you can drive on off. I'm sure Cecilia will give me a ride home later."

"If you don't stay the night."

I scoffed and playfully swatted at Michael. Then I shoved myself out of his SUV. He wished me luck and I closed my door, grinning at him through the window.

And just as I turned around, the front door burst open.

"Clint!"

I looked on in horror as the man I loved fell to his back on the porch. I heard a door open in the distance as the world around me tunneled. All I saw was Clint lying on his back, blood dripping down his face. Flashes of him lying at the bottom of that ravine bombarded my mind. Until I heard that fucking voice.

"Get up and fight me like the man you think you are!"

His father.

I watched in slow motion as Cecilia rushed out onto the porch. She was missing a shoe. Her hair was disheveled. Her dress had been ripped off her shoulder and she looked as if she'd been crying for hours. I saw her drop to the porch beside Clint. I stood there, frozen, as Clint's father appeared in the doorway. His fists were balled up. He had blood splattered all over his face. His eye was swollen shut. His lip, split. He had the fire of Satan in his eyes.

And I watched as Cecilia helped Clint back up onto his feet.

Michael stepped up beside me. "Hey!"

I jumped at the sound of his voice. Because I had no fucking clue when he'd gotten out of the car. Time toppled over on itself. I watched Michael push away from my side, sprinting for the porch. I followed behind him, finally pulled out of my trance. The world moved in regular motion again as the smell of blood, sweat, and tears filled the space around me. Michael moved behind Clint, steadying him as he stumbled back. And while Cecilia smoothed her hands over his chest, I reached up to cup Clint's cheek, pulling his eyes to mine.

"Can you hear me? Are you okay?"

"You won't get out of this another time, son."

His father reached between all of us, ripping him away from our grasps. I lunged for him, trying to get him back as Michael held me around my waist. Cecilia screamed for him to stop. Screamed at his father for him to let Clint go. I reached out for him, kicking and trying to get out of Michael's grasp.

But if he wouldn't let me use my body, I sure as hell would use my words.

"Let him go!"

My shrieking voice filled the night as Clint's father held him tightly by the collar of his shirt.

"Let him go, you coward! I'm tired of you hurting him. Abusing him. Beating him to a pulp. You're the sorriest excuse for a father I've ever seen in my life, and mine left me when I was just a little girl!"

Michael put his lips to my ear. "Calm down. He's going to hurt you. He's drunk. I can smell it. Calm your voice, Rae."

But I didn't listen. "He's still recovering from the crash, you piece of shit. I'm going to call the police and have you thrown in prison to rot!"

The sounds of his father laughing at me fell against my ear. As Michael settled me back down onto my feet, he strengthened his grip around my waist. I reached out for Clint. I watched as his father's eyes fell onto his son. Cecilia cried in the background, slumped against the front door as that man drew his fist back. I reached my hand out, screaming with all my might. My fingertips wiggled for the back of Clint's shirt, so I could pull him out of the line of fire of his father's fight-ending punch.

Then, Clint brought his knee up, nailing his father straight in his groin and taking him to the ground.

The world fell silent as he growled out in pain. Cecilia's cries stopped. Michael's grip loosened. And my shrieking ceased. I watched as blood dripped down Clint's face. His neck. Soaking his shirt as it poured from his nose, which I knew his father had rebroken. Clint stood there in front of his father, letting his blood drip onto the top of his damn head. And once his father looked up, Clint sighed.

"You really are a piece of work, Dad."

Then, Clint struck his father with a blow of his knee that knocked the man out cold.

Everything fell silent. Everything stood still. Time itself yielded to what had just happened. Clint's father fell face-first onto the porch. Passed out in his own alcohol-laden drool. And as Michael released me from his grasp, I scurried to Clint's side, gripping his arms and slowly turning him toward me as shock and anger rolled over his features.

"Baby, can you hear me?"

I rubbed my hands up and down his arms, trying to pull him out of his trance. I heard Cecilia gasp for air, as if she'd been holding her breath. I heard her walk out onto the porch, dropping to her knees next to his father. I watched his eyes dart around. He slowly came to as he tried to get a bearing on his surroundings. He looked at me. At Michael. At his father, lying on the porch. He brought his hand up to his nose before he winced, with tears streaming down his face.

"Baby, talk to me. Can you hear me?"

He shook his head. He stumbled back away from me, holding his hand out. I tried to get to him, but he stopped me. I tried to reach out for him, but he wouldn't let me wrap him up like I had planned. He wouldn't let me pull him close, like I had planned. The words danced on the tip of my tongue. The words I knew he needed to hear.

He beat me to the punch, though. With words that shattered my heart right there on his fucking porch.

"I can't do this."

His words were such a soft whisper, I thought I'd misheard him. Until he said them again with strength.

"I can't do this, Rae."

I paused. "Do what?"

He looked away. "Us."

"What?"

"This."

"Excuse me?"

"I need you to leave."

I looked up at him, hoping this was all a dream. "You can't be serious right now. You need help. You need a—"

His head whipped around to mine. "I need you to leave. Now."

"Clint, I—"

"I. Said. Leave!"

And as the roar of his voice filled the space around me, wrapping me up in the greatest nightmare of my life, he took a step toward me. His fists were balled up at his sides. I felt someone yank me away from him, and I stumbled down the stairs. Cecilia cried as she sat by his father's unconscious body. Blood poured down Clint's face as he stared at me with lightning in his eyes. I wanted to reach out for him. I wanted to press my lips to his ear. I wanted to whisper to him how much I loved him, and reassure him I wasn't going anywhere.

I hadn't prepared for him wanting me to leave, though.

And I had no words for the true desire of his heart.

Thank you for reading PROMISE ME. Don't miss STAY WITH ME, the next book in Rae and Clinton's love story, and be sure to join my email and SMS lists below to don't miss any of my future books!

Want to read an exclusive novella from Clinton's point of view? Check out CLAIMING ME, book 1.5.

Get an SMS alert when Rebel releases a new book:
Text REBEL to 77948

REBEL HART

Rebel Hart is an author of Dark Romance novels. Check out all the books in her #1 bestselling series Diamond In The Rough. And don't forget to join her Readers' Group to chat with Rebel and other fans: facebook.com/groups/rebelhart

NEVER MISS A NEW RELEASE:
Follow Rebel on Amazon
Follow Rebel on Bookbub

Text REBEL to 77948 to don't miss any of her books (US only) or sign up at www.RebelHart.net to get an email alert when her next book is out.

authorrebelhart@gmail.com

CONNECT WITH REBEL HART:

ALSO BY REBEL HART

For a full list of my books go to:

www.RebelHart.net

Printed in Great Britain
by Amazon

85882472R00205